MW01205292

THE

RED

PARKA

by

Joseph B. Hodgkins

The Red Parka

Copyright © 2022 by Joseph B. Hodgkins

All Rights Reserved

The Red Parka is a work of fiction. Names, characters, events, and incidents either are the products of the author's imagination or are used fictitiously. Certain restaurants, businesses, hotels, retail stores, locations, long-standing institutions, agencies, and public offices are mentioned, but the characters involved are wholly imaginary. Otherwise, any resemblance to actual persons, living or dead, is entirely coincidental.

ISBN (paperback): 978-1-7363849-6-1

ISBN (e-book): 978-1-7363849-7-8

B RAGDON
OOKS

BOOKS BY THE SAME AUTHOR

The NoMO Killer

The Reverend Elizabeth Williamson

& Church Gagne Crime Drama Series

Murder in the Apothecary

Lizzy's Jazz Joint

All titles are available in both e-book and paperback formats at amazon.com.

Search under the title or *Joseph Hodgkins*.

IN MEMORY

JAMES R. LAPPEEGAARD

1926 ~ 2015

Jim loved his wife of over thirty years, the Reverend Dr. Ruth E. Mohring, his children and grandchildren, the Navy, "Frisco," Freemasonry, clowning, and mystery novels.

HAPPY LAPPY

PROLOGUE

Monday, May 28, 2012

San Francisco

My husband, Denis, is running errands while I sit on the deck. At first, I tried to read, but my mind wandered to the roses. Even now it looks like they'll be spectacular this summer, but my thoughts won't rest there. They continue drifting, mulling over gloomier matters . . . our time together.

***

I met him nine years ago while attending a creative writing workshop he was chairing. I stopped to talk with him afterward, and then we went for coffee. It turned out to be one of the most enjoyable evenings ever. Denis seemed like a charming, considerate man. He listened attentively and made me feel like I was the most important person in the world. It was his eyes—captivating. It didn't hurt that he was handsome and well-dressed. Later, he walked me to my car. Holding the door open, he asked, "May I kiss you goodnight?" But he didn't wait for a response. We kissed for a long while, and when we parted, Denis's hand, which had found the small of my back, stroked my bottom. Driving home, I wondered, *Was that on purpose or inadvertent?* I didn't know.

In any case, I couldn't fall asleep right away. The next day, I was disappointed when he didn't call. The following day, I still hadn't heard from him. Finally, I realized we hadn't exchanged phone numbers. Recalling the university where Denis taught, I rang him.

"I'm glad you called," he said. "I was about to send out a search party. By the way, I've finished your book. It's top-notch." We talked about my novel, and it was clear Denis had read it. "I hope you're working on a second. So where should we go on our first real date?"

"I don't know . . . I'm easy."

"Oh, I hope so," Denis bantered. "If you don't think it's too lowbrow, we could go to a movie and have pizza afterwards."

"Just like high school sweethearts," I said, matching his flirtatious manner.

"I don't know, because I grew up in Paris, where it probably would've been an art film and a bistro. But I have a suggestion that might add pizzazz to our date. Why don't you come commando?"

"*What?*"

"You know—no bra, no panties."

"I wasn't asking for a definition. Are you serious?"

"Why not?" There was a long pause that soon became uncomfortable. Avoiding the issue of my underwear, I suggested a few movies.

Later, leading up to our date, that conversation sprang to mind repeatedly. Denis's idea had been titillating, and once the evening arrived, I was still tussling with his suggestion. Ultimately, I acceded. When he picked me up, I was sure my skirt, lack of a bra, and blush gave me away.

I suppose I'll be fine. After all, Mom taught me to sit, bend, and kneel like a lady.

Denis was a gentleman during the film. But then at Uncle Vito's, he put his hand on my knee, moving it higher bit by bit. I'd been waiting for something like this, albeit not anything so public. After a while, he asked, "Would you like to wait until later?" I shook my head no, and in a few minutes, I was thankful for the pizzeria's hubbub. That night I took Denis home, and we've been a couple ever since.

We were married in 2003 and were happy for the first few years. But then our relationship started to deteriorate, and by the fall of 2010, Denis had begun an affair. In September 2011, I spoke face-to-face with the student who claimed she'd been only seventeen when he seduced her. Honestly, it was hard to doubt or cast blame, because when my husband turns on his charm, women don't stand a chance. I hadn't, so I couldn't hoodwink myself.

Then I had an affair as well. It wasn't much of one, lasting barely three months, and eventually I convinced myself it was a natural reaction. *So now we're even*, I told myself, but I worried, *Was I justified? I don't know . . .*

In late January 2012, all hell broke loose. A cliché, but clichés exist for a reason. I had confessed a couple of weeks before, and it was a mistake. I'd been forewarned by girlfriends who'd cheated. They unanimously agreed: "Don't tell him. Once you do, you can't unring the bell. Make it up as best you can—chiefly with sex." My literary agent put it less elegantly. "Screw his brains out, do all those nasty things he bedevils you for, and hope he never catches on!"

When Denis found out, he raved on and on about how terribly I'd treated him. He insisted he hadn't had an affair himself and eventually left the house. I had no idea what would happen, but it turned out to be the calm before the storm. When Denis returned, he didn't say anything at first but gave me an attractively wrapped package. My despondency lifted but quickly returned, because the box contained items from a sex shop and a pet store.

"What the hell," I blurted out.

And then Denis calmly unleased a harangue of invective that reduced me to tears. My husband used every vile word he knew to describe my actions and what he thought of me.

"What happens next is up to you. Go upstairs. Make up your mind. If you're leaving, get your suitcase, and I'll be done with you. If you're staying, get your naked ass back down here and start making amends."

I stomped off, flipping him the finger. "Don't you dare talk to me like that. You're a bastard!"

***

It's early afternoon, and Denis still hasn't returned from his errands. When he does, we'll be leaving for a Memorial Day barbecue at the Howells'. As I wait, I replay our relationship from the beginning once again. I feel better for a while when I start there, because it was the best time of my life. I was free and happy then. But now it's the worst of days, and I'm trapped and miserable.

and a list of the victims' possessions—their clothes, mobile phones, wallets, keys, and so on. The entire building was dusted for fingerprints, revealing dozens of smudged prints but nothing conclusive.

***

Gabi met with the victims' landlords, Mr. and Mrs. Carlton, at their two-family house. A couple in their seventies, they'd owned the home and resided on the ground floor for many years. The twosome reported that the girls regularly had women and men friends over, and, from time to time, their men friends spent the night. But the Carltons had never met any of their visitors. The couple had heard the twins leave their apartment around nine o'clock on Wednesday morning the twenty-third but hadn't seen or heard them thereafter. The landlords were upset about the girls' deaths but couldn't offer any other useful information

CHAPTER TWO

Monday, June 25, 2012

As Susan Johnson's flight from New York to San Francisco reached cruising altitude, a business-class attendant poured her a glass of champagne. Susan, a 2005 honor graduate from Harvard College, was an attractive young woman, with coloring favoring her mother's Irish side—green eyes and red hair. The timing of her trip couldn't have been better. Normally, business class would've been an extravagance, but Susan sought pampering after the stress she'd been undergoing.

To begin with, on June 2, there had been the death of her favorite uncle, her mother's brother, Brag O'Brien. Susan had been named executrix of his estate and was flying to San Francisco to settle his affairs. Winding things up would provide a welcome distraction from Susan's other calamities.

Those had begun when Susan was unexpectedly sacked from the bank where she had worked for six years.

Until then, her career had developed well. She had been at the top of her class of twenty-five in the commercial training program when it concluded in 2008. Following that, Susan had hoped to land a position in the prominent national accounts division, which was regarded as a fast-track assignment and offered the chance of becoming vice president in three years.

But then James had arrived to see her boss, and Susan was called to the office. Apparently, James was too impatient to wait for the trainees' assignments to be made. He sought to hire her as his assistant, wanting her to start the next day. Susan wasn't certain what to make of the offer, but it didn't seem like she had a choice—a conclusion her line manager confirmed after James left.

It was rare for a trainee to be chosen to work directly for an executive of James's stature. Susan recognized that a man with his influence could do marvels for her career.

James was an executive vice president and inarguably one of the three most powerful officers in the bank. He had been hired to head the asset recovery area and reported to the president. In the past, the division hadn't been regarded as offering a desirable career path. However, that had changed; the topsy-turvy economy of recent years had created unprecedented loan losses. Many once-profitable banks—including theirs—had teetered on the brink. These losses had lingered and provided James's division with ample work. And James had the kind of charisma that made you want to follow him into battle. He was in his late thirties, tall, dark haired, with refined features and well-tailored clothes, and it wasn't a secret he was married.

Susan had been powerfully attracted to him nevertheless. She recollected the sexual tension that had existed between them from the beginning, a condition that had probably played a disproportionate role four years ago when she accepted the position in his office. Susan had assumed James had chosen her because of her accomplishments, but now she wasn't certain. She ought to have recognized that she had lost her ability to keep their relationship professional and see what James was really like.

Ten days ago, James had callously destroyed her career. "What can I do?" he'd told her. "It's downsizing."

She was stunned. Their bank had weathered the storm, and a lot of the credit had been given to her—at least according to the performance reviews James had prepared. Now she grasped that the excitement of becoming his mistress had prevented her from seeing the truth. She was still reeling from his disingenuousness.

"We've been working ourselves out of jobs ever since the economy started to turn around," James had continued. "You had to know this was coming. We haven't had any large cases in months."

"Bullshit," Susan snapped, and their conversation deteriorated from there. She wasn't used to failure and didn't take it gracefully. She left his office with six months' severance and a metaphorical pat on the head. *Fuck him. It's about our recent conversations. It's about him leaving his wife. James wants me out of the way because I'm becoming too demanding.* So in the end, her boss, mentor, and lover were all gone.

Susan continued to ruminate wistfully as they flew. She saw the irony of being fired in his office. The place had been special for them; they'd frequently made love there. Susan recalled how nervous she was the first time. It was late one afternoon several months after she began, and they were alone. James had gone to his door, closing and locking it, and then returned, saying, "Why don't you undress?"

"What?"

"You know, take off your clothes."

"Are you out of your mind?"

But James continued coaxing. In the end, they'd made love on his couch, and their relationship was sealed.

Susan roused when lunch came. Afterward, she managed to put James out of her mind and started thinking about settling Brag's estate. She would be staying with Linda Sanchez, her uncle's significant other.

Linda and Brag had met when he visited her art gallery near Fisherman's Wharf. Brag was an accomplished amateur photographer who, after selling his tavern, tutored young folks gratis, and he'd stopped by to view a showing of his former students' photography. He and Linda became friends, and Linda offered to put together an exhibition of his work, but she couldn't get him to agree.

Later, after Brag's wife died, Susan's mother suspected Linda of being a gold digger. Susan first met Linda when Brag brought her east to a family reunion. The gathering was tense because of her mom's misgivings, but despite that, Susan liked Linda, and after seeing the couple together, she had no doubt they were in love. When Linda called about Brag's death, Susan was surprised her uncle's partner hadn't been named as his executrix, but if Linda was upset, she didn't reveal it. "You were his favorite," she'd said. "He appreciated how you always kept in touch. Brag recently revised his will, and all his affairs are in order. I'll show you where everything is and will give you a hand if you'd like."

Susan listened to music, read, and dozed for the rest of the flight. After landing, she took a cab, as Linda had said she'd be unable to pick her up. Linda had mailed Susan a house key along with directions to a neighborhood Italian restaurant, where they would meet for dinner.

***

" 'Evening, ladies." The restaurant's owner welcomed them as they arrived.

"Marco, this is Susan, Brag's niece from New York."

"Nice to meet you," Marco said, before greeting Linda. "I still can't get over Brag's sudden passing. I keep looking for both of you at your table, so I'm glad you're back." When they were seated, he uncorked and poured their wine before leaving them to peruse their menus.

"I'm sorry I couldn't meet you this afternoon, but I was tied up at the gallery," Linda said.

"Don't worry about it," Susan replied. "I was through baggage claim and in a cab before I knew it."

"This was our favorite restaurant, and I haven't been able to return until tonight. I'm glad you're here. I've been so lonely since Brag died; it was unexpected. He awakened me in the middle of the night with a pain in his chest. I called 911, but he died in the ambulance." Linda teared up. It was clear she was still having a tough time. "Brag kept in tip-top shape, ate properly, and exercised three or four times a week. Everyone thought he was in his late fifties."

"I'm sorry . . . I know how much you loved him. We don't have to stay if you'd like to go home. I can fix something there."

"This is fine, because I'm trying to return to a normal routine. You've had a long trip, so let's stay and relax this evening, all right?"

After dinner, they walked home. The house, painted a pale primrose with hospital-white shutters and trim, was a three-floor Victorian on Russian Hill.

"It's a wonderful house," Susan observed. "I noticed this afternoon how Brag's photos are displayed throughout. They're great."

"They are. What isn't hung is stored on his computer in the small office next to your room. Look through them whenever you want. You'll see how top-of-the-line they are."

"I don't understand why Brag was averse to sharing his photography."

"I'm not sure, but I don't think he was self-conscious or insecure about his talent. It was just private—something he did for himself." As Linda opened the front door, she continued, "You know, they bought this large house expecting a family, but it never worked out. I don't know why they didn't adopt. Your aunt Ruth was a pediatric nurse at San Francisco General. I wonder if that gave her comfort?"

Linda settled Susan in the large third-floor guest room. Susan was tired and disoriented, so she retired early. Nonetheless, she started reading the copy of Brag's will that Linda had provided.

Brag had sold his Irish pub twenty years ago and invested the proceeds well. He and her aunt had accumulated a sizable liquid estate of about $5 million. This was in addition to their house, which they'd bought long before San Francisco's real estate became some of the costliest in the country.

The disposition was straightforward. Linda had inherited the house and $1 million. Susan had received another million, and she and her brother would split the rest of the estate.

Feeling drowsy, Susan put the will aside and fell asleep to the sound of foghorns in the harbor.

***

The next morning, Susan slept in. By the time she came downstairs, Linda had already gone to work. Susan made coffee and read the front page of the *Examiner*. They had agreed to meet at the gallery for lunch, so when she left the house, Susan followed the sounds of cable car bells for several blocks. She sighted a Powell and Hyde car, rode it to the end of the line—

getting off across from the Buena Vista Café—and then walked to Fisherman's Wharf.

Linda's place, named Dock Side Gallery, was on the south side of Jefferson, facing the piers. This wasn't a trendy spot, but Linda had been located here for years and had a favorable lease. Brag had told Susan that in the beginning, Linda sold the usual collection of paraphernalia carried in tourist shops. However, it turned out she had an eye for undiscovered artists that established galleries wouldn't carry. She began showcasing more and more of them until the original store had all but disappeared. Notwithstanding her location, the artists were loyal, the shop prospered, and Linda earned a decent living. In recent years, she'd taken on a small group of photographers.

"Did you find everything you need?" Linda asked as Susan entered. "I thought you'd like to sleep in because you looked so tired yesterday. Sorry, I couldn't wait—it's my week to open."

"Everything was fine."

"I ordered a couple of salads and sodas from the deli. If that's okay, we can sit in the back office and review the will? After lunch, when my assistant, Derrick, arrives, we'll go to the bank and pick up the original from our safe-deposit box."

***

That afternoon they went to the bank, and following that, Susan meandered around the wharf before catching a cable car back to Russian Hill. Linda had given her directions to a greengrocer, and she picked up what they needed for dinner. As evening approached, Susan readied everything, set the table on the back deck, and sat outside reading the *Examiner*. She noticed that the paper continued to cover the warehouse murders, as they'd been dubbed, but it didn't seem like the investigation was proceeding rapidly.

During dinner, they nearly finished off a bottle of Sonoma merlot, and while Susan cleared the table, Linda started reminiscing. "Over a hundred people attended the funeral—a lot, considering he was retired. Even though your mother returned home right away, I was happy she came west, because our relationship bothered Brag."

"I thought you had reconciled your differences."

"Mostly, but it took time. We're polite to each other but not close."

"Now I wish I'd come," Susan interjected. "I felt bad when I was fired . . . if I had only known. I was wrapped up in my career and that son of a bitch James, and for what?"

"Don't worry. You're here now when I need someone. Do you want to talk about him? I listen well."

"No, not now . . . in a while. I'm just not ready yet. But tell me about Brag, because Mom didn't talk about him much. How did he end up out here and acquire a pub?"

"After being discharged from the army, he was restless and hitchhiked west. In the early sixties, he bounced from job to job. By then Brag had met your aunt Ruth. Before they were married, he found a job at an Irish pub in North Beach. Its owner, Paddy Kelly, a third generation San Franciscan, was a character. He affected a thick Irish brogue and acquired the sobriquet Tis Himself, since he constantly incorporated that nickname into his speech. Eventually, Patty changed the pub's name to TIS. Brag never left, and when Paddy sold up, he made Brag an offer he couldn't turn down. When Brag retired in 1990, he paid it forward to a longtime employee, Jorge Martinez."

"So when did your relationship change?"

"It grew after Ruth died. Before long, we were in love. It startled me, because I never expected to fall for an older man. We were twenty-five years apart. At first, Brag seemed to feel like he was cheating on Ruth. Nevertheless, I slept over frequently. Then one evening, I noticed Brag had taken out Ruth's picture from where he'd hidden it in a bedside table. I'd found it earlier, gleaning that he'd put it away because he didn't want Ruth to see what we were up to. As a result, I knew Brag was finally at ease with us, and I moved in the next day."

"That's so adorable," Susan chuckled.

CHAPTER THREE

Thursday, July 12, 2012

Traffic was backed up as Joe drove home from work, and he let his thoughts drift. Laura frequently came to mind throughout his day, and his ruminations were pleasant as he recalled how they'd bought a two-story, three-bedroom house on Russian Hill.

But before long he became pensive, recalling her death in 2006. She was forty-two then, and they'd been married twenty-one years. Laura, a teacher, was stopped at a traffic light on her way home from a PTA meeting when an out-of-control eighteen-wheeler rear-ended her at the bottom of a steep hill. The police estimated the truck was traveling at over seventy miles an hour, but the trucker suffered only minor injuries. He called for help, but Laura died without regaining consciousness. Joe had tried to fathom how it could have happened, but in the end he'd had to accept that the other driver had simply dozed off at the wheel.

Traffic remained heavy, and his thoughts wandered to his relationship with Gabi. Joe had been on the force for twenty-nine years and Gabi about seventeen. They'd been partners in the Homicide Division for many years. Joe was a big-picture guy, and Gabi was detail oriented. She'd moved up quickly and earned the rank of detective sergeant. He'd repeatedly encouraged her to take the lieutenant's examination, but once, at drinks after work, Gabi had finally been honest with him, saying she would rather remain his number-two, working behind the scenes. Joe had been delighted and never brought it up again. When the SCU was formed ten years ago, Joe had been recruited as a team leader and brought Gabi along as his partner.

Finally, his thoughts meandered to this afternoon's update with their captain, Ben Weber, about the warehouse murders. Joe and Gabi worked well with their boss, even though it would be hard to find three people who were less alike: the tactician, the strategist, and the politician. It was no secret that the captain hadn't earned his position based on his record as a detective. But it was important to let him feel that he contributed, and Joe didn't mind as long as the man didn't interfere with the real investigation. Overall, he'd been a satisfactory boss. He always had their backs, could acquire the resources they sought, and ran interference for them with HQ and the mayor.

This afternoon's briefing had gone well. Gabi had taken the lead because of her eidetic memory, command of details, and ability to delve into the weeds.

"Captain, I've prepared a file memo that details our investigation," she began. "The forensic lab's toxicology report disclosed no traces of narcotics, alcohol, or date-rape-type drugs. There were no useful fingerprints or other evidence, such as fibers, hair, and so on. The CSU investigators agreed with our conclusion that at least two people were needed to effectuate the murders. We checked our local and national databases for similar MOs. We recovered passwords for all their digital devices and reviewed their mobile phone records (no landline), credit and debit card transactions, banking accounts, text messages, emails, social media, and the like. We conducted in-person interviews with the parents of the sisters, their landlords, and the warehouse's owner. And we followed up with all viable tips received on the tip line. We obtained a list of the victims' instructors and advisers for the prior school year. The university reported no disciplinary problems with any of them. Criminal background checks are in process, but nothing out of the ordinary has turned up yet. Frankly, we haven't made the progress we had hoped for."

The captain's first contribution was to nod and observe, "After all, it has been one and a half months."

CHAPTER FOUR

Saturday, August 18, 2012

Susan and Linda had settled into a routine. Linda managed the gallery while Susan handled household activities, which gave Susan time to work through Brag's collection of photographs. She had booted his PC and found the database he'd built for them. She'd quickly determined that cataloging this information had probably taken Brag several years and most likely accounted for how he'd spent his time after Ruth died.

This afternoon, Linda was working at home to lay out an exhibit of photographs taken by schoolchildren. It was scheduled to open after Labor Day, and Derrick had offered to work the gallery this weekend for her. Linda had hired Derrick as a part-timer when he was still in high school, and he'd turned out to be honest, excellent with people, and a quick learner. Several years ago, to ensure Derrick stayed with her after graduation, Linda had made him a full-timer and later given him ten percent of the business.

While Linda was working, Susan came down from Brag's office. "It's a shame we can't display his work. I've been looking through the photos, and they're tremendous. It occurs to me Brag wanted people to see them. Why else would he organize and catalog them?"

"I agree. The last pictures he took were at the wharf on Wednesday, May twenty-third. He intended to put together an essay about life there, featuring tourists and locals going through their daily routines. I have his film in the kitchen, and after it's developed, we could choose several prints to display with the students' exhibition. The photo shop can make enlargements, and I have all the mats and frames necessary to assemble them. What do you think?"

"Let's do it. It'll be an appropriate tribute, since he loved to work with the kids."

Linda retrieved the film, and they took a trip to drop it off at the shop. When they returned home, Susan began making a chef's salad for dinner. While setting the table, Linda asked, "Do you have any plans about how long you're going to stay? I'll hate to see you go, but once you have your court papers, you can do everything else with Brag's lawyer by fax or email. And you don't need to go through his personal effects now. It can be done anytime. I'll leave them in his office for whenever you're ready. Plus it will guarantee you'll visit."

"I'm unresolved. I'm in no hurry to return home, since there's nothing there for me but bad memories. And I'm not ready to be alone yet either. I don't mean to impose, but could I stay on longer?" Susan sniffled.

Linda hugged her. "Of course you can stay. Do you want to talk, or do you just need a hug?"

"Both."

"It's all right. You don't have to keep it in. I'll finish dinner—sit here."

They ate their salads silently. Susan knew she was repressing a lot of pent-up emotion. *I can't hold it in much longer.* Finally, Susan put down her fork and began speaking her mind.

"At first, I felt terrible about being the other woman. But as James told me about his wife, I came to believe he was married in name only. It doesn't speak well for my morals, yet I thought I could live with it. James was terribly controlling, and I did anything he liked. He was depraved, and I'd be embarrassed to tell you the humiliating things I did. The few people who knew about James and me thought he'd eventually leave his wife; I know I did. I wanted us to be together openly, not sneaking around. I thought he loved me and wanted the same thing. Now I'm convinced their marriage wasn't a sham after all. He deceived and manipulated me, and James never meant to leave his wife. I can't believe I was so gullible. At first, I was hurt, but now I'm mad as hell!"

***

It was August 31, but since Joe and Gabi had met with the captain, there had been no breaks in the case. Everyone kept picking away without progress. The SCU team continued to follow up on the university's list with criminal background checks. Undergraduate classes had started on August 29, but according to the university, the detectives couldn't begin their interviews until Wednesday, September 12. Gabi would be meeting with the administration to schedule one-on-ones with the faculty, advisers, and students.

Joe settled in for another unproductive day, but when the morning's mail arrived, there was a letter for him with no return address. He handled it carefully, made a copy, and took it to the forensics lab. When he returned to his office, he waved Gabi in to review it with him.

Joe:

Excellent job identifying the girls. I knew you'd eventually discover the IDs hidden among the equipment. Did you find the small scar on Carol's right buttock? Stick with it!

Vlad

Vlad's references to the hidden IDs and Carol's scar authenticated the letter; only the police knew those details.

35

By the end of the day, the lab had turned everything around except the DNA analysis. There weren't any usable prints or other evidence on the 8½-by-11 paper or the envelope. The lab reported that the letter and address label had been printed by computer on standard stock sold at big-box and stationery stores. Captain Weber had already left, so Joe emailed him a PDF scan.

As they were leaving that evening to start the Labor Day weekend, Joe noticed that Gabi seemed distracted. When he mentioned it, she replied, "It's nothing. This case is upsetting me; that's all."

That didn't ring true, because one of Gabi's strengths was her ability to avoid personalizing cases, but Joe let it pass. He spent the long weekend sleeping, walking, reading, and watching baseball and returned to work Tuesday morning recharged. Gabi was upbeat as well. "I got it! It came to me when I was changing for bed last night. I nearly called you, but then I thought it was too late."

"What . . . ?"

"I'd filed it under *Dracula*, not *Vlad*. That's why I couldn't remember it. That was what was bothering me on Friday."

Joe knew what Gabi was talking about. She remembered things, even after many years, with great precision. She simply needed to see something briefly and could recall it as accurately as if she were viewing a photograph. Her recollection was usually instantaneous, although Gabi occasionally had short-term lapses—scarcely a few seconds. Friday had been a major brain fart.

"Okay," Gabi continued. "I knew *Vlad* rang a bell, but I couldn't recall what. I was frustrated until I remembered a PBS show from years ago about Dracula that contained a segment on Vlad. At the time, I was intrigued. So I researched him, but I'd filed what I discovered under Dracula, the main character of Bram Stoker's novel. Stoker based his character on an amalgam of historical and legendary figures, of whom Vlad Dracula was a main component. He was born in the mid-fifteenth century in modern-day Romania and was the Prince of Wallachia. Vlad was a cruel tyrant, and his sobriquet became Vlad the Impaler because of his favorite way of dispensing with his enemies. For centuries impaling was a form of execution, and the victims usually died within two to five days. Ironically, it had been developed as a less cruel method than crucifixion."

"So it's sort of a copycat murder, and the time of death fits," Joe commented. "Also, I think Vlad's letter implies he knew at least one of the victims. It's time to talk to Dr. Sandler. I'd like to have a profile before we do the interviews at the university."

***

Dr. Ellen Sandler, a PhD from Stanford, had joined the FBI's Behavioral Analysis Unit shortly after it was founded. She'd been a lead profiler for twenty-five years. After retiring in 2000, Ellen joined the SFPD. Joe had been skeptical of profiling until he worked with her. He'd quickly learned that if you gave her enough information, she delivered better profiles than the generic ones routinely provided.

"Sandler," the profiler answered when Joe called.

"Ellen, it's Joe Cancio with Gabi. You're on speaker."

"Hi, I've been waiting for your call on the warehouse murders."

"I think we've developed a partial profile of one of our unsubs, the leader. I hope it's enough for you to work your magic on."

"I'm in all day."

"Gabi will stop down later."

"Thanks. Let's see what we can do. See you then, Gabi."

Immediately after Joe hung up, his phone rang. " 'Morning, Captain. I'm with Gabi. We're brainstorming the case."

"Glad I found you together. I read your email. Arrogant son of a bitch, isn't he? I've been thinking, perhaps we ought to bring Dr. Sandler in now. We don't want to leave any avenue unexplored. How do you feel?"

"Agreed. We're already on it."

***

On Wednesday afternoon, September 5, Dr. Sandler left Gabi a voice mail saying she had a preliminary profile of the leader finished. They met the following morning. "I'm convinced your unsub is a high-functioning sociopath. I know Joe's aversion to generalities, but he's probably a thirty-plus white male. He's well educated with an extremely high IQ and may be married to an attractive, successful woman. Children are optional. All of this is part of his camouflage.

"High-functioning sociopaths have hardly any conscience but are charming and clever. Their actions seem genuine and sincere, but gradually, lies and deceptions reveal their sociopathic nature. A high IQ helps them plan, manipulate, and exploit others. Common characteristics are lack of empathy, narcissism, sexual deviance, affairs, entitlement, quick tempers, lying, and criminal behavior. There are additional ones, but focus on these. Frequently, they are victims of child abuse. Your unsub must've been under extreme stress to commit such brutal murders. I think they're revenge, but probably not against your victims specifically. Do you have any questions before I go on?"

"Why do you think he might have an attractive, successful wife? Wouldn't that be unnecessary competition for him?"

"Excellent question. I think his ego requires constant support. A trophy wife would appeal to him and reinforce his sense of entitlement. Initially, her success would be an added benefit, increasing others' envy of him. But eventually, it would become a threat and stressor. His crime—besides being sadistic—has a clear undertone of sexual cruelty. If they've been together a long time, he will have used his skills to make her into a sex slave. His wife's environment is intolerable, a weird world she doesn't understand and hates. But if she's a good girl, she thinks everything will get better. That's the only way she can see to improve her situation."

"Sounds like torture."

"It is. I've been thinking about his MO, and notwithstanding your local and national searches, I don't think these are his first kills. Here's why.

"Before I left the BAU, I'd been working on advanced theories in profiling. At a conference in Montreal, I met a Frenchwoman, Bridgette Dubois, who worked for the Police Nationale, which is France's civilian arm of law enforcement. Although she was an *inspecteur*, Bridgette was also functioning like a profiler. She encouraged me because she'd already been playing around with similar concepts. Specifically, she thought there was a successful, professional killer who'd been operating in Europe for years. Bridgette believed the killer escaped detection because he never used the same MO twice. We shared a belief that her unsub's intelligence was probably off the charts. Her conclusions were like mine: if obvious characteristics such as weapon, sex, age, type of victim, and so forth don't lead anywhere, then subconscious motivations and characteristics ought to be used. But determining these motives is difficult. We both thought traditional analysis was inflexible, tending to merely look at the obvious. Ergo, your unsub and leader is covering his tracks well, using multiple modi operandi. If you don't turn up routine motives, you'll need to dive deeper.

"You've already recognized that using Vlad as a nom de plume can help identify your unsub. The Vlad analysis you've done is top-shelf and focuses on his cruelty. However, don't overlook that his murders shock and horrify, demonstrating that he's unaccountable to society. This attitude suggests a second avenue—namely, the relationship between Fredrich Nietzsche's concept of the Übermensch, or superman, and Fyodor Dostoevsky's protagonist, Raskolnikov, in his novel *Crime and Punishment*. I call it the Raskolnikov syndrome. These unsubs know they're extraordinary and above the rules that govern us. Their crimes are designed to demonstrate that superiority. They have little or no guilt or remorse. I think you have two-character assimilations going on—Vlad-Dracula and Nietzsche-Raskolnikov. Thus, it isn't a leap to concentrate on the university's faculty. Here're a few additional thoughts. Look at a literature professor first because of Stoker, Dostoevsky, and Nietzsche. Next, to history, because of Vlad the Impaler—not exactly a household name. If he's in your group of interviewees, your unsub can't wait to match wits. Look for stressors; they're the same as in the normal population: death, health issues, bankruptcy, unfaithfulness, loss of job, and so on. Stress him further by putting these interrogations last. And don't underestimate him—be wary. He's dangerous."

Gabi and Joe met later and reviewed the analysis. Joe decided that while their other detectives spoke with the students, they would question the faculty and advisers. Their emphasis would be on the English and history professors, scheduling them last in the day. Gabi suggested dragging their feet so that those interviews spilled over into Monday the seventeenth. "It'll give them something to ruminate about all weekend."

***

Earlier in the week, Linda and Susan had picked up the contact sheets and a DVD from the photo shop. Over the weekend beginning September 14, they intended to choose the prints they wished to have enlarged. So after breakfast on Saturday, when Linda left for a manicure, Susan stayed behind and began reviewing them.

On May 23, Brag had captured a day in the wharf's life, and in his notebook he'd recorded data about each exposure. As a result, it was easy to trace his movements and identify each photo. There were shots of the inner harbor's docks; the Golden Gate Bridge; the bay; street people, including a wheelchair-bound vet holding a sign reading FAMILY KIDNAPPED BY NINJAS NEED $$ FOR KARATE LESSONS; the homeless; and the Jefferson Street area, where a nautical shop boasted a statue of an old salt in front. The crowd scenes on Jefferson attracted Susan's attention. They were the most ordinary of all but nonetheless kept reaching out to her.

After a while, Susan took a break and looked through today's *Examiner*. As she perused the paper, it dawned on her what'd caught her eye in those scenes. She went to the stack of papers awaiting recycling and retrieved one that contained what she sought. Then Susan took everything up to Brag's office, and when Linda returned, she called down, "Come up. You have to see this."

Linda came in, and Susan showed her the paper and the photo on the computer. "Oh my gosh."

"That's what was intriguing me in the Jefferson Street pics."

Even though it was late Saturday afternoon, they called the police's tip line. Brag had photographed the twins just before noon on the day they disappeared.

***

Gabi and Joe had finished all the interviews late Friday afternoon except those with the history and literature professors, which had been postponed until Monday. Then on Sunday morning, Joe received a call from their

team's investigator, who'd covered the tip line on Saturday, reporting that one call seemed promising. Joe took down the callers' details and made an appointment for Monday afternoon. He knew where they lived on Russian Hill because it wasn't far from his house.

On Monday morning, September 17, Gabi debriefed the detectives, who had questioned the students last week. While she did that, Joe tackled his first appointment—John J. Howell, PhD, a history professor. He'd lectured at the university for over forty years, and the administration reported there'd never been a whiff of trouble with or about him. Howell's class roster for his freshman world history survey course had included the twins, whom he knew casually. He couldn't provide any additional information and showed no interest in the crime beyond what would be expected. Dr. Howell had been married fifty-plus years to the same woman and had two children and four grandchildren. He was soft-spoken, considerate, and an attentive listener. Moreover, the professor was over seventy, walked with a cane, and lacked the physical strength and agility to carry out a gruesome crime. Joe didn't spend a lot of time with him.

Afterward, Joe called Gabi to hear about her debriefings. He knew that Denis Rodolphe, DPhil, the English professor, was waiting for him. It wouldn't hurt to delay the inquiry longer.

Gabi revealed that she'd discovered an inconsistency about him. Whereas her review of the English professor's background with the faculty dean had turned up nothing, a graduate student had provided alarming information about Rodolphe. This student had occasionally dated one of the twins, which was why he was being questioned. Apparently, there'd been a scandal during the fall of 2011. Rumors alleged that Rodolphe had had an extramarital affair with a freshman woman who was underage. The scuttlebutt was that Rodolphe had told this woman a divorce was imminent. It blew up after Rodolphe's lover telephoned his wife, who later confronted the girl on campus, causing an embarrassing rumpus. The young woman had been so distraught that she left school, and her father threatened statutory rape charges. Somehow the school smoothed everything over, and Rodolphe wasn't officially brought before the administration's disciplinary committee. The university hadn't informed the police either.

"Wow! I'll cover that this morning. Explaining this should amp up his stress level. Anything else before I talk to him?" Joe asked.

"No, that's about it."

"I think this interview will go longer than I anticipated. Afterward, I'll grab a sandwich, then head over to Russian Hill to speak with the tipsters. See you tomorrow."

Joe reviewed what Gabi had found out about Rodolphe from their background checks and the faculty dean. Rodolphe's father's family had emigrated from France to New Orleans during the mid-eighteenth century. By the mid-nineteenth century, they'd amassed a fortune in shipping and stevedoring. They were clever enough to liquidate their assets prior to the Civil War, park them overseas, then repatriate them before the postwar railroad boom. Their wealth became incalculable and remained so. Rodolphe's mother was from an old Virginia family, albeit now on hard times.

Both parents were purported to be philanthropists and high-level career diplomats, serving in France and subsequently Russia. Rodolphe had been born in Paris. He was schooled there until his parents were transferred to Moscow, where he graduated from high school. By the time he went to college, he'd achieved a native proficiency in both languages. Rodolphe graduated from Princeton with honors in their creative writing program. Following that, he studied at Oxford University, obtaining both Master and Doctor of Literature degrees in 1995. Then Dr. Rodolphe lectured at the Sorbonne for three years. He returned to the States, teaching at the Lawrenceville School near Princeton, New Jersey, until 2001.

Rodolphe had been hired by the University of San Francisco ten years ago to develop a world-class creative writing and comparative literature program. Although his literary output had been limited to criticism—especially of Russian novelists—he'd presented a businesslike model that appealed to the hiring committee. Additionally, he had the charisma necessary to attract students, faculty, and visiting authors. According to the faculty dean, Rodolphe's IQ was 200, and there hadn't been any formal proceedings before the university's disciplinary committee. Rodolphe was in his early forties and was married to a successful mystery novelist, Cameron Sinclair, who was ten years his junior. There were no children.

Joe was an excellent interrogator. In this case, he meant to ask open-ended questions and encourage Rodolphe to do the talking, letting him feel comfortable and in control. The more the man talked, the more likely he would be to make a mistake. Joe would be perfectly happy if Rodolphe thought he were merely a flat-footed cop. Then Joe would broach the rape allegation to see how he reacted.

He knocked on the professor's open door. The office was tidy, with shelves of books written in English, French, and Russian, and Rodolphe was sitting at his computer, correcting papers. "Doctor, it's Detective Lieutenant Cancio, SFPD."

"Come on in, Detective. I've been expecting you."

"As I'm sure you're aware, we're investigating the murders of two university students, Carol and Carla Rowe. They occurred on or about the Memorial Day weekend. We've been talking to students or faculty who knew them. We understand you did."

"That's not accurate. Carol enrolled in my comparative literature class. Obviously, I knew her, but I had scarcely a nodding acquaintance with her sister, Carla."

"May I ask what your relationship was with Carol?"

"Nothing beyond what you'd expect with an excellent student. She consulted me on her second semester paper. It was going to account for a lot of her final grade."

"How many consultations did you have? And where?"

"Maybe three or four times, here in my office."

"Did you leave the door open?"

"Of course."

Smart. Acting oblivious to the implication in the question, Joe thought, and continued, "How did Carol do on her paper?"

"I gave her an A. She wrote about how society suppressed or crushed women who dared to defy social norms, especially sexual mores. She analyzed several nineteenth- and early-twentieth-century novels. Carol chose *Madame Bovary, Anna Karenina, The House of Mirth,* and *Rebecca.* At first, I wasn't convinced about *Rebecca,* but she made her case. I don't know if you're familiar with them?"

All going according to plan. Rodolphe's bloviating, Joe thought to himself, and carried on. "I'm confused about one thing. Normally department heads like yourself don't teach freshmen-level courses."

"That's easy," Rodolphe said, warming to the question. "When I was hired, I was given a mandate to develop a first-rate program. I sought to ensure they had a firm background and a high-quality experience."

48

Joe reviewed Rodolphe's antecedents with him, and there were no irregularities.

"One thing I'm curious about is that your writings are limited to criticism, whereas your background would suggest you've been well steeped in creative writing. It strikes me as odd that it's your wife who has the successful career writing fiction. When we did our background checks, I recognized her name because I've read several of her mysteries. I think they're terrific. It must chafe at you."

"Not in the least, Detective," Rodolphe responded, perhaps a bit peevishly. "My wife is immensely talented, with a real penchant for what she does. Suffice it to say we both respect each other's fortes and enjoy sharing common literary interests."

Well rehearsed, Joe observed. *He's probably asked that more often than he would like.*

"So I've chosen to limit my writing to criticism, as you put it," Rodolphe continued. "This—by the way—is consistent with our university's policies. They don't subscribe to the publish-or-perish philosophy adopted by many schools. I consider myself a manager tasked with advancing the goals of our school, not a beneficiary of patronage while I pursue a writing career."

Utter bullshit. "I notice many of your books are about Russian literature and are in Russian. I think one of my favorite authors is Dostoevsky—in English, of course."

"As you know, Lieutenant, I'm fluent. It's a shame you can't read him in the original text. In fact, I'm working on a project about Raskolnikov right now . . . You know Raskolnikov?" he asked, and Joe nodded yes. "I call it the Raskolnikov Conundrum. The short version of it is that Raskolnikov fancies himself a superman; think Nietzsche's Übermensch. He's above all moral law, since he's superior, and commits

49

murder to prove his thesis. But over time he succumbs to guilt and remorse, hence the book's title, *Crime and Punishment*. Ultimately, Raskolnikov seeks redemption and salvation through Sonja. Now here's what I'm intrigued with:

"What if Dostoevsky believed Raskolnikov's original thesis? It would support an argument that evil lives and walks the earth.

"What if friends or editors suggested Dostoevsky change the book because the public wasn't ready for it?

"What if Dostoevsky didn't have the balls to stick to his guns?

"It's a different world today. You certainly know that. You work with serial killers and see horrible crimes all the time. Maybe now we're ready for the truth. That's what I'm investigating through as many original source documents as I can. I'm not certain where it's going yet, but I don't think you'd try to dissuade me from the notion that evil exists."

Blah, blah, blah. "Interesting," Joe observed.

"I'd be glad to send you a copy when it's finished."

"I'd appreciate it. There's another thing I need to ask you about, though. Our investigation has developed contradictory information that I would like you to clarify. When we spoke with the faculty dean regarding your record, he said there weren't any problems." Joe went on to describe what he'd learned from Gabi. "Is that correct?" *Let's see how you handle this.*

Dr. Rodolphe appeared to be gathering his thoughts. Finally, he said, "That's correct—there was a rumor. But I never had such an affair. Because of her outstanding high school record, Melisa Williams was invited to take my graduate-level creative writing class. I had no idea about her age. It was irrelevant. Looking back on it, I realize she had a terrible crush on me. I didn't think much of it but was nevertheless flattered that an eye-catching young lady found an *alte kaker* like me attractive. I've concluded Melisa was convinced that if my wife were out of the way, we might hook up. Then she called Cameron with a preposterous story of an affair. You must've heard how Cameron reacted—obnoxiously, to say the least. Melisa also reported it to the university and told her father." Then Rodolphe described what Gabi had already recounted to Joe about the outcome. "It was a nightmare for me."

He handled it deftly. But there's no empathy for what Melisa or Cameron went through. Perhaps Rodolphe gave away more than he intended to about his attitude vis-à-vis women. I don't have a positive feeling about this guy, Joe thought, and continued, "Lastly, do you have an alibi for the Wednesday before Memorial Day through the following weekend?" *That ought to stress him out.*

"You have to be kidding."

"I assure you I'm not."

"That was over three months ago . . . let's see. We didn't go away that weekend. We went to Dr. Howell's for a barbecue Monday afternoon . . . probably about three. Cameron was home most of the time, working on her new book. During the period you're asking about, I ran lots of errands, such as gas, food shopping, beer for the barbecue, those sorts of things. I usually put everything on a credit card, so you can probably track my movements throughout. Other than that, I don't know what to tell you."

Joe made a big production of taking notes on Rodolphe's alibi. "Thank you, Professor. That about covers it for today."

Rodolphe had unquestionably noticed the suggestion that there might be further interrogations, but he handled it gracefully. "Glad to help, Detective. If you need anything else, you know where I am."

***

After Joe wrapped up the interview, he called Gabi. They agreed to meet for breakfast the next morning at Sears on Powell Street. Then Joe grabbed a quick lunch and headed to Russian Hill to see Susan Johnson and Linda Sanchez.

He arrived about three o'clock, and they both met him at the door. On the way upstairs, Susan explained why she'd called. "As I said to your officer on Saturday, we've discovered a few of my uncle's photographs that include the victims. They were taken around the wharf on May twenty-third." She went on to describe where, when, why, and the delay caused by Brag O'Brien's death. Joe offered his condolences.

When he saw the pictures, there was no doubt what Linda and Susan had uncovered, although Joe didn't know how he could use the prints yet. The photos unquestionably pinpointed where the twins had been that morning and at what time, and Susan had prepared a DVD, five-by-seven prints of all the photos, and a scan of the relevant notebook pages. As Joe left, he said, "If I need the original negatives, I'll let you know."

Driving home, he mused that Susan was bright and articulate, not to mention one of the finest-looking women he'd met in a while.

After supper, Joe reviewed the prints again. Something was bothering him, but he couldn't put his finger on it. He went back to the photos a few times with no luck. *Maybe Gabi will see something tomorrow.*

When Joe arrived at Sears the next morning, Gabi was already there. They ordered breakfast, and Gabi said, "Tell me; I can't wait to hear about your interview with Rodolphe."

Joe gave her the big picture and shook his head. "You know my hunches. They're rarely wrong. Twenty-plus years of experience tells me that Rodolphe's our guy. He didn't give anything up, but he's dirty as hell. It's a feeling based on his attitudes. Rodolphe is self-centered and insensitive, possibly a misogynist. Also, I think he has the hubris to believe he could pull off a murder to validate his Nietzsche/Dostoevsky research. I don't know how we're going to round him up yet. We don't have enough evidence for search warrants, but there are several things I'd like you to do.

"First of all, search the national and local law enforcement databases again, using his name this time. Make certain to include New Jersey and the Princeton area. Also talk to Princeton University and the Lawrenceville School.

"Next, call Rodolphe for the information on those credit cards he used around Memorial Day. Say we're trying to eliminate him as a person of interest. Get an email from him with permission.

"Then let's start a low-key investigation into the statutory rape allegation, because he's still within the statute of limitations. We'll try to nail his ass on that charge. I've already heard his side of the story, so we won't contact him again—keep him in the dark.

"And finally, question his wife and Melisa Williams. It'll be a surprise and ought to be another stressor when he finds out."

"Makes sense," Gabi said. "What did you find out from the women who called in the tip?"

"They provided photographs of the wharf area on May twenty-third. I'll fill you in on how this all came about later. I brought the enlargements along. I'd like you to look at them and give me your thoughts. You'll see several in which the twins appear. Here's a copy of the photographer's notebook also. It gives places, times, and so on about each photo."

Gabi studied the pictures for a while, comparing the notebook to the photos. "You're bothered by something. Nothing to do with the girls, though. Am I right?"

"Yes."

"It's the van . . . It's in four shots. I don't know what it means, if anything."

"Dammit, Gabi, that's it. I knew something was there, but I didn't tell you because I didn't want to influence your thoughts." Joe thumbed through the photos several times. "I'm sure it's a Ford Econoline 150—probably ten or twelve years old. I used to have one like it. I'll work on the van while you're dealing with the searches, credit cards, and interrogations. Let's meet with Dr. Sandler ASAP."

"Fine," Gabi responded, but she was curious. *Joe rarely gets into the weeds. What's with the van? That's Gabi work.*

***

They were able to see Dr. Sandler the next morning and reviewed their findings with her. "Well," Ellen started, "I think you've checked a lot of boxes on our sociopath's demographic scorecard. You've uncovered classic character traits. I think Rodolphe is your unsub also. We should probably call him a person of interest now. I agree with you that pursuing any legal action would be premature. All you have is a plethora of quasi-circumstantial evidence.

"So where are we? If he's our guy, repressed anger stokes his hatred for women. The murders were triggered as a result of pressure caused by numerous small stressors or a major traumatic event. Two such

CHAPTER FIVE

Thursday, September 20, 2012

Joe reviewed the enlargements when he returned to the office. One was clear enough for him to read the last two numbers of a California plate. Gabi searched the Division of Motor Vehicles' online license plate database for Ford Econoline 150 vans with tags having those partial numbers. Unfortunately, nothing surfaced. Next, she searched for vans stolen over the last several years. There were twenty-five, and Gabi delegated those to her and Joe's investigators for follow-up. If necessary, the final step would be to canvass Bay Area used-car dealers, junkyards, auto salvagers, and similar businesses.

Gabi stopped by Joe's office, reporting on the van search and interviews. "I spoke to the university's admissions office, and they provided Melisa Williams's phone number and home address in Palo Alto," she said. "I left a message, and I'll tackle Cameron Sinclair next."

The Rodolphe-Sinclair residence was in the wealthy Pacific Heights area. It no doubt appealed to Rodolphe's old-money, elite, and entitled pedigree, and spoke volumes about their wealth. Gabi called a friend at the phone company, who—on the sly—provided Cameron Sinclair's mobile number.

Ms. Sinclair seemed confused by the call. Gabi explained that new evidence had come up concerning the allegations Melisa Williams had made a year ago against her husband, and as a result, the police had opened an inquiry. Sinclair said she couldn't help and suggested Gabi contact her husband. She was surprised to learn that Gabi's partner had already spoken with him. "Well, I can't add anything else. You ought to talk with the Williams girl."

"I've already reached out to her," Gabi said. It was clear that Cameron Sinclair didn't want anything to do with this investigation. "Look, Ms. Sinclair, you aren't in any trouble. You're not a person of interest. You're simply a material witness." Then Gabi pressed, changing her tenor. "I can obtain a subpoena and compel you to come to HQ for a statement."

"May I bring a lawyer?"

"Of course," Gabi replied, but didn't say anything else.

The silence was so long that Gabi thought they'd been disconnected until Sinclair finally said, "Fine, but I have conditions."

"What are they?"

"I won't do it at home. I can't take the chance my husband will come in. His hours at the university are flexible. Plus, I can't risk a nosy neighbor. Next, I won't do it at HQ. I'm not a criminal. I insist on a neutral public place. A coffee shop or the like—something you choose. But don't make it where my husband might stumble upon us. You have no idea how upset Denis would be if he knew I'm doing this. But if it'll help put this behind us, I will. Lastly, and please don't take offense—if you're not the lead detective, I'd like the lead to question me. Would you tell me who it is?"

Gabi was suspicious of what was behind her request. She'd Googled Ms. Sinclair earlier and discovered she was a knockout. *Sinclair's angling for a man*, Gabi reckoned, but she answered, "It's Detective Lieutenant Joe Cancio."

"I'm doing a book-signing, but will be available after October 4, and won't need a lawyer."

Joe chose to call Cameron right away; there was no point in playing games, and they agreed to meet on Friday, October 5. Joe suggested the lobby of the Kensington Park Hotel because it was out-of-the-way. Sinclair knew it and agreed.

Later, Gabi told Joe that it had gone easier with Melisa. She was coming to HQ on Tuesday, the twenty-fifth, since she didn't want to do it at home with her father around.

Before Joe left for the day, he made a couple of phone calls. First, he updated the captain. Then he called Linda Sanchez, apologizing for not answering her question about displaying the photo that included the girls. "I have no objection. The picture you chose only shows them from behind. And the rear end of the van has been cropped from the finished print." They chatted for a few minutes, and Linda invited him to Saturday's opening.

***

Friday was a paperwork day. Gabi reported that nothing had shown up with the law enforcement searches she'd run under Rodolphe's name. "I talked to Princeton—nada. Then at the Lawrenceville school, I spoke with a woman in personnel. She remembered Rodolphe because he was very popular, no problems. But something struck me as odd. The woman recollected that Rodolphe's mother had phoned the head of school, inquiring about a position for her son. His parents were big donors, and it seemed like she was using their influence."

"Huh. Doesn't seem like Rodolphe would need assistance landing a job with his résumé."

"No, but it gets curiouser. The only open spot was for a French instructor. Why would he change disciplines, and why was he there?"

"I don't know. Let's file it away for the time being."

Saturday arrived, and Joe realized he was ambivalent about attending the gallery's opening. He wished to see Susan, but there was no work justification for him attending. He was afraid she might think it odd. By now, Joe had become convinced that whatever he'd thought was developing was purely a fantasy. After all, they had met and seen each other just twice. Their hand-holding was probably nothing but her empathy for the pain he'd shared with her. Nevertheless, Joe meant to play it out.

He arrived midafternoon. The gallery was crowded, and the guests seemed to be enjoying the show. Then Linda saw him and waved. She was busy being the perfect hostess—passing champagne and so forth. It looked like Derrick was working his tail off as well.

After an hour or so, without Susan appearing, Joe prepared to leave. He found Linda and made his excuses.

"Oh, don't go now!" she said. "Susan will be disappointed, because she's on her way. I called and told her you were here. Please stay." When Linda saw Joe's uncertainty, she laughed. "You don't have a clue, do you? Well, I'm not convinced Susan does either." But then she added, "She had a terrible time with that good-for-nothing James. He exploited her badly; don't take advantage!"

Linda might've had too much champagne, since she seemed ill at ease with her spontaneity, but it showed she cared. Joe had already sensed that he needed to tread lightly with Susan. If his inklings were correct, Susan had been dominated, manipulated, and abused, and that was familiar territory for him. But one thing Joe had learned being a detective was patience. It would all come out when Susan was ready—not before.

"I would never hurt her. But I'm confused. Do you think Susan likes me . . . that way?"

"Yes."

Susan arrived soon after this exchange. "I'm glad you came," she said. "I asked Linda to call if you did." Soon the two of them were chatting comfortably, and before Joe knew it, it was five.

"How about an early dinner? We could walk over to Scoma's."

Susan nodded yes. "I haven't been there."

When they left the gallery, Susan took his hand again. Joe didn't think about it this time; he simply went with it.

"It's a San Francisco landmark," he said. "There're better restaurants, but old-timers swear by it."

Scoma's wasn't crowded, so they were out in less than an hour. Joe was thinking about what they could do when Susan preempted him.

"Would you like to come back to the house? Linda probably won't be home until ten o'clock."

After arriving, they sat in the den, and Susan brought bottled water. Even though this turn of events was unexpected, Joe thought it felt natural. Nonetheless, he chose caution because of Linda's admonition. They continued to sit quietly for a while until Joe finally mustered his courage.

"I'm nervous."

"Me too," Susan admitted.

"It's so soon . . . It's been a while, though."

Susan took his hand and started upstairs. "For me too," she said, then she laughed. "Let's practice a few times until we get it right."

Before they knew it, Linda was calling from two floors below. "Susan, I'm home."

"We're up here."

"We're . . . ?"

"Joe's here."

It wasn't long before Linda reached the third-floor landing. "Congratulations! Cover up. I'm coming in." She opened the door and came over and sat on the edge of the bed. "Have you been up here all evening?" Susan nodded, and Linda continued, "Come down, and we'll toast. But I'm going to make tea because I'm tired of champagne."

"Give us a little more time," Susan pleaded.

As Linda left, she called over her shoulder, "Half an hour."

"You're shameless," Joe chuckled.

"And you're complaining why?"

Later, they sipped tea. Linda was happy with how the exhibit had gone. The guests had enjoyed the children's photography. A few regulars had offered to purchase several of Brag's photos for surprisingly generous amounts. But Linda wasn't convinced she wanted to sell them; that hadn't been what Brag was about.

They continued chatting with Joe until he finally said, "It's getting late, so I'll head home."

Walking to the door, Susan said, "Linda is going to work the gallery tomorrow. Why don't you come for brunch around one? We can do something in the afternoon." Her tone became teasing. "'Sorry if I wore you out."

***

When Melisa arrived on Tuesday at ten o'clock, Gabi asked if she could record their interview, and Melisa agreed.

"I know you want to talk about my affair with Dr. Rodolphe, but I thought this was all behind me. It was a difficult time, because nobody believed me."

"This isn't idle curiosity," Gabi said. "New information has surfaced that supports your claim. No reports were filed with either the school or the SFPD. So we need to talk."

"That's odd. I filled out a detailed one for the school's disciplinary committee. I'm aware they didn't notify SFPD, because they believed Rodolphe and took the position there was nothing to report."

"That may be, but whatever you filed is missing. We learned of your allegation from a graduate student we interrogated in an unrelated case. Would you tell me what happened? My partner spoke to Dr. Rodolphe recently and heard his side."

"It's simple," Melisa said, "I was a seventeen-year-old freshman in the fall of 2010 who fell in love with a charming older man. Shit, he was old enough to be my father. It happens all the time. But to the best of my belief, Denis didn't know I was underage. It never came up, but if it had, I would've been happy to let him assume I was legal."

"Would you describe your relationship for me?"

67

"You want details?"

"Just what you're comfortable with."

Melisa was unenthusiastic but finally began. "My mom died five years ago. Dad's been great, but I miss her. I would've liked her guidance through this period. During the summer before I went to college, I had my first real boyfriend. But I was naive, and he was just as clueless. We made out a lot and started petting. It was fun, but that was it.

"Then enter Denis Rodolphe. I was enraptured when he spoke to me. One day I made a bullshit excuse to go to his office; I still remember it clearly. We chatted about this and that, then Denis asked, 'Would you like to do something for me?' I would've done anything he wanted, and we didn't even bother to close his door. Soon I was crouched in the leg well of his desk, but before we'd finished, a woman graduate student came in. They talked for a while, and I remember thinking it was funny and was afraid of giggling."

"It didn't bother you that he was married?"

"Denis assured me that his marriage was only one in name. He claimed that he hadn't been able to get it up until I came along."

"Yeah, right!"

"But I was enamored. We had sex all the time. He schooled me, and in the beginning, I was comfortable with what we did. But by the time I called his wife, I didn't like where Denis was pushing me. Our relationship was becoming weirder and weirder."

"How so?"

"Is this necessary?"

"I'm trying to understand how depraved he was, that's all."

"Well, he wanted me to start doing other guys. Guys he chose."

"Have sex with them?"

"Yes. Once Denis got something in his head, he was unyielding. He picked this naive boy in our class. The guy was nice enough but clueless about women, probably a virgin. I had no interest in him, but Denis kept on and on, talking about all the things I could do."

"Did you?"

"Eventually. I'm not proud, because I know I hurt him."

"Do you have any way to prove that you had an affair? The details aren't important. It's the consummation before you were eighteen that's at issue."

"Yes—I have a few nude photos and one other that might be relevant. They're on my phone; you can tell the date from the file name, and I know they were taken before my birthday."

"May I see them?"

"I don't know," Melisa said, vacillating. At length, she scrolled through her photos, then handed the phone to Gabi. There were two frontal shots of Melisa and Denis in a full-length mirror. Another showed Melisa alone, nude from the waist up. The last one was odd—a picture of a rumpled bed with four pair of panties laid out. They were all taken in Rodolphe's master bedroom with distinguishing furnishings and sundry items in the background.

"These could be the proof we need—"

Melisa put up her hand. "Please, you can't use them, at least not the nudes. I won't have my father see them."

Gabi chose not to argue. "Explain the odd one. Maybe we could use that one instead."

"I spent a long weekend at his house. Cameron had been called away to a last-minute book-signing, so we took advantage of it. Denis wouldn't allow me to go outside, but I became uncomfortable when he insisted that I go around the house naked. It was bizarre. Talk about being objectified."

"And the panties . . .?" Gabi probed.

"They were Cameron's. I'm embarrassed because Denis cajoled me into wearing them. Before we left, he returned them to his wife's dresser drawer. It was . . . icky. I'll email you that picture if you'd like."

"Please."

"Here's another gross thing. Before I left, I wanted to change the sheets, but Denis wouldn't hear of it. When I asked about Cameron, he said, 'She'll never notice.'

"I ought to have bailed on him then. Finally, I stopped pursuing my allegations, since I didn't want my father to learn about our debauchery and sodomy. It would've been too much."

"Is there anything we need to know about your phone call and subsequent meeting with Cameron?"

"Denis and I had only seen each other about once a week over the summer. That wasn't what I wanted, so I meant to resolve it and called her in September 2011. When I did, Cameron lost it and started yelling, 'I service him very well, thank you. Keep your fuckin' hands off him. No one believes you anyway—you're obsessed!' and then she hung up. I realize now that I hadn't been thinking clearly. I mean, what was the point? When my father found out, he said, 'She sure as hell ripped you a new one.'"

"What about your confrontation?"

"It was unexpected. We met about ten days later, and I thought she was going to start screaming again. But Cameron simply wished to talk. She apologized, saying she'd been confused. I was also, and we were a sight—both blubbering. We went to an unused office in the student union building. It struck me how much Denis had manipulated her. I didn't think she deserved what he'd done. I said I was sorry that I'd caused so much trouble. We started crying again and ended up hugging. 'Denis has royally screwed us,' Cameron said as we parted."

***

After Melisa left, Gabi wondered about the similarities between the young woman and Cameron. Was Rodolphe's modus operandi preying on vulnerable, beautiful, intelligent women?

- Melisa's vulnerabilities had been her naivety and the fact that she was mourning the loss of her mother. Had she been a diversion, or was Melisa still in play? Had Melisa's defection been an unanticipated temporary setback? Or had she de facto short-circuited the bastard and escaped?

- What was Cameron's vulnerability? Did it have something to do with her sexuality? Moreover, what was Rodolphe's endgame? He'd been working on her since before they were married. Was she destined to be his pièce de résistance?

Gabi also thought about how the two women might be aligned in the future. Did Rodolphe want two subjugations running concurrently, or was he choreographing something more intricate, like a long con? Perhaps even an elaborate ménage à trois?

I'm confused. I wouldn't want to play chess with this son of a bitch.

***

The following day, Gabi reported that Rodolphe's credit card transactions were as expected and updated Joe on Melisa's interview.

"I'm surprised she agreed to be recorded so readily," he said. "Send copies of your recording to Ellen and me. And let's see if we can meet with Dr. Sandler."

Before Gabi left, she said, "I've been wondering if his type of victim might be vulnerable women, and if Rodolphe still has plans for Melisa."

"I agree that it's his type," Joe replied. "But I'm skeptical about Melisa being in his upcoming schemes. Don't overestimate Rodolphe's prowess. Most of the time the simplest explanation is the best one. Odds are it's what it appears to be—that he's finished with her. But let's see what Ellen says."

They were able to see Dr. Sandler before they left that evening. She thought the questioning had gone well. Joe told her Gabi was sending her a copy of the recording.

"Great. I'll brainstorm all this material," she said. "Let's meet Monday afternoon. I hope to be able to give you direction for your interview with Ms. Sinclair. Is that it for now?"

"No," Gabi said, and explained her ideas.

"When Gabi mentioned this to me," Joe interrupted, "I cautioned her about overestimating his chicanery. Now I'm having second thoughts."

"It would be a greater blunder to underestimate his skills," Ellen said. "I would never disregard a hunch of an experienced investigator. This isn't an exact science. It's subjective—more like an art. No two cases are the same. I wouldn't rule anything out with Rodolphe."

On Monday afternoon, they met with Dr. Sandler again. "Here're my thoughts," she said. "There're perverted actions disclosed in the Williams recording. And as Gabi suggested, I'm also bothered that Rodolphe might have maneuvered Melisa and Cameron into physical contact, albeit simply a hug.

"Nothing has made me change my opinion that Rodolphe, conspiring with at least one other, is your suspect. If anything, he's more conniving than I realized. I don't think anything he does is by happenstance. He exists in a penumbra, treading back and forth between reality and fantasy. Rodolphe knows the difference between good and bad, but he doesn't give a damn. I haven't seen a psychotic break yet, and that's great news. It gives us time to work on his wife.

"Regarding her interview, keep it simple. Your goal is to have her accept how dangerous her situation is becoming. Try to obtain Cameron's cooperation by making her an undercover agent. Also, ask her these questions." Ellen handed Joe an envelope. "In case she's skeptical, I've prepared a listing of them on my PD letterhead. Ms. Sinclair needs to know I'm for real."

"And how am I supposed to pull this off?" Joe asked, after glancing through Ellen's questions. "Sinclair will storm out if she doesn't slap me first."

"I didn't say it would be easy. These queries are important for my analysis. Go slowly, and if it's obvious that Sinclair is becoming offended or agitated, tell her she can speak with me. But based on her conversation with Gabi, I'm betting Sinclair will be comfortable with you. Assure her you can provide protection at a moment's notice. Tell her about Sister Mary Magdalen."

They left shortly thereafter. On the way back to the office, Gabi asked to see the questions. She read them quickly and said, "Jesus . . . you're kidding me. And by the way, who's Sister Mary Magdalen?"

"She runs a safe house for former street girls and abused women. It's a long story—tell you later."

CHAPTER SIX

Friday Afternoon, October 5, 2012

When Cameron arrived for their meeting at the Kensington Park, Joe was already seated at an out-of-the-way coffee table, facing Post Street. Once she was settled, he said, "I hope this is all right. John, the manager, promises that we won't be disturbed after he brings our orders."

"It's fine," Cameron responded, then asked, "How do you know him?"

"My wife and I used to come here for weekend getaways." Their cappuccinos arrived, piled high with frothed milk and sprinkled with cocoa powder, and were accompanied by a plate of homemade chocolate biscotti. Cameron sipped her coffee, dabbed froth from her mouth, and waited. Joe began straightaway. "Here's where we're at. I had already scheduled an interview with your husband regarding the warehouse murders case before Melisa Williams's allegations against him resurfaced. We've since opened an inquiry into those, and my partner has already questioned Melisa. Your husband is now a person of interest in both cases, and I'd like to talk to you about them."

"May I say something first?" Cameron asked.

"Sure, go ahead."

"I don't know how I can help. Concerning Melisa Williams, you know that we talked and put things to rights—as much as we could. I agreed to this meeting because your sergeant threatened a material witness subpoena. I'm a public person and believe there's such a thing as bad publicity. I'd like to avoid it and don't relish a perp walk into your office. So, since I have nothing to conceal, I'm here. Moreover, I could've hired a lawyer and fought. But even with spousal privilege, I was uncertain of the outcome. I'd be surprised if Melisa's recollection and mine differ much. About the warehouse murders, they were four months ago. I haven't followed them at all, and I don't recall ever talking about them with Denis. I didn't even know my husband was acquainted with the girls."

"Okay, it's important you understand the murders, how they were committed, and so on," Joe continued. "We've released a few details but held back a lot. Would you tell me exactly what you know?" Cameron did, and it wasn't a great deal. "All right, I'll tell you as much as I possibly can and trust that you won't disclose it. Do you agree?" She nodded yes. "First, do you have questions?"

"Do you honestly think that Denis committed these murders?"

"Yes. We've started to develop a profile for the leader, your husband. We believe he is a high-functioning sociopath." Joe launched into a description of the details. "Someone with an IQ around 200 and highly educated, with a background in literature—"

Cameron put up her hand, stopping him. "I'm no expert, but I've run across sociopathic traits in researching my books. I'd prefer not to hear them again. I can't imagine why you'd think Denis is like that. It's pure conjecture, based on a few superficial resemblances."

Joe continued with a description of the crime. "Does any of this ring a bell? Is there anything you can add?"

Well, Cameron thought, *only the first time when Denis punished me by making me hump that damnable suction-cupped dildo he mounted to a stool. How he put his hands on my shoulders when I became hung up and forced me down until my butt thumped bottom, watching me all the while. That sure rings a bell!* But Cameron was too embarrassed to tell Joe, and she wasn't certain any of this was germane. So she sidestepped. "I can't process this all at once. Let's talk about Melisa first; it's easier."

"Fine, I have a recording of her interview. Her statement covers intimate episodes with your husband that might be upsetting; may I play it? If the part about your meeting with Melisa reflects your recollection, you can stipulate."

"I'm not a child, Detective." Cameron listened, and when the recording finished, she said, "Regarding all this, I agree with Melisa's description of our call and meeting. But how do you think I feel, hearing her talk about going down on my husband? And I don't know what to say about her doing that guy in her class either." *Other than Denis badgering me to seduce a little girl*, she said to herself. "Moreover, about my underwear, it makes me feel unclean. And now I recall having sex on the morning in question before I left, and I did change the sheets afterwards. I must've forgotten about it, even though I noticed telltale signs when I returned.

"But you! You want me to believe all that bullshit. For God's sake, you coached Melisa into saying that."

Joe took his phone, scrolled through the photos, and handed it to her.

Cameron took a look and, in a few moments, said, "I'm sorry I called you a liar. May I have another cappuccino . . . please?" Her voice had become meek, and she avoided eye contact.

Joe gestured for John and ordered coffees. "I'm convinced something about the murders is familiar to you. Will you tell me?"

"No," she sniffled.

"Would you at least confirm I'm right?"

Cameron continued sniffling but eventually nodded yes. After the coffees arrived, she said, "You're implying that I'm living with a monster and don't even know it. Hell, you're not implying: you're saying it outright. We've had a good marriage for most of the time. Like everyone, we've had some difficulties. I love Denis, and I admit I'd do about anything for him. A while ago, I made a mistake, for which I paid dearly. Things are nearly back to where they were, and I won't jeopardize that. I know the traits you're attributing to my husband, but he's not like that. Denis isn't abusive and has never raised a hand to me. I don't feel threatened by him—not at all."

***

Joe noticed that thus far Cameron's mood and demeanor had changed several times: professional, confident, quarrelsome. But now she was meek and submissive. Recognizing that this was perhaps revealing of her current state, Joe pushed harder. "I'll tell you what I think has been going on. You won't like it. After that, I'm going to ask you a few important but intimate questions. Will you stay with me?"

"Yes, Detective."

"I think you have been, and continue to be, abused both emotionally and sexually. All with your passive consent. I would bet it started on your first date, then increased so slowly thereafter that you hardly noticed. It's now becoming unbearable, but you feel helpless to change it. You astounded your husband by lashing out at Melisa. Also, I think you had an affair. And if you aren't already in danger, you will be. You need help, and so do I. Let's work together."

Cameron jumped up, spilling her coffee.

"Screw you; you're a bastard. Do you think I would tolerate that? I'm out of here."

Cameron had scared the hell out of the few staff who were about. John rushed over to help Joe clean up.

Afterward, when Joe began to gather his belongings, he realized Cameron hadn't left. She was pacing the lobby but soon returned to the table. "Sorry for the mess—not for calling you a bastard. Let's hear your questions."

Joe hadn't liked Cameron's meek and submissive mien, but the defiant Cameron was genuine, and her rebellious, feisty side boded well for the future. He explained that Ellen had offered to continue the questioning if Cameron became uncomfortable.

"I'm okay with you . . . and with a buildup like that, these better be good."

"If you want to stop at any time, say so, all right?" Cameron nodded yes. "Fine, do you want to read her letter?"

"No."

"Let's do the easy ones first. Have you threatened divorce? If so, was it over the Melisa situation?"

"No."

"Since your marriage, have you had an affair? If so, was it specifically caused by the Melisa episode, and did you tell Denis?"

"Yes."

"Yes, because of Melisa, or did you tell him?"

"Yes to both."

"Will you share any details and when you told your husband?"

"No, except that it was for a little over three months in duration, ending in December 2011. I told Denis this January."

"Was it for revenge?"

"I don't know, Detective. I was confused."

"Was this the mistake for which you paid dearly?" Joe asked. But when Cameron didn't answer, he continued, "Does he like you to dress without undergarments, specifically panties?"

"Yes."

"Has he asked you to have sex with others?"

"What does that have to do with anything?"

"Do you and your husband practice deviant or aberrant sexual behavior? If so, does anything in the Melisa tape mirror your activities?"

"If it's consensual, not life-threatening, and so on, I'm not going to debate whether it's deviant or not," Cameron said. "But I understand what you're asking. The answer is yes."

"Will you share details?"

"Lieutenant, now you're pushing, and no, I won't. It was consensual, and that's all you need to know."

"Do you want to take a break? The questions become more intimate."

all, are underage street girls. It's run by Sister Mary Magdalen, who's a nun at the Sisters of Perpetual Adoration Abbey and is an ex–street girl herself."

"Joe, you're scaring me."

"I'm trying to," he said, reaching out for her hands.

They sat for a couple of minutes before Cameron said, "I ought to go now. I'll keep in touch—promise."

Joe gave her his business card along with Dr. Sandler's and Gabi's. "Call any of us twenty-four hours a day."

After Cameron left, Joe was in a hurry to head home, shower, and see Susan. But he didn't know that she and Linda had been boutique shopping along Post Street, and that as they passed the Kensington Park, Susan had seen him holding hands with Cameron through the hotel's lobby window

CHAPTER SEVEN

Friday Evening, October 5, 2012

After returning home, Joe took a long shower to relax. Interviews with victims of abuse were demanding, and he was sympathetic to the pain they dredged up. Before their meeting, Joe had been convinced Cameron could provide information, and she'd admitted as much, even though she hadn't been completely forthcoming. So now she would have qualms about her husband, and Joe bet they'd grow. But it was time to put Cameron aside and call Susan.

When she answered, it sounded like she'd been crying.

"Are you okay? Is something wrong?" Joe asked.

"I don't think you should come over. I'm too upset."

"What happened. Tell me . . ."

"Maybe we shouldn't see each other anymore. It isn't working."

"Why? I thought we had a good thing going."

"Me too."

"So what's changed?"

"I know we didn't have an understanding; it has been so fast. But I felt like we weren't going to see others."

"We weren't."

"So why were you at a hotel on Post Street this afternoon, holding hands with another woman? What was that all about?"

"Oh good lord, Susan."

"You're not answering me."

"I'm coming over."

"Don't—"

"Susan, I am. We can't leave it like this."

When Joe arrived, Susan led him to the living room and sat stoically in a straight-backed chair, hands folded in her lap.

"The woman you saw is a material witness in the warehouse murders case," Joe began. "I questioned her at the hotel, since she insisted on neutral territory. It was a rough interview, and I upset her. Plus I'm concerned for her safety. I was trying to calm her down before she left. That's what you saw. It was work—nothing else."

"Who was she?"

"Her name is Cameron Sinclair."

"The novelist?"

"Yes. Her husband is a person of interest in the warehouse murders."

"Well, maybe if you had talked to me about what you were doing, I wouldn't have jumped to a hasty conclusion. I know you talked to Laura about your job, and I've been waiting for you to do the same with me."

"I've kept the grisly details of this case from you on purpose. But I'll tell you if you're ready. And why is Laura coming up now? Of course I talked to her, but we were married a long time. I'll share how I feel, but if you accuse me of objectifying you, I'll lose it."

"I won't . . ."

"I love the way you make me feel. You're bright, fun to talk to, and gorgeous to boot. And in bed, outstanding. I love everything about you."

"You're not just saying that?"

"I mean it. Can we please hug? We can't keep sitting on opposite sides of the room."

"All right, let's go upstairs, but only to cuddle." There was still hesitancy in her voice, but at least Susan was willing to take a step toward reconciliation. Upstairs they lay on her bed, and she nuzzled against him. "There're a lot of things I want to tell you about James and me. I'm ashamed of what I did."

"I thought this was about us."

"It is. But if you like the way I am in bed, it's because James taught me. I can't unlearn it. Are you okay with that?"

"Yes, I know what you're talking about. You don't have to explain. You never have to do anything you're uncomfortable with again. Shame on him. None of it was your fault. I hope what I've said makes you feel better."

"It does, and I get it about your job. But this isn't solely about you; it's about me. Why are you making this so hard? You don't understand. I need to tell you." And then Susan did, crying until she was exhausted.

At length, Joe asked, "Did James hurt you physically?"

"No."

Susan fell asleep soon afterward.

The next morning, they slept in, but Joe was up first. Linda had made coffee and left the newspaper on the kitchen table. Joe was having a cup when Susan appeared fresh from the shower, combing out her wet hair and wearing only a towel around her waist. Noting Joe's surprise, she said, "What? I was trying for a Hawaiian look. Did I miss it?" She began mimicking a hula dancer's gyrations.

"No, I think you have it down pat," Joe laughed. "I swear, Susan, when you swivel like that, you could bring sight to the blind."

"It's a gift. Seriously, though, I had to take a shower—wash James away. I didn't feel like we could make love again until I did that. Does it sound silly?"

"Not at all."

Susan took off her towel and tossed it to him. "Are you coming back to bed or what?"

***

Joe spent the weekend putting together his thoughts from the two interviews. On Monday morning, he and Gabi discussed them with Captain Weber, who observed, "The warehouse murders investigation is taking time, and we may never develop enough to indict. So can we pull the trigger on Rodolphe using the rape? It seems like Melisa could put him away with her testimony and photographs. Perhaps we ought to cut our losses and get him off the streets?"

"It's a sound suggestion, and I'm tempted," Joe replied. "But as it stands now, there're a few problems. I don't think she'll produce those nude photos voluntarily. And then she's determined to stay out of this. We can't establish the date of their first tryst without Melisa taking the stand. But even if she does, I'm concerned about her as a witness. And Rodolphe has unlimited means. He'll hire topflight lawyers to destroy her. And if Melisa performs poorly, I'm not confident we'll prevail."

"Is there anything else?"

"Yes. It has been about two weeks, and we're not having any luck finding the van. Would you approve OT for the uniform division to start canvassing auto salvage lots and the like? And second, would you contact your press sources? Ask them to expand the tip line to include the van. We're running out of ideas."

The captain agreed, and Gabi began organizing the salvage yard survey and following up with their investigators, who had been tracing the girls using O'Brien's photos and notebook. The counterman in a nautical gear and clothing shop had confirmed they'd been there, and Joe believed this was the last known sighting of either of them.

Joe sent Ellen Sandler the summary of Cameron's interview. On the ninth, the newspapers carried an update of the case, including the van's information, and Cameron called.

"How are you doing?" Joe asked.

"I don't know. I'm ambivalent about spying, yet little things I've noticed over the years keep surfacing. They're bothersome, but I still have trouble perceiving Denis that way. I told him about our meeting. He was furious and went on and on about how stupid I was to do it without an attorney. Honestly, I think he was mostly pissed that I had the balls to do it on my own. I packaged it as if I had tried to cover his back and so forth. I didn't discuss the warehouse murders because I couldn't work it in. But here's one thing: I saw the revised tip line regarding the van this morning. It was easy to bring it up at breakfast, because we typically look through the papers then and it's not unusual to exchange tidbits. I can't say Denis reacted to it, though."

"That's great. Be careful. Don't do any more than you feel comfortable with, and I still want to hear from you regularly, okay?"

"All right."

CHAPTER EIGHT

Tuesday, October 9, 2012

What a fuckin' bombshell Cameron had dropped this morning. How the hell had the cops stumbled across the van?

Denis was annoyed when Cameron chattered on the phone and fussed around the house all day. That wasn't like her, because even when she was engrossed in writing, she always found an excuse to go out. Denis didn't have classes today, so he wanted to call Zack, their handyman and his partner in crime. But he needed a burner phone from his small stash in the basement's ceiling and was unwilling to risk discovery with Cameron about. *Shit—I need to talk to him.*

Denis and Zack had been careful. Weeks before Memorial Day, Denis had given Zack cash to purchase a van in Nevada. Afterward, Zack had kept it under a tarp behind his isolated cabin, which was located south of San Francisco in the San Juan Bautista area. Finally, he'd snatched plates from an abandoned car, using them on the van during the caper. But despite their precautions, it was time to ditch the van.

When Denis came to bed that night, he was still riled at Cameron. *Fuck, she's always underfoot!*

The next day, Denis had only morning classes and was home by midafternoon. Cameron wasn't there, so he retrieved a burner and called Zack.

"Hey, Doc, how you doin'?"

"Not well; we've got problems with the van. Come to San Francisco ASAP and locate a junkyard with an auto crusher. But don't use the van. Afterward, go home, pick it up, and bring it back to the yard. Text me where and when to meet you, and let's wrap this up within a week. Questions?"

"No, I'm cool."

After that, I'll deal with my other problem, Denis thought.

***

After talking with Zack, Denis reflected on their relationship. He had known his partner about eight years. Denis and Cameron had bought their home early in 2004. Following that, Denis asked a hardware store to recommend a handyman. The counterman had suggested Zack, even though he lived out of the area. Denis arranged for him to come to the house, and when he did, Cameron joined them on the deck. She wanted to see the guy who'd be working at the house. Shortly afterward, Cameron left, mouthing behind Zack's back, "Okay."

"I think it's two days' work," Zack had told Denis. "I can probably start by the middle of next week."

Later, Denis learned that Zack had owned a small, successful landscaping and handyman business until a nasty divorce cleaned him out. That's when Zack moved to his cabin. He'd slowly rebuilt his life, and now he worked for cash. He still did a fair amount of work for loyal customers in the Bay Area, but to make it worth the trips, he needed to schedule them carefully and stay overnight with friends. It was far from a perfect scenario, but he seemed to make it work.

Over time, Zack started staying in a guest room at Denis and Cameron's home whenever he worked for them. There'd been only one glitch. It happened when Cameron was naked in their bedroom after a shower. Zack thought she'd already left the house and came in to change a faulty outlet. It was an awkward moment.

Later, Denis surmised that Zack hadn't retreated quickly enough for Cameron's liking. She was peeved and wanted Zack out of the house. Denis convinced her to give Zack a second chance. Denis didn't care how Cameron felt; he didn't want to screw up a fine working arrangement. Zack seemed contrite, so Denis didn't bother to say anything about it to him.

But Denis's curiosity about Zack's divorce had been piqued. Apparently, his marriage had blown up overnight. The wife of the hardware store's counterman, who worked in the courthouse and was an insatiable gossip, reported that Zack hadn't even had a lawyer. Zack's court filings contained a relinquishment of any right to see his wife's daughter again, which the courthouse worker opined was tantamount to a restraining order. That wasn't a typical term in a divorce, so there had to be something else. If Denis wanted to make sure of Zack's help in future less-conventional projects, he needed to find out what it was all about.

So late one afternoon while sipping Jack Daniel's whiskey on the deck, feigning a buzz, Denis probed. "So tell me, why were you so screwed over in your divorce? I hear you were taken to the cleaners."

Zack hadn't expected such a plain-spoken line of conversation. "Well, it was a difficult situation, and I'd rather not talk about it."

"You shouldn't feel that way, Zack. We're friends. And I'd like to know more about you," Denis coaxed.

"Doc, let's leave it at this. I'm not telling you, because I value your friendship. It would hurt me if I lost your respect."

"How can you say that? We're friends, and friends don't bail on each other. I thought you trusted me. Didn't I have your back when

Cameron caught you checking her out? I didn't tell you how pissed she was. Cameron wanted you gone, and it took an effort to convince her otherwise."

"That's not right. It isn't what happen—"

But Denis interrupted, "Well, that's the way Cameron looks at it. Frankly, I don't give a shit." Then Denis lowered his voice conspiratorially. "You gotta admit, she's an eyeful and even better in bed than she looks. She was inexperienced at first but eager to learn. One of my best students. You get my drift?" Denis was flying on trusted instincts now. "Look, I'll share with you; I'll take the risk. No matter how great looking she is or talented in the sack—sometimes I need a change. It all becomes so routine. Since we've been married, I've had plenty of women. The campus is a hunting ground—I'm not bragging, but I get laid whenever I want. Cameron has no idea. She thinks I'm faithful. I'm trusting you, since this could destroy my marriage."

"Doc, I'd never tell her; you know that. But this is hard, because I could go to jail for what I'm about to say. It's the hold my ex has over me."

"It can't be that bad," Denis said, egging him on.

"All right . . . here's what happened. I had a happy marriage. My wife was attractive, and our sex life was fine. But as you said, I became bored. She had a daughter by her first marriage, Janet. She was sweet: barely ten years old with a pretty face, blonde hair, and long legs with a cute butt. I kept fighting inappropriate thoughts. Janet had accepted me right away, calling me Papi. She liked to snuggle when we watched TV. It became a regular thing because her mother, a practical nurse, worked four to midnight at the hospital.

"Things went along like that until one afternoon, I came home early from work. My wife had already left for her shift, and Janet was at

94

the kitchen table doing her homework. I was tired and went upstairs for a nap. I was under the covers in my briefs when Janet came up to see if I was okay. She sat on the edge of the bed, chatting about her day. Then she kicked off her shoes, slid under the bedclothes, and cuddled. At first it seemed normal, but then Janet became . . . curious. I ought to have stopped her. So that was the beginning, and before long we were doing nearly everything. This went on for months, and I felt guilty but couldn't stop. If she'd protested, acted scared or despondent, maybe I could've gotten a grip. I've said too much."

"Shit, I hear you, Zack. It was her fault for being so curious. You didn't rape her. I don't have a problem with any of this. Focus on how you showed her an awesome time. Her next boyfriend should thank you."

"Jesus, Doc."

"So what happened next?"

"One evening, Janet and I had fallen asleep naked on top of the covers. Without warning, my wife came home early and walked in. She was apoplectic, spasmodic. I'd never seen anything like it before. There was no point in bullshitting her, and I was gone the next day. In exchange for not going to the police, my wife took everything, and I agreed not to see Janet again."

"I've never done anyone that young." *But I've fantasized.* "Cool, we'll talk again."

***

By the summer of 2005, it was time to reveal his idea to Zack. Denis was counting on Zack's cooperation because of what he'd already shared about Janet. That conversation had occurred about six weeks before, and they hadn't talked since. Denis's plan was to embrangle Zack. He envisioned executing it when Cameron was away on a book-signing trip.

"Hi, Doc," Zack answered when Denis called.

"I'd like you to come to San Francisco as soon as you can. Probably for three to four days. I'll pay you for a week to make it worth your while."

"Cool. What's on the agenda?"

"Landscaping, but more important, another idea. I've been working on what we talked about the last time you were here."

"Fine, but I'm not clear what you're referring to."

"Not on the phone."

Zack arrived within a week, and they began planning a rose garden that Cameron wanted built around the pool. She was actively involved in making all the decisions. Zack said the area was sunny and roses ought to do well but suggested supplementing the soil with clay, sand, and humus. This was easy, since their detached home was far enough away from neighboring houses to allow a small backhoe in between. Cameron went about her normal routine throughout. Thus, the men had time to discuss Denis's primary plan.

"It's simple," Denis explained. "While Cameron's away, we'll abduct a girl about Janet's age and bring her back here. But she must be chosen randomly. We'll integrate the abduction scheme with the construction of the rose garden. Let's finalize it now, and then we won't meet again until go day. It isn't difficult. Any questions?"

"Wouldn't it be easier with a rototiller?" Zack asked, not grasping the full implication of the plan.

"We can't simply take her home afterwards . . . understand?"

***

Before noon on Tuesday, October 16, 2012, Gabi and Joe met with Ellen Sandler. "You've been busy," she told them. "I've been through Melisa's tape and your notes on Cameron's. Both interviews provide a trove of information, and I revisited my notes as well.

"Let's deal with Melisa first. You've correctly surmised that Melisa was vulnerable because of her mother's death and her naivete. She has provided significant insight into how controlling Rodolphe is and how far his corruptions have developed. I continue to share Gabi's concern that Melisa is still in play. He didn't anticipate the kerfuffle, but he'll make it work for him. The clue is in Cameron's interview, when she hints that Denis has already suggested a lesbian routine. The irony of a Melisa-Cameron tryst would appeal to him. Another benefit might be influencing Melisa against testifying. If she does, you ought to be able to put him away. I suspect Rodolphe hasn't recalled the photos yet. They're his Achilles' heel. He has been passive towards Melisa, since he doesn't see her like a threat. But when he remembers those photos, her life will be in danger, so stay close.

"Regarding Cameron's questioning, she's revealed more of his depravities. I think Cameron is insecure about her sexuality. It's her vulnerability and will unfold as you get to know her. Now here's the most interesting part: Rodolphe has a grand plan, albeit flexible. I think Gabi's onto it, and Cameron is a work in process. She's going to be his masterpiece, and everything he does furthers her metamorphosis. Rodolphe's motivated like some art thieves. He'll stash her away, then enjoy her whenever he wants. It's worse, though, because like a pimp, he'll discard her when she's no longer attractive. It doesn't bode well for her, but I think Cameron's starting to realize what her husband may be like. Her situation is deteriorating and becoming insufferable because she rebelled twice: the confrontation with Melisa and the affair. Her affair could've been the stressor that pushed him towards the twins' deaths, because the timing is right. Enough time for things to come to a boil and to make plans.

"Here's my revised profile. Rodolphe is intuitive, easily spotting women's vulnerabilities. Combine his talent and intellect, and you have the picture. Rodolphe can keep multiple balls in the air simultaneously. He sets things in motion, tracks reactions, and pushes where and when he can. We may be focusing on the Übermensch theme at the expense of Dracula's. Broadly, Raskolnikov is the intellectual persona to Dracula's emotional one. Rodolphe may move back and forth between them and probably has varying degrees of each personality at any time. Those personalities are each driven by a different force. The Nietzsche/Raskolnikov persona is driven by the need to show his superiority, proving he can get away with murder. It's an intellectual exercise and is the personality where planning, manipulating, and clear thinking comes from. The Vlad/Dracula persona is cruel. It's driven by emotions of anger and hatred towards women. When stressors accumulate to the breaking point, Vlad emerges. That's when Rodolphe is most dangerous.

"So think about Dracula. He walks the earth in search of victims. Dracula is portrayed as devil-like. When he sucks a victim's blood, he sucks out their soul, leaving behind an undead but lustful creature. There's a strong sexual component. Don't forget: you need to read between the lines. Stoker couldn't write the way an author would today, because it would've been too shocking. In its day, *Dracula* pushed the limits."

"And Rodolphe thinks he's like Dracula?" Gabi asked.

"Probably; Vlad's his sobriquet. Here's where I think Rodolphe becomes eerie. What does he think about a person's soul? We always portray it in idealistic ways. It dwells in our hearts, in our minds, or both. But what if he believes it resides elsewhere, in our center of lust, in our genitalia? Why not? Our sex drive is fundamental? It's corporeal rather than introspective or metaphysical. There're clues that support this. If a woman's undergarments are her genital armor, then they are metaphorically protecting her soul. Not wearing panties is obvious—no armor. But Melisa's putting on Cameron's panties is a subtle attack. I'm suspicious he made her masturbate in them, because Melisa says, 'It was icky.' He's corrupting and weakening Cameron's armor. Thus, she becomes defenseless. Following that, Rodolphe steals her soul, killing her figuratively or worse. Spooky."

"Do you have a better read on what caused his sociopathy?" Gabi interrupted.

"As I said before, sociopaths are frequently victims of child abuse themselves. It can be a combination of mental, physical, or sexual. He's striking back, and it's all about control. In this case, sex and violence are a means to an end. You need to put him away."

"And was his abuser a woman?" Joe asked.

"Possibly, but if so, it isn't clear who she is yet. Clues about that might pop up during your investigation. Plus you asked me about Cameron using your first name. It's a positive sign. She accepts your sincerity. She won't flip on her husband just yet, but Cameron's moving in the right direction."

"Before we go," Joe said, "we've come up empty on all our domestic searches with law enforcement as well as our questioning of Princeton and the Lawrenceville school. Maybe we'd have better luck in France. Rodolphe lived in Paris before moving to Moscow. Also, he taught at the Sorbonne from 1995 through 1998. Could your friend Bridgette Dubois check that out for us?"

"I don't see why not. I'll give her a call. Also, I'll ask her to check with the Russians, because the French have better relations than we do."

"Great. Gabi's going to try a back door with the Brits as well."

***

Zack's text message came early on the morning of October 19. He was on his way to San Francisco with the van. Denis met him at noon, a block away from a small, ramshackle auto salvage yard on the outskirts of the city. He asked Zack if he'd taken care of everything.

"Yes."

"Including wiping down the van?"

"Yes, but we need to hurry. This is a one-man show, and the junkyard guy goes to lunch about noon. He left before you pulled up, so we have about forty minutes."

"All right," Denis replied. "The yard's unlocked and unguarded, right? No CCTV?"

"Yeah, just a nasty chained-up dog. I brought raw hamburger on the off chance it gets loose." Zack slowly drove around the jumble of parts and cars until he was at the rear of the yard near the car crusher. Denis followed. They still had thirty minutes. Zack checked; nothing had been left behind in the van. He removed the plates and put them in his satchel before getting in to Denis's car. "All set."

Denis hesitated. "Looks like we have time left. I'm paranoid. Let's wipe the van down again. We'll clean like hell for ten minutes, then leave even if we're not finished."

"Okay."

Denis took two rags from his trunk, and they went at it. When they'd finished and were on the way out, they threw the hamburger to the dog. Denis and Zack were back on the street in ten minutes, having seen no sign of the proprietor.

"So what now?"

"Let's have lunch and celebrate. How would you feel about Sausalito?"

"Cool."

"After lunch, we'll ride to wine country. We need to plan our next adventure and reconnoiter. I'm thinking of a mother-and-daughter combo. They can put on a little show first."

Zack perked up. "Neat, but keep the ole lady in her midthirties."

"What? No granny sex?" Denis laughed. "Okay, we'll do it your way.

"When we return, stay at our house for a couple of days. Do busywork, and maybe Cameron will give you another show. Then we'll buy a junker and you can head home with it. It'll all look normal."

By two o'clock, they were seated at an Italian restaurant. After lunch, they were on their way again, and before long Denis turned off the main road. He knew where he was going; years ago, he and Cameron had visited friends at a nearby cabin in the woods.

"This will be perfect for our purpose," Denis said, pulling to the side of the road. "We'll go the rest of the way on foot."

They started trudging through the woods, following a narrow path, Zack leading. When they were far enough away from the side road, Denis pulled a .22 LR semiauto pistol from under his sweater and put two rounds in the back of Zack's skull. Afterward, he picked up the brass, Zack's wallet, and so on, slipping the lot into a three-gallon ziplock bag from his car's trunk.

Zack was the other problem I couldn't deal with earlier!

When Denis arrived home, he had a glass of wine with Cameron. "I was thinking. We should do something this weekend. Something we haven't done in ages. How about taking the ferry to Tiburon tomorrow? The weather looks pleasant—midseventies and sunny—and we could have lunch at Sam's. We had a lot of fun doing that back in the day. What do you say?"

Cameron happily agreed at once. After she went to bed, Denis cut up the van's plates, broke down the gun, and wiped off everything before rebagging it. *I'll drop this overboard halfway to Tiburon tomorrow.*

CHAPTER NINE

Monday, October 22, 2012

The van and Zack had been dealt with. Despite that, Denis thought it prudent to continue contingency planning. On September 21, in response to Cancio's interrogation, he'd already sold $1 million in securities and transferred it to his Swiss account. Today he sold an additional $1.5 million and transferred it to the same account. Notwithstanding his precautions, something was irking him, yet he couldn't put his finger on it. So Denis sat on the deck, thinking everything through.

He assumed the bother was about Melisa. *But why? It's nothing but a side show. It's a "he said, she said." There's no evidence. However, the police are taking it seriously. Why else would they question Melisa? I ought to pay closer attention and get professional advice.*

Denis called his lawyers in New Orleans, a high-powered firm that his family had used for generations. It was a better choice than their San Francisco firm, because there was no chance of any accidental disclosures to Cameron. He rang Bernie Kaplan, head of the corporate group, and Heather, his secretary, put him through. "Bernie. I need a favor. Nothing to do with the family business. I'm in an embarrassing situation and need to speak with one of your criminal litigators."

"When can you come down?"

"Anytime. I want the best—a street fighter. I don't care about age, where they went to school, or seniority. None of that bullshit."

"That bad."

"Probably not, but I don't want to fart around. It's annoying if nothing else."

"All right, Heather will call you," and Bernie rang off.

Cameron had been working on her next book. Denis stuck his head into her study. "I think I'll be going to New Orleans shortly. See the family legal brain trust. I'll be gone a day or two."

"Do you need me to come?"

"No, it doesn't have anything to do with us. It's about one of the shipping companies where I'm a director."

"Let me know," Cameron said, returning to her writing.

Denis went back to the deck. He felt better having a course of action. *Now to the murders.*

***

Their first murder, in August 2005, had been well designed and carried out when Cameron was away. Denis and Zack did it under the camouflage of her landscape project. Beforehand, Denis had picked up a few of the commonplace items they needed. Following that, Zack tagged the rosebushes at a nursery near his home and arranged for a small backhoe rental, soil, and so forth in San Francisco, all consistent with the project. Then Zack found a semirural location between San Juan Bautista and San Francisco. It was the type of place where parents didn't worry too much about their kids' safety.

On a Monday afternoon, they parked on a side street near the community pool and waited until a young girl came by. After making sure no one was around, Denis and Zack grabbed her, then gagged and bound her before putting her in the trunk. They were back in Denis's garage in less than two hours and carried her to the basement. When they stripped her, she was so scared she peed her undies. Denis was angry and kicked her clothes across the basement, where they landed by the washing machine. Then he yanked her up by the hair, growling, "If you obey, we won't hurt you." She tried like hell to please them but sobbed herself to sleep every night, wanting to believe they would let her go.

The soil and backhoe were delivered on Friday. On Saturday morning, Zack turned over the garden, mixed the soil, and graded it. That afternoon he dug a grave, then gathered up everything they had used in the basement and threw it in the hole. While Zack did that, Denis bound and gagged the girl before holding her nose until she died. Afterward, they tossed her in the grave, and Zack filled the hole and graded the spot again. Sunday morning Zack policed the basement, and Cameron arrived home that afternoon. She was delighted with the progress. And there was never a peep from law enforcement.

***

Heather interrupted Denis's analysis to confirm an appointment with Haniff Seaton for ten o'clock on Thursday morning the twenty-fifth. He made a reservation for a nonstop flight on United for Wednesday afternoon and another for a room at the Omni Royal Orleans hotel. Denis could concentrate fully now.

***

Earlier this year, the twins had been different. Denis liked the complexity of the planning. As a general precaution, Zack and Denis had agreed not to keep any records of each other's names, addresses, and so forth. They'd policed their residences for any telltale paperwork and only used burner phones. Their first abduction, using Denis's car, had taught them that a van would be easier—just a quick push through already opened side doors and it would be over.

Zack acquired the van early and kept it out of sight. Over time, he purchased the other materials away from their homes, shopping at big-box stores when possible and paying cash. Then Zack reconnoitered warehouses all around San Francisco before choosing one. He canvassed it thoroughly, establishing that it would be vacant when they needed it to be, and found a point of entry through a rear window. In case he couldn't locate a key inside, he bought a new slam lock for the front door. Later, Zack stayed in a San Francisco motel during the week before the Memorial Day holiday. Then he broke into the warehouse, cleaned up the debris, and fitted the window with a piece of plywood he'd found inside. He even located a key, so the new lock wasn't necessary. Finally, the metal poles, flanged floor fittings, and so on were hidden under tarps.

Denis hadn't met with Zack for nearly eight weeks. Then, finally, it was the Wednesday before Memorial Day: go time. Cameron was occupied with her new book and wouldn't be aware of Denis's movements.

He left his car in a public parking lot near the ferry piers, where Zack picked him up. They'd known the wharf area would be crowded with tourists, so the plan was to troll until they spotted their quarry. Once she was isolated, they'd seize, bind, and gag her, then pile tarps on top while they searched for number two.

That was before Denis spotted the twins. He'd always thought they were hot. Zack started following them, and it was easy for him to avoid being noticed because of the traffic and crowds. Meanwhile, Denis thought it through. *I don't know them well, so there's little to arouse suspicion. I'm convinced I can lure them into the van voluntarily—a small risk compared to grabbing two women against their wills. And I can't ignore the danger of driving around searching for a second woman while the first one's in back.* "Zack, it'll work," Denis finally announced.

They followed the twins to a shop with a carved statue of an old salt, in yellow foul-weather gear, outside the door. The sisters went in, and Zack doubled-parked. When they came out, Denis faked surprise at seeing them, and the girls smiled. They came right over and started chatting through Denis's open window. "We're going to Point Lobos for lunch at the Cliff House," he told them. "Do you have time to join us? Our treat."

They didn't hesitate and climbed into the rear of the van, sitting on the pile of tarps. Zack started driving toward the warehouse. "Sorry," Denis said, "I didn't mention it, but we need to make a quick stop to pick up a table my wife ordered. Is it okay?"

"Sure." The girls continued chattering about their morning, paying no attention to where they were going. When they arrived, Denis opened an overhead garage door, and they were still talking as Zack backed into the warehouse.

Zack and Denis had trouble controlling the twins at first, until Zack gut punched one while Denis grabbed the other by the hair. Then they bound the women's wrists behind their backs. One of them sobbed, "Why are you doing this to us?"

"Because we can. Do what you're told, or we'll kill you— understand?"

By Friday afternoon, Carol and Carla, who had hardly slept, were dog-tired. That's when Denis and Zack bound the sisters' wrists once more, gagged them with their panties, erected the shafts, and mounted the twins thereon. They died about noon on Monday. Denis hid their clothes and IDs behind abandoned equipment where the police would eventually find them. And lastly, they packed the van and cleaned up before Zack headed for San Juan Bautista, and Denis returned home in time to leave for the Howells'. Cameron seemed not to notice that he'd been in and out all weekend.

I feel comfortable that I've covered everything about the murders. It must be the Melisa drivel, Denis concluded.

***

Before he left for New Orleans, Denis mailed a second taunting letter to Joe Cancio. He dozed on the flight until he woke up with a start. Finally, he had recalled what'd been nagging him about Melisa. *It's those four fuckin' photos I took when she stayed at the house. Her "keepsake," she said, and I'm in two of them. Shit!* And the bedroom could be easily identified as well. Although he wasn't a techie, Denis assumed the phone could be analyzed to establish their date. *I won't mention these to Seaton. I can always recall them later if necessary. I'll fess up to an ex post facto knowledge of her age if I must.*

***

Thursday morning when Denis arrived at Seaton's office, he was escorted to a small conference room. Denis had already Googled him. He was from Saint Kitts, midthirties, Harvard educated. His curriculum vitae was impressive—unmistakably a heavy hitter in criminal litigation. He'd been admitted to the Louisiana and California bars but had practiced all over the country. Impeccably dressed, he was imposing: dark, tall, and soft-spoken, with a touch of an island accent. Seaton's voice was charismatic, but so low a listener had to pay close attention. Denis concluded this was by design. And Seaton was all business.

"Dr. Rodolphe, I would like to go over a few basics. You're consulting me on a criminal matter. It's a different situation than a corporate or civil one. Please don't tell me if you're guilty of criminal charges. It doesn't matter what I think, but it does matter what I know. I can't knowingly permit you to lie under oath. Do you understand?"

"Yes."

"Have any charges been filed, or do you expect them imminently?"

"No."

"All right. I'll need an additional retainer of ten thousand dollars."

"Okay. I brought my checkbook."

Seaton went on to discuss attorney-client and spousal privileges, how they would communicate, search warrants and how to contact their local SF office should that happen, and so on. "Any questions?"

"Not yet."

"So tell me . . ."

Denis recounted the allegations Melisa had made and explained that there was current police interest. He admitted to the affair but lied about it being before Melisa's eighteenth birthday. He described the rest of their affair accurately but omitted any mention of the photos. He stuck to the truth as closely as possible. "Our affair continued until Melisa called Cameron in September 2011. That resulted in a quarrel between them in the student union." Denis explained that the university's disciplinary committee had taken no action and hadn't reported Melisa's allegations to the police. Then he disclosed Cameron's recent interview with Detective Cancio.

"I don't like it that your wife spoke to the police without counsel. And why are they reopening an investigation? Have you left out anything about letters, texts, photos, or the like that they could have discovered?"

"No," Denis answered, sticking to his story.

"Well, notwithstanding the 'he said, she said' nature of the allegation, it's a serious situation. You should know that in today's world, there're no longer just fines and community service for these types of nearly legal, 'consensual' offenses. If convicted, you're looking at jail time. It may seem like a technicality, but judges and prosecutors aren't flexible anymore. Having said that, there doesn't seem to be any hard evidence, the university absolved you, and we should prevail.

"I'll be in SF before Christmas, and if nothing happens prior to that, let's meet. I'll only charge you for my time, since I'll already be there."

***

That afternoon, Denis was on a flight back to San Francisco. He used the time to review his situation. As he evaluated his meeting with Haniff Seaton, he felt ambivalent. On the positive side, Denis liked Seaton and thought he was in capable hands, but on the negative side, Seaton hadn't told him anything that alleviated his anxiety. *I can't fool around with this.*

There remained two items Denis needed to deal with. First, if the shit hit the fan, a go plan was necessary: getaway money, somewhere to go, fake IDs, burners, offshore brokerage and bank accounts, and so on. Such a change wasn't daunting for him. After all, Denis had lived abroad, was multilingual, had unlimited wealth, and had already started transferring money to his Swiss Bank account.

Second, Melisa and her photos. *One thing's for certain, I'm not going to jail over that deceiving little bitch!* Denis silently carped, and by the time he landed, he had a plan for her. Denis intended to visit the hoodlum in the Tenderloin District from whom he'd purchased the .22 LR semiauto he'd used on Zack. Before he'd gone the first time, Denis had discovered that this area was the most dangerous in San Francisco. Notwithstanding the risk, Denis had driven to its center and parked near a group of loitering ruffians. He recalled approaching them, saying he needed a gun and asking who could help. They looked at him incredulously. After verbal abuse and inquiries as to whether Denis was a fuckin' cop, the largest thug frisked him and checked his ID. Then he was led into a dilapidated bar, where several other hoodlums were hanging. "Who's this asshole?" one said.

"Calls himself Doc," his escort responded.

In the far corner was a multiracial racketeer sitting at a round table. A .45-caliber semiautomatic lay on the table close to his right hand. Denis repeated his request while the mobster evaluated him.

"Bring your ass over here, motherfucker."

The man was called Tyree. About two weeks after their meeting, he produced a gun for Denis along with fifty rounds of ammo.

Following their first meeting, Denis had searched the *Examiner*'s online archives and discovered Tyree was a small-time impresario of crime. He dabbled in prostitution, extortion, gambling, drugs, and so on. There was no question Tyree was the person who could help with Melisa.

Today, Denis parked and approached the corner bar, where he'd met Tyree before. He was greeted by a chorus of "Hey, Doc," and after a superficial pat-down, he was told to go on in. He and Tyree talked for about fifteen minutes before the gangster said, "All right, Doc, give me a couple of days. I'll call you."

Denis wrote a new burner number on a napkin and left. A few days later, Tyree called. "I'll be in the office all afternoon. Bring five thousand dollars."

When Denis arrived, Tyree began, "Here's what we can do. I have two associates familiar with the area. They'll surveil her and determine where and when it's best. My understanding is they are to mug her and steal all her possessions—everything except her car keys. You want her roughed up but not enough to require medical attention, correct?"

Denis nodded yes.

"Can they have a little fun with her?"

"Yes, but no rape."

"These guys are pros and won't overdo it."

"All right."

"That'll be ten thousand dollars. Give me half now."

Walking out, Denis chuckled silently. *Well, if this isn't 'the beginning of a beautiful friendship.'*[1] *It's certainly an odd one.*

CHAPTER TEN

Late October 2012

Nearly three weeks had passed since they'd met with Ellen Sandler. Bridgette Dubois had turned up nothing with the Police Nationale, the Paris police, or the Sorbonne, and an Interpol request to Russia hadn't received a response. Gabi spoke with a friend at the CIA, who contacted an associate at MI6, with no luck. That Brit then talked with both MI5 and Scotland Yard—nothing there either. Thus, the investigation continued to crawl.

During the lull, Joe spent time with Susan. He began talking about details of Melisa's case. He showed her the photo and played the recording.

Susan's reactions were complicated. She was happy he was confiding in her and sympathized with Melisa. But the audio dredged up bad feelings about James as well. So Joe waited a while before telling Susan about Cameron's interview. When he did, she took it in stride, yet cautioned, "Cameron needs help and support. I know how important it is, because I have you. But Joe, you can't be that person."

"I know. It's not professional, and I can't become involved."

"That too, but it's not what I mean. Cameron's a threat to us."

Joe looked puzzled.

"Don't look at me that way," Susan continued. "Don't you think I can spot my competition?"

"Susan, it isn't that way."

"Are you confident? It might be if you don't keep your distance."

"You don't have anything to worry about. But I've been thinking about her situation, and Sister Mary Magdalen might be the solution even if Cameron doesn't go to her safe house."

"Okay, that makes sense. And don't forget, you still need to tell me about Sister Mary."

It was Linda's weekend to work the gallery. So on Saturday, Joe thought it might be a suitable time to tell Susan about Mary. When she came down for breakfast, he suggested walking to the ferries and crossing to Sausalito. Susan thought it was a fine idea, made sandwiches, and brought bottled water for an impromptu picnic. They took cushions, ate lunch on the rocks along Bridgeway, and watched the city from across the bay. Afterward, Joe said, "Mary is a nun at the Sisters of Perpetual Adoration Abbey. She also runs a safe house for former prostitutes and abused women. I learned her story during an investigation."

***

Mary had run away during the summer of 2002. She was thirteen then and should've started high school that fall. Arriving at the bus terminal in San Francisco, she was scared and hungry, had less than twenty bucks in her jeans, and was easy prey for LeRoy, who hung around the terminal looking for girls precisely like her. He took Mary under his wing. They went to a coffee shop and talked, and she felt protected. He offered food and a bed, but she didn't realize LeRoy meant his own bed until they arrived at his rooming house. Mary wasn't a virgin, so she went with the flow; it seemed like a small price to pay for security. LeRoy took care of her, grooming her for her new role—a role she didn't grasp until one morning after sex when he said, "It's time to buy clothes for your new job."

Mary was confused.

LeRoy explained.

"You're fuckin' crazy!" Mary shouted. "I won't do that."

That's when LeRoy exploded, hauling her out of bed, slapping her around, dragging her downstairs, then tossing her into the street—naked. LeRoy locked her out until she begged to be taken back. Sister Mary Magdalen was turning tricks that afternoon.

LeRoy had a stable of ten girls who took turns servicing him. Mary figured that to survive, she needed a strategy to outsmart him. So she honed her craft, using her turns with him to show off her skills. As a result, Mary became LeRoy's favorite, wrangling the best street corners. Next, she spruced up her image, converting her clientele to high-enders who drove expensive cars and dressed well. Over time, Mary discovered that many of them seemed lonely. So she personalized their relationships, encouraging conversation, learning about their families, and so on. Her johns left bigger tips and visited more frequently, and her business—as Sister Mary now thought of it—took off. But she fell short of generating enough money to break free and begin a legitimate enterprise.

So she revised her scheme, proposing to set up in a hotel, because it would be more comfortable and safer than her johns' back seats. There would be no cops to hassle them either. When Mary approached her men, saying she wouldn't mark up the hotel's rates, they got a kick out of it because it appealed to their entrepreneurial predispositions. Mary would also ask for ideas, and the men would joke about participating in a joint venture. Finally, Mary would ask them what they thought a fair price was. Their suggestions turned out to be greater than Mary had envisioned, and soon all was running smoothly. LeRoy had no idea, Mary easily kept his cash flow intact, and her profits grew.

***

Susan was puzzled. "I don't understand how she pulled it off. LeRoy was a no-brainer—Mary was a top producer, so he left her alone. But what about the other girls? Someone should've grown envious and ratted her out."

"She's a woman of charisma and presence, but I'm not merely talking about her sexuality. Sister Mary had easily become the de facto leader of the girls, looked out for them, and wasn't stingy when she began to accumulate cash. If they required anything, she was there.

"Then Mary needed to open a bank account, because she'd been keeping her cash under the mattress. But she encountered a hurdle because in the post-9/11 era: proper ID was required, and Sister Mary didn't have any. So she found a branch with a down-in-the-mouth manager, and after a private meeting, including some TLC, she walked out with an account."

"Well, it seems like a simple solution," Susan observed. "Women have been bartering their bodies forever. How is this any different than a city girl who can't pay the rent rewarding a guy in kind for buying dinner?"

They strolled around Sausalito for a while, then sat in Viña del Mar Park.

***

Everything was fine for Mary for quite a while. Her johns treated her well and referred additional clients, and soon Mary had over $50,000 in her savings account. It wasn't difficult to succeed; she had sound relationships with her men, many of whom saw her like a daughter. Apparently, role-playing daddy's little girl was a hit.

But change was on the way: Mary had been evolving spiritually. She had no idea why, but she recognized it. As a result, Mary started visiting the Sisters of Perpetual Adoration Abbey, riding the bus to their lady chapel. Eventually she met Sister Agnes, the abbess, and they became friends.

It all came unglued when one of LeRoy's youngest girls was caught holding back. He made an example of her, rounding up the rest of his girls and beating the thief so badly that she died on the way to the hospital. LeRoy didn't even give a shit about the girl's lost earnings.

After that, Mary was done, but before she left, she vowed to avenge the dead girl.

First, she put together a go bag with plenty of cash, stashing it in her hotel room. Next, it was time to deal with LeRoy. An ongoing feud between him and several other pimps gave her the cover she needed. So she bartered sex for a chef's knife at a local diner, then sneaked hand towels along with the knife into LeRoy's room, hiding them underneath his mattress. When her next turn came around, Mary took him to bed early. He was a happy man until she pulled the knife from under the mattress and castrated him in a single slash. Mary yanked a towel from under the bed. "Here, apply pressure. It's gonna hurt, but it'll save your life." Then Mary dialed 911 and left after telling LeRoy, "Blame one of the other pimps, because if you squeal on me, I'll come back and slit your throat." Mary returned to her hotel, cleaned up, and caught the bus to the abbey. Sister Agnes granted her sanctuary, and she had been there since.

***

As they walked to the ferry, Susan said, "Even though LeRoy deserved it, I can't imagine how much repressed rage Sister Mary must've had to do it. I'm overwhelmed by her violence, and it makes me squeamish. I hope she received help from the church."

Later that evening, having coffee at the kitchen table, Joe told Susan how he'd met Sister Mary. "I caught LeRoy's assault case in 2006 while Gabi was on vacation. I reviewed the uniform officers' report.

They'd obtained a brief statement from LeRoy. He'd told them what Mary had commanded him to say, and the brass was willing to accept everything at face value. They didn't want to waste time on an assault between pimps. But a few things bothered me, the most significant being that it was too personal for a business dispute. It made better sense that the attacker had already been in the room and in bed with LeRoy. Since he had no history of homosexuality, the inescapable conclusion was that one of his girls had attacked him. And it looked premeditated.

"Notwithstanding HQ, I visited LeRoy in the hospital. He refused to identify his attacker, steadfastly sticking to his story, and said that he intended to return to NYC, where it was civilized. So I followed up with his girls. They didn't know anything and were in a panic, since LeRoy wasn't around to protect them, and other pimps were circling. That was another thing that supported my theory. What pimp would've launched an attack on LeRoy without a plan in place? I tracked down all the girls except one. Secretly, I hoped she was thousands of miles away. I ought to have left it alone, but instead I questioned the girls a second time. Something new turned up. I was talking on a street corner with two of his girls who were turning tricks. When one approached a slow-moving car, the other whispered, 'Meet me in a half hour.' I learned that the missing girl had been with LeRoy the night he was attacked, and no one had seen her since. It was rumored that she'd gone to an abbey. I easily identified it as the Sisters of Perpetual Adoration. I never learned why that girl finked on Mary.

"But I had second thoughts about continuing. LeRoy wasn't going to testify. And I was unclear about sanctuary if that was the girl's plan. I knew I couldn't arrest her without involving HQ, and they wanted it to go away. But by now I had to meet her, so I spoke with the abbess. She confirmed that the girl was there, requesting sanctuary. 'She's beginning her postulancy and is remorseful about her past life. Can't you leave it at that?' I insisted, suggesting that the abbess join us. But Sister Mary wanted to see me alone. She told me her story and offered no justification for what she'd done, putting her future in my hands. We sat silently for a long time until at length I gave her my card and asked her to call if she wanted to talk. Then Mary walked me to the door and simply said, 'Thank you.'

"Arguably, I let a violent criminal off, albeit her victim was a killer. But Sister Mary wasn't a threat to society, and at trial she could reduce any jury to tears. I knew other cops who'd played judge and jury, but I'd always been by the book. Had she played me like a Stradivarius? Somehow it didn't seem like that, but I was bewildered, because I didn't have a choice. I didn't understand what had happened, but I felt good. And I was convinced I'd done the right thing. I wrote it up in accordance with the first responders' reports. Then I discussed it with the captain, and we agreed to close the case as unsolved."

"I'm happy you shared this with me. It means a lot," Susan said, coming around the table to hug Joe. "Whatever happened to LeRoy?"

"He beat a hasty retreat to Harlem. He's probably singing a cappella on the corner of One Twenty-Fifth Street and Seventh Avenue," Joe chuckled.

"Odd, isn't it? From what you said, LeRoy doesn't seem like the type to run. Why didn't he stick around and fight for his business?"

"I'm not certain, and by all accounts he was a mean son of a bitch. When I interrogated LeRoy, he was still terrified, and it went well beyond his physical injury. I think he had looked pure evil in the face and was horrified. Don't laugh, but I believe somehow Sister Mary conjured up all the demons of hell. All the rage and hatred she'd kept inside was exorcised with one stroke of that knife. And I keep seeing an apparition of a naked blood-spattered Mary Magdalen, standing over LeRoy, holding a knife to his throat."

***

There'd been no word from Melisa or Cameron. Although Joe and Gabi had left it up to the women to call, they were becoming impatient. Despite that, they intended to wait a bit before reaching out to them. Then another arrogant letter arrived from Vlad.

Joe:

Excellent job discovering the van. Keep up the outstanding work!

V.

It had been mailed from the same location. The paper and so forth were the same. Joe sent it to the lab but didn't expect any better results than before. He noted the informality of the signature, thinking, *I'll mention it to Ellen.* Gabi reported that it had been a month since they'd expanded the van search with the uniform division, but nothing had turned up. So they agreed to call it off and rely on the tip line.

***

On November 6, Gabi called Melisa, who said, "I was mugged last Thursday."

"Are you all right? What happened?"

"I was beaten up but could drive to the emergency room. They checked me over. Just scrapes and bruises. The pricks sure took their time feeling me up, though. My breasts are still sore."

"So the hospital released you, then?"

"Yes."

"I'm glad that's all that happened. Did you report it to the police?"

120

"Of course."

"Do you think you could identify them?"

"No, it was dark."

"What'd they take?"

"Almost everything: my bag, jewelry, even my small change, but they left my car keys."

"So that's how you got to the hospital. Tell me they didn't take your phone. You know how important those photos are."

"They're gone. The one I emailed you is all that's left. I'm sorry, but it never occurred to me this could happen. I've been thinking about the attack, though. Am I being silly or paranoid? Do you think Denis could've arranged all this to recover those pictures? And having me groped would appeal to him—sick bastard."

Gabi was a few steps ahead of Melisa. Something was off about the attack; most muggings were smash-and-grabs, and it sounded like Melissa had been roughed up on purpose. "I don't think you're silly. If you're up to it, I'd like to visit," she told the young woman, and they agreed to meet on Friday.

After Gabi rang off, she briefed Joe, who also thought that Rodolphe might've arranged the attack. Next, they called Dr. Sandler. "So Rodolphe finally remembered the photos," she said. "Maybe Melisa will be safe now."

Joe asked her about the truncated closing of Vlad's second letter.

"Rodolphe's playing with you, vouchsafing his comradeship. That's consistent with his profile. Pay no attention."

Later that day, reflecting on the investigations, Joe didn't like the conclusions he was drawing.

What did they know so far?

- Melisa had been an unwilling witness, and the photos were probably destroyed by now. Without them, the district attorney wasn't inclined to indict, as the case was only a matter of "he said, she said." It was DOA.

- The warehouse murders case was almost as hopeless. There was a profile that suggested Rodolphe was a high-functioning sociopath. Otherwise, there was just the circumstantial evidence that he had known one of the victims. Then the van had disappeared, and the international inquiries had yielded nothing. And they hadn't identified Rodolphe's accomplice yet. Cameron wasn't one hundred percent aboard yet either, and there was still the issue of spousal privilege. It seemed like Rodolphe had stalemated them at every turn, and there was no doubt he was managing his end well. But Joe wouldn't accept that this case was DOA yet. *Rodolphe's confidence and arrogance will eventually lead to a blunder, if he hasn't made one already. I'm confident a mistake will show up eventually, and I can wait.*

CHAPTER ELEVEN

Thursday, November 8, 2012

Before noon, Denis received a text from Tyree telling him that his order was in. He didn't have any classes that afternoon, so Denis took an envelope containing $5,000 and left. When he arrived in the Tenderloin, he was greeted by the loiterers, patted down, and waved in. Tyree was in his usual place with a .45 next to his right hand. "Hey, Doc," he said, "the whole thing went the way you wanted it to. But her tits are gonna be real sore."

"Excellent." Doc chuckled as they traded envelopes. "I'll have another project for you shortly—fake IDs."

Denis hoped Cameron wouldn't be home when he returned. He needed to deal with Melisa's shit. But her car was there. *Damn it, she's always in the way.* Denis locked Melisa's things in the car's trunk, and then they went out to dinner.

***

That evening, Cameron thought Denis seemed out of sorts, but she scarcely gave a shit anymore. Once they got home, she went to bed straightaway. When Denis came up later, Cameron was curled up with her back toward his side, pretending to be asleep. She continued to feign sleep but couldn't drop off. Instead, Cameron brooded about the root of her problems.

They'd developed slowly after she'd become sexually active at fifteen. She turned out to be uninhibited and insatiable. Everything seemed fine at first, and Cameron continued to mature, becoming a "ten" in the eyes of most men. With her looks and appetite, she should've been the epitome of every man's fantasy. However, it didn't work out that way, and Cameron eventually inferred that she made guys feel inadequate. That wasn't how she felt, yet in the end, she became insecure and ill at ease with them. So Cameron tamped down her urges.

Then Denis had come along, and everything changed. On their first date, he saw through her, and the early years were wonderful. Denis never judged, and she felt liberated. But their relationship wasn't purely sexual. They loved being together. Denis encouraged her writing, and she began her second book.

All of it seemed to delight Denis, but Cameron hadn't recognized yet that she was a possession. Denis had acquired a perfect trophy wife, and he liked showing her off and watching other men become envious. After a while, their relationship began deteriorating. The sex became kinkier; he pushed Cameron hard, at first cajoling, then manipulating. Later, Denis had an affair, and there was the rumpus with Melisa. When Cameron confronted her, it was partially to see what Melisa had that she didn't. Then Cameron had an affair, but even after it blew up, she stayed and made amends. Denis punished her, and she was a good girl. And eventually their relationship improved.

Over time, though, he had become creepier, colder, and rougher. Cameron's wishes never mattered, and Denis took her whenever he liked. It would've been a victory for her to avert a climax, but Cameron's physiology didn't work that way, because even with minimal stimulation, Denis always got her off. It galled her how he controlled her body. And lately Denis had become unrelenting about having Cameron seduce a little girl and bring her home for them to share. But despite her objections, Denis had drawn Cameron into his planning. It even became a topic of dinner conversation. Inexplicably, she was considering a compromise—a barely legal girl.

The upshot was that her past insecurities returned. Now Cameron needed Denis's approval for everything. Her public image, what the world saw as a happening, striking, and professional lady, was nothing but a facade. Cameron's unseen self was like a picture of Dorian Gray.[2] She hated it all, was despondent and miserable again, and needed help. Cameron thought about Joe. *I ought to call him.*

***

When Denis came down the next morning, Cameron was already out shopping, so he retrieved Melisa's things, finding all the items he'd expected. Denis deleted the photos from her phone, smashed it, and burned it in the grill. Later, he gathered up its remains and the rest of Melisa's possessions and scattered them among four or five trash cans around the city. All the loose ends were now tidied up.

Nevertheless, Denis couldn't relax. What if the police wouldn't accept Melisa's mugging as a random event?

He decided he would continue making plans to disappear. He needed an attorney with contacts to overseas brokers and bankers. Also, another talk with Tyree. He envisioned slipping across the northern border and making his way to French-speaking Quebec, where he could hole up. And Cameron wouldn't be coming with him.

***

On the thirteenth, Gabi went to Palo Alto to meet Melisa, mainly to give her moral support and assess her injuries. But that week was hectic, as Gabi was in court for several days, so she and Joe couldn't meet until Thursday for a briefing.

"Her face showed the remains of a scrape from falling during the mugging," Gabi reported. "But this wasn't a simple one. An unsub lifted her off the ground from behind while the other one worked over her stomach, kidneys, and breasts. It wasn't just about retrieving her photos, and I'm convinced these guys were pros."

***

Cameron was hesitant about calling Joe, so she put it off until Friday afternoon, the sixteenth.

"I was hoping you'd call. It's been a while," Joe commented.

"I know. I don't have anything to report, but I didn't want you to worry. Could we meet and talk anyway?"

"Sure."

"How about where we met before?"

They agreed to meet on Monday afternoon. Driving over, Cameron mentally reviewed their prior meeting, recalling the questions she'd been evasive about. Revisiting them would be a suitable opener. Cameron was becoming comfortable with Joe, so she decided that she'd be straightforward. *Anything I tell him is probably same ole, same ole anyway.*

***

Before he left for the Kensington Park, Joe had called Sister Mary Magdalen and asked if she would talk with Cameron. "Will she be a guest?" Mary asked.

"Probably not. I don't think we're there yet."

"No problem. Whatever you need."

While driving to the hotel, Joe had also thought about the upcoming interview. Notwithstanding his uncertainty over what Cameron wished to talk about, he had an issue to discuss with her. He and Gabi hadn't focused on the unsub's accomplice yet. It wasn't an oversight; it was because they didn't have anything to go on. But now that Cameron appeared to be more cooperative, maybe she could shed light on his identity.

When Joe reached the hotel, John had already arranged for cappuccinos and biscotti as before. Cameron arrived and began without small talk. "I didn't answer all of your questions last time."

"I know, but I need all the help I can get now. We're going no place fast."

"All right, you asked me if Denis did anything that rang a bell about the warehouse murders, and I avoided your query because I was embarrassed. I still am." Joe reassured her, and she continued. "I told you that I paid dearly for my affair. Denis punished me for months afterwards. It was humiliating. It's confusing because I was powerless." Then Cameron told him about "making amends," including dildo riding and puppy play using a collar and leash: sitting, heeling, and crawling after a ball while wiggling her butt and such. "You understand?"

"Yes, take your time."

"I can't believe I just told you all that stuff. It's sick, Jesus. But it's the business with the dildo that rang a bell." She told him how Denis had forced her down the first time. "It seems like a forerunner to the twins."

At last, I think she's turning the corner. "I think you're right: Denis impaled you. But look, Cameron, you don't have to go any further. You're not the first woman who has fallen under the thrall of a master manipulator. Humiliation and control are his stock-in-trade. Don't beat yourself up. I know someone who can help. We'll talk about her before you leave."

"Okay, but there's more," Cameron said, and went on, telling him about Denis's obsession with her seducing a little girl for them. "It's the last straw. I don't think I can do it anymore. But you need to understand about me, the way I am about sex." Then, among tears and anger, it came out. "I don't want this. But who will believe me? We look like a perfect couple. Denis never physically abuses me. No bruises or black eyes. No broken bones or trips to the emergency room. And do I want this out in the open? Christ, I don't know. I'm in a bad place."

When she had calmed down, Joe asked, "Do you want to leave home?"

"No, not now; I need to put a plan in order. The situation hasn't deteriorated to that point. Even though Denis is becoming rougher and rougher during sex, I don't feel physically threatened yet."

"You know all you have to do is call whenever you want out."

Cameron nodded, and Joe continued, "Here's what I think you should do. I spoke to Sister Mary Magdalen about you. I didn't mention your name, only that you were a woman in trouble. She's willing to meet, talk, and offer you any support she can. Sister Mary was turning tricks at thirteen and has seen and done things you can't imagine. But don't be put off by her prior vocation. Also, she's the least judgmental person I know. Will you let her counsel you?"

"Fine, before I leave we'll figure out dates. But I want you there, at least to introduce us. Will you set it up?"

"Yes, but I have another thing before you go, all right? I told you we're positive the murders were a two-man job. There's the leader, your husband, and a helper. Probably a fit person, handy with tools. Maybe in the construction trades, or a manual laborer. Is there anyone like that in your husband's life."

"Zack," Cameron said, "but he hasn't been around lately. I know Denis has been trying to reach him. Apparently his phone is out of order or shut off." She filled Joe in on their relationship with Zack. Cameron didn't know his last name but knew he lived about a hundred miles south of San Francisco. She was able to provide the name of the hardware store that had made the initial recommendation. Afterward, Joe arranged her lunch with Sister Mary on the twenty-first at Scala's Bistro.

Later, Joe reviewed Cameron's interview with Gabi. "Cameron's beginning to think he's our murderer, but she's hanging in there."

"Will he have to assault her before she makes the break?"

"I hope not. We have some positive news, though. Cameron has identified a possible accomplice, Zack. But I have an uncomfortable feeling about him, since he can't be reached. I think Rodolphe may be doing damage control." Joe told Gabi what little he knew about Zack. "Try to locate this guy. Make him your priority."

***

First thing Tuesday morning, Gabi tackled tracking down Zack. Contacting the hardware store, she spoke to the manager who had made the initial introduction to Rodolphe. He hadn't seen Zack in six months, but he provided the following information: Zack's last name was Wheeler; he lived south of San Francisco; his wife had been a practical nurse, but the manager didn't know where; and there'd been a messy divorce. Then Gabi discovered that there were at least four common given names associated with the nickname Zack. As a result, her DMV search turned up a plethora of hits, so Gabi decided to trace Zack's ex-wife first. She would likely have an address that would narrow their search. After a couple of calls, Gabi learned that San Francisco General had a record of employing Gwen Wheeler until 2004. Her emergency contact was Zackery Wheeler. She had left a forwarding address in San Jose. Her file also contained a request from the Good Samaritan Hospital in that city for an employment reference.

Gabi obtain Gwen's mobile number through her contact at the telephone company. When she called, she explained to Gwen why they were interested in Zack and concerned for his safety. Gwen didn't seem overly cooperative, asserting she'd had no contact with Zack in several years and hoped she would never see or hear from him again. Gabi pressed, offering to drive to San Jose. Finally, Gwen agreed. Her next day off was the day after Thanksgiving, and they agreed to me at a local McDonald's. Before they hung up, Gwen said, "Under no circumstances are you to contact my daughter."

Gabi's antennae went up over Gwen's concern about her daughter. So before leaving that evening, she contacted the county records clerk for a copy of the divorce filings. When she arrived to work on Monday, they were on her desk. There were boilerplate reasons for the divorce, but strangely, Zack had agreed to what was tantamount to a restraining order regarding Gwen's minor child, Janet.

Odd. What's this all about?

***

During Thanksgiving week, Denis retained an international lawyer, James Steinberg, meeting with him on the twenty-first. Lawyer Steinberg was well known to the San Francisco elite, yet they had never met. Rodolphe had ideas about repositioning funds overseas, and Steinberg encouraged him to call several CEOs of EU family–affiliated businesses to explore his stratagem.

***

Joe's meeting with Cameron and Sister Mary was scheduled for noon on the twenty-first. He arrived about twenty minutes early, and Mary wasn't far behind. She was usually dressed in jeans and a flannel shirt, with no makeup and a spectacular disregard for her hair. But today it was professional attire, and Joe commented on how attractive she looked. "I clean up well, don't I?" she chuckled, and they both laughed.

When Cameron entered, she was nervous. They all made small talk for a while, but Joe soon excused himself, thinking that Mary had called it—a habit would've put Cameron off. Now they just looked like business associates at lunch.

Sister Mary and Cameron continued to chat, and finally Mary said, "Joe tells me you need help. What can I do?"

"Did he tell you what's happening?"

"Only in the broadest terms."

"Well. I don't know where to start; it's confusing."

"Would it reassure you if I shared more of my story?"

"Yes."

"Joe must've told you how I ran away from home and ended up with a pimp."

"Yes, but he never said why you left."

"My father beat my mother. Then when I got older, he turned the belt on me. After a couple of years, I took off."

"Didn't anybody notice the beatings?"

"No, he was a wily bastard, beating us where the bruises wouldn't show. He never broke any bones either." Then Sister Mary told Cameron an abbreviated but guarded version of her story, saying simply that she had fought with LeRoy.

"So you escaped to the abbey. Did you find peace there and learn how to forgive yourself?"

Sister Mary considered her answer for a moment. "Yes, but it's a two-part, intertwined process. Peace comes if you're remorseful and ask for the Lord's forgiveness. Yet when you've hit rock bottom and have nothing left, it almost comes naturally. Nevertheless, work at it every day, and don't forget the Lord's grace is always with you. But forgiving yourself is harder, because we can't accept that we're victims. Even if merely subconsciously, we want to be accountable for our actions. So we accept God's forgiveness but not our own. I don't understand why we think we're more demanding than the Almighty is. That's how I look at it, but you might feel differently."

"Prayer?"

"It's what I do and my ministry. Has Joe told you about that?"

"Yes, but how did you put the money together? Joe said the church didn't provide the funds."

Sister Mary laughed. "A story for another time. You'll enjoy it, because it was truly inspired with just a touch of divine irony."

They talked until nearly three o'clock. Then Cameron settled the bill, and as they left, Sister Mary said, "Let's talk again."

That's fine. I like the sister, Cameron thought as she exited the building.

***

132

On her way home, Sister Mary reflected. She'd been less than candid when telling Cameron what had happened when Joe came to the abbey. She'd said that after talking with her, Joe had concluded there wasn't enough evidence to charge her with anything. Cameron had seemed to accept it, yet it wasn't really what happened.

Joe had asked her what she knew about the attack on LeRoy. Almost at once, Mary had become confused. She'd prepared an alternate narrative for the police, but as she spoke, something changed. To this day, Mary couldn't adequately describe it. She recalled how slowly her heart beat, but that wasn't the most surprising part of what she experienced. Mary remembered warmth diffusing through her, accompanied by a feeling of tranquility. Joe's face seemed to radiate kindness. His eyes were gentle, and they relentlessly coaxed the truth from her.

They sat for a long time. At length, Joe said, "I'm satisfied. Here's my card; call if you want to talk again." Mary accompanied him to the front door, thanking him. His face seemed normal now. She wondered, *Is he confused too*? Returning to her cell, she collapsed on the bed, mystified and overcome with tears. Sister Agnes heard and came to hold her. At last, Mary was able to sob, "I'm so happy."

"Oh, my dear."

"You don't understand."

"The Lord works in mysterious ways and chooses the most unlikely people," the abbess explained.

"No, I don't mean me."

"I know. It's terrifying yet wonderful when you've seen the face of God," Sister Agnes whispered, hugging her postulant closely.

It took Mary days to distill what had happened. Finally, it became clear. The Lord had heard her confession and forgiven her. And now she was ready for the next chapter of her story. A story that had already been written.

Sister Mary hadn't told Joe her full experience yet either.

CHAPTER TWELVE

Friday, November 23, 2012

On Friday, Gabi left for San Jose early. There wasn't much traffic on the day after Thanksgiving. She was at the McDonald's an hour before her ten-thirty meeting with Gwen, which gave her time to gather her thoughts. Her goal was to verify Zack's home address and current phone number, the last time Gwen had seen him, what'd caused the sudden divorce, whether she knew about Denis Rodolphe, and so on.

After Gwen arrived and got coffee, she asked, "Why are you worried about Zack's safety?"

"There's a murder investigation underway. A material witness was mugged and beaten up last week. We think our unsub contracted for it."

"To keep them quiet?"

"Yes."

"Well, as far as I'm concerned, a beating is too good for that son of a bitch. I don't care if he lives or dies. I've lost contact anyway. Don't know if I can help you much."

Gabi pushed. "I'm sorry you feel that way. I thought you were speaking metaphorically. Zack must've treated you badly."

"Yeah . . . he treated me badly all right, but I probably don't mean it. I loved him right up until the last. I never saw it coming. The bastard abused Janet and cheated on me. For Christ's sake, she was ten. I walked right in on them, naked, asleep, and cuddled up on top of our bed. I was gobsmacked. Obviously, this hadn't been their first time, and it was also clear Janet had been 'consenting.' I yanked her from his arms and dragged Janet back to her room. When I returned to our bedroom, I demanded he agree to an immediate divorce, give me everything, and never see Janet again. Then I told Zack to shut the fuck up and leave, otherwise I was going to the police. I never saw him afterwards except to sign the papers. A year or so later, Zack sent me a handwritten note. He said he was sorry, gave me his address and told me his phone number was the same, and said, 'If you're ever in a jam, you know you can call.'

"That was it, nothing else. I never called him. Here's a copy of the note; I wrote his mobile number on it."

Gabi let Gwen calm down for a moment. "You've been through a lot. Can you fill in some information for me? You know, when you were first married, your first husband's name, Janet's birthday, when you married Zack, his relationship with Rodolphe, and so on?"

Gwen said she'd never heard of Rodolphe but supplied the other details.

"One last thing, if it isn't too painful: How did all this play out with Janet? Was she in bad shape? Did your daughter need therapy?"

"It's bizarre, and we're still working through it. After it happened, I took her to my gynecologist. Her virginity was intact, but Janet had signs of anal sex. I begged the doctor not to report it. Thankfully, she didn't. I'm an RN now, so I'm aware of all the symptoms that Janet should've been exhibiting but wasn't. It was just her anger at me, and we fought all the time. Janet kept yelling that she wanted Zack to be her first. Then after a while, she seemed calmer. She joined the women's field hockey team, doubled down on her school work, and started horseback riding. It was complicated because Janet had been abused, and that broke my heart, but she was also the other woman. I tried to get her into therapy, but she refused, and I ended up with a shrink. Things seemed to change again for the better when she was sixteen. I was confused about what had happened, but I didn't ask. If you met Janet today, you wouldn't have a clue about what she has been through. Now she's a freshman at San Jose City College and doing well."

***

Monday morning, November 26, Cameron called Joe and summarized her meeting with Sister Mary. "I'm glad you introduced us," she told him. "She was helpful, and we're going to meet again. But nothing has been arranged yet."

In the early afternoon, Gabi and Joe met with Dr. Sandler. Ellen agreed there was probably nothing else to gain from Melisa and that Rodolphe was likely behind her attack. Joe reported that they had identified Zack as a probable coconspirator, noting his susceptibility to Rodolphe's blackmail, his appetite for young girls, and that Zack had the skills Rodolphe required. Then Gabi reviewed her interview with Gwen. "I don't understand Janet's reactions. It goes completely against anything I've ever heard. How could she cope so well during and after his abuse?"

"I don't know," Ellen said. "I can't say without talking to her. Victims cope differently. Did Janet figure out a way to survive, even if subconsciously, by convincing herself that she loved Zack? A variation of Stockholm syndrome, maybe? But regardless of what Janet says, she wasn't capable of consent. Additionally, notwithstanding the usual PTSD symptoms, there're no absolutes. Think of all the soldiers returning from battle who can handle it. I think Janet has no guilt, since it seemed normal to her. And she appears to have loved Zack. Perhaps Janet replaced her real father, who abandoned her, with him. After it blew up, she took her repressed anger out on her mother. When things improved the first time, she transferred her aggression away from mom to sports and schoolwork. I'm guessing it was by design. More significant, when Janet was sixteen, something happened that altered her life. I would bet it was an adult romance in which she willingly surrendered her virginity. Honestly, I think she's doing fine. It also seems like Janet has closure with the Zack saga. Mom, on the other hand, is still struggling.

"Wrapping up," Ellen concluded, "Rodolphe's attempts to call Zack could be a ruse. Or perhaps he's cleaning up loose ends. Even if we can't see it yet, his plan is unfolding. That makes me worried for Cameron's safety."

Later, Gabi came into Joe's office. "Guess who called and wants to talk? Gwen Wheeler's daughter, Janet Edwards. That's her birth father's last name. She doesn't have classes on Tuesday, so she'll be here tomorrow morning at ten thirty."

"I wonder what that's all about?" Joe replied.

The next morning, the twenty-seventh, when Janet arrived, she was dressed as if she were going to work. It occurred to Gabi that either by design or instinct, she was making certain she was taken seriously. "Mom doesn't know I'm here, and I'd like to keep it that way. I don't want this interview recorded either." Gabi assured her she wasn't being recorded. "I didn't know about your meeting with Mom, but she was upset when she came home. It must have dug up everything, and she called a girlfriend for support. I wasn't paying much attention until I heard about Zack being in danger, then I started eavesdropping. If you didn't notice, Mom hates him and probably wouldn't give a damn if Zack came to harm. I, on the other hand, don't feel that way. I'm worried and am here to help."

"Yes, we're concerned," Gabi said, and explained. "The information your mother gave us ought to pinpoint our search. But unfortunately, his mobile number is out of service." Janet took out her phone, scrolled to a contact, and handed it to Gabi.

"Is this the number and address you have?"

"Yes." Then Gabi asked if she were willing to talk about her relationship with Zack. But Janet was reluctant at first.

"Is it necessary?"

"I think so. I ask because I'm trying to understand your family dynamic. Frankly, I'm amazed at how well you handled it. Most victims of abuse manifest symptoms like PTSD. I'd like to hear your story. But if you're uncomfortable, we can skip to brainstorming how you might help."

"Fine," Janet said, "but we must be off the record until I say we can go back on. If you try to indict Zack, I'll deny everything I'm going to tell you." Gabi nodded her agreement.

"Your mistake is in thinking of me like a victim. I don't know why, but it felt natural. Not exactly in a sexual way, because I was too young." Janet continued with her story, concluding with when her mother had burst in on them. "I loved Zack and wanted to live with him."

"I understand," Gabi said. "Let's start with what your mother told me about your life after Zack left. If you feel it's accurate, you don't have to talk about it further, or you can tweak it." She reported what Gwen had said.

"It's accurate; I was a first-class bitch. But I need to clarify the second change. It's complicated. I'm still off the record?"

"Yes."

"I was sixteen and interested in men. I had dated occasionally, but nothing serious. So I was ready to take the next step. Yet I was looking for something besides a hook up. At the same time, I recognized that I hadn't resolved my relationship with Zack and needed to bring that to closure. Eventually the obvious solution dawned on me. So I located Zack. I knew there were risks and that sleeping with him might screw me up. It seemed like it was worth it, though."

"You went to him, didn't you?"

"Yes. I knew where Mom kept his note with his address and phone number. So in June 2008, I spent a weekend there. It came together easier than I envisioned. Mom went away for a four-night hospital off-site. They provided bus transportation, so I was left with her car, even though I had only a provisional license. Once her weekend plans were settled, I called Zack and arranged to drive to San Juan Bautista. He waited for me in his same old pickup, at a secondary road leading to his cabin. We talked at the kitchen table until I went to the bedroom. I admit I was anxious, but I ought not to have been. Afterward, Zack said, 'I'm sorry: I don't deserve you.' "

"Did it give you what you needed?"

"Yes. Before I left on Sunday afternoon, we had supper at a burger joint on the highway. When I was leaving, Zack said, 'Janet, you need to move on. Don't worry about me. I'm okay with where I'm at now. But if you ever need me, just call.' I told him I understood and headed for home." Janet paused. "Unless you have other questions, we can go back on the record now. What can I do to help you find Zack?"

"Did Zack ever talk about a wealthy person he worked for in San Francisco? He probably went there for a week or so at a time and stayed with his customer?"

"Zack didn't say much about work. But he mentioned a wealthy doctor who would help him if he needed extra cash. Zack called him a 'stand-up guy.'"

"Was he a medical doctor?"

"I assume so, but Zack didn't say."

"So he could've been otherwise—a professor, for example?"

"I don't see why not. All I know is that Zack called him Doc."

"We'd like a look inside Zack's cabin. We might be able to determine if there's a reason for concern. If there is, we can collect a DNA sample and fingerprints for our database."

"That's easy. I can tell you where a key is hidden outside, because Zack showed me."

"That won't work for us. We need a search warrant. Otherwise, anything we uncover can't be used in court. We don't have enough evidence to apply for one."

"Does that mean Zack might be prosecuted?"

"I don't know. We're unclear how Zack is involved. It's possible he was coerced. Our suspect won't hesitate to eliminate him. That's why we're concerned."

"You mean *kill* Zack . . . right?"

"Yes, but let's not focus on that. We think Zack has valuable information. If you file a missing persons report, it might give us enough to obtain a search warrant."

"Okay, can I do it now?"

"No, it's within San Juan Bautista's jurisdiction. You'll have to file it there, but we'll effectively quarterback it."

Before Janet left, Gabi spoke to the chief in San Juan Bautista. He agreed to work with them, suggesting that Janet come to their HQ tomorrow because he'd be on duty. After they rang off, Gabi told her, "I don't think you'll have any problems with the chief. He seems cooperative. Present yourself as Zack's stepdaughter and let me know when it's filed, so I can plan with them."

***

On Thursday, November 29, Gabi and Joe updated Dr. Sandler on Janet's interview. "You were correct about her two personality changes," Gabi began. "And the second one was after a weekend with Zack."

"It makes sense. She kills two birds with one stone, becoming a woman and achieving closure with him," Ellen said. "This fits together. In 2002, Zack steps over the line and abuses Janet. Despicable though it was, we now know it wasn't violent or cruel. Fast forward ten years. Zack participates in two cold-blooded killings. What's changed along the way? Obviously, the divorce in 2002. It was a stressor, but more important, Rodolphe enters the scene in 2004. I'm still convinced the warehouse murders weren't his first kill. With merely a clue, he could've wheedled Janet's story out of Zack. Was Zack blackmailed into a prior killing? Maybe a young girl like Janet? That would appeal to Zack's tastes and make his first time easier. You've already searched the databases using the modus operandi. Why not search on Zack's type: attractive, Caucasian, blonde, and around puberty? You only need to go back eight years to when he met Rodolphe."

When they returned to the office, Gabi requested searches of unsolved abductions from 2004 to the present. She reduced the rest of the criteria to all girls taken in northern California between the ages of nine and sixteen.

***

The SJBPD chief called the next afternoon. "Sergeant, I have the search warrant. I expanded it to include bank and credit card records as well as Wheeler's mail. It wasn't a problem with the judge, because we've been friends since grade school. Where Zack lives there's no mail delivery, so he has a post office box. We won't have any problems there either, since the postmaster's a friend of many years as well. I don't mean to tell you your job, but let's execute this tomorrow. Saturday isn't a problem for us. I don't think we should overlook the obvious."

"You mean that Zack's dead inside the cabin?"

"Yes. Is his stepdaughter coming?"

"I'd like her to."

"Will you prepare her? Just in case."

"Janet's a smart young lady. I think she's already figured that out, but I'll talk to her. What time?"

"Nine. It shouldn't take you more than an hour and forty-five minutes on a Saturday."

"Okay, I'll call you back to confirm."

Then Gabi called Janet. "You know we might find Zack inside?" she cautioned.

"Yes, but I'm coming anyway."

While Gabi was on the phone, Joe pursued a thought triggered by their meeting with Ellen Sandler. What if the suspects had used Rodolphe's house? It would've been easier than using a warehouse or the like. So Joe called Cameron. "I have an update. We've identified Zack, and we have his full name, address, and mobile number now. I'll let you know what turns up. I need a favor too."

"Sure."

"Do you keep your calendars? I'm looking for the last eight years."

"Yes, on my laptop. What do you need?"

"I'd like to know when you've been traveling—alone. Let's say for three days plus."

"What you're asking is when Denis was home by himself, right?"

"Yes?"

"Are you onto something?"

"Maybe."

"All right, give me a few days. I'll be traveling, but I can start with 2004 through 2008 before I leave," Cameron said, and rang off.

Gabi told Janet who to contact at the sheriff's department. "If you have any problems, call me."

Then Gabi reached out to the chief in San Juan Bautista. After she finished, he said, "I'm sorry it ended this way for Janet. She seems like a nice young lady. I think Janet was close to her stepdad, even though she didn't see him often. At least the family has closure now. If Janet wants to plan for his burial down here, I can help. I'll call her to express my condolences."

"She'll appreciate that, Chief. Would you like periodic updates?"

"Please, and if you need help, call."

Joe asked how Janet had taken the news. "About as well as we could have expected. I think she anticipated this outcome. She'll tell Gwen."

***

Janet wasn't looking forward to telling her mom, but it might lead to cleaning up their emotional mess. It was time to put that behind them. Her mother was fixing tea in the kitchen. "Mom, I need to talk to you," Janet said as she walked in.

"All right . . . what's the matter?"

"Sergeant Müller called me this morning."

"I didn't know you knew her."

"I do; I'll tell you afterwards. Let me get this out. The Marin County Sheriff's Department found Zack's body in the woods two weeks ago."

She filled her mother in on the rest. By then, Janet was crying. Gwen reached across the table and, taking her daughter's hands, said, "I'm sorry for you, honey. I was afraid it would be something like this when the police came knocking. I'm sad too."

"Do you mean that? I thought you hated him."

"Yes, I mean it. It's complicated, but I still have fond memories . . . they survive."

"Do you still hate me?"

"Janet, I never hated you. I hated what the two of you did to us. It took me a long time to put that in the rearview mirror. You were a little kid, and it wasn't your fault. Damn it! What was the matter with him? Zack ought to have known better! You and I became so entrenched in our feelings, we couldn't move on. I should've been able to because I was the adult. In the end, you broke the cycle. You seemed to put your anger aside when you doubled down on sports and schoolwork, but mostly with the change when you were sixteen. I never asked, but I noticed. We ought to have talked then. Sad that it's taken this long."

"I want to talk about when I was sixteen. I saw Zack. That's what happened."

"Was that the long weekend in June? When I was at the hospital's off-site?"

"You knew? You never said anything."

"I Googled the distance. The mileage on the car was a giveaway. I wasn't certain, but I was suspicious. You seemed to be putting your past to bed . . . Is that a bad choice of words?"

"Probably, but that doesn't mean you're wrong. It was my first time."

"I thought it might be. How do you feel about it now?"

"It was kind of bittersweet. Afterward, we knew there was no unfinished business. Nothing left to say. Nothing left to do. Is this conversation weird or what?"

"Oh, it's weird, all right. Not your typical mother-daughter talk. It's time we had it, though. Stay here; I need to get something we should read together. It's a letter Zack sent. It was inside another envelope, and it's dated after your visit." Gwen went into the living room and collected it. It was sealed and had OPEN IN THE EVENT OF MY DEATH written on the outside. "I didn't tell the police about this. I was confused, but I guess it's okay now." She opened the envelope and pulled out a letter.

> *Gwen:*
>
> *I ought to have reached out a long time ago. I'm sorry for all the pain. I never thought this could happen to us. I was happy and loved you. I knew it was wrong. But I lost my moral compass, and I don't have it back yet. Janet was never to blame. I hope she understands that. I don't know any way to make this right.*
>
> *Since I left, I've continued to make mistakes. I can't seem to extricate myself from a cycle of bad judgments. I'm scared that I won't be around much longer. My health is fine. It's not that, but I have an overwhelming feeling that it's all ending. I'm sad, because I'm not ready yet.*
>
> *I don't have much, but what I have, I don't want to squander on a lawyer. So here are my wishes. I made*

a copy which is in my safe-deposit box. Both copies are notarized and witnessed. Don't be upset with the disposition. You have a great job, a career, and a pension. I'm not worried about you. You're strong. You're a survivor. I'm trying to give Janet a better start in life than I had. I leave her everything. If she's a minor when I pass, I want you to handle this. If Janet's old enough, she can do it.

I love you both.

Zack

Then he listed his possessions, such as his cabin, truck, savings account, checking account, and so on, and there was a safe-deposit key.

They stayed up late and talked. Gwen intended to reach out to the Marin County officials to see about having Zack's remains cremated. Janet called the chief, asking for help in arranging a graveside memorial and burial in San Juan Bautista. Then they talked about whether Janet should see a therapist. Finally, Gwen said, "Don't overlook the obvious. Zack always used to say, 'If it ain't broke, don't fix it.' It's a phrase they used in the trades. You've done so well, and I'm proud of you. I think you have it together, no matter how you did it. Maybe it's best to leave it alone. Think about it; it's your call."

***

Susan and Joe had a pleasant weekend despite the Christmas crush. On Saturday, December 15, Joe bought a tree, and later they did some household shopping. On Sunday, over supper, they talked about holiday plans. When they were finished, Susan said, "You never did tell me the rest of Sister Mary's story. How about now?"

"Why not? It takes a while, though? I'll make coffee." When it had been made and poured, Joe began. "After our interview at the abbey, I didn't see her until early 2008, when she called, inviting me to lunch. Mary was nervous because she wanted to talk about that meeting. Then she told me that after I'd left, she couldn't stop crying for a long time. She'd been confused and wondered if something otherworldly had happened. Eventually, she accepted that her tears were happy ones because I'd given her a second chance and vowed not to squander it. As a result, Mary developed a plan that was to be her ministry, but before she undertook it, she wanted my blessing."

***

Mary had pondered over what her ministry might be and now envisioned establishing a safe house, one that would provide shelter and medical care for escaping prostitutes and abused women. If the house was successful, she hoped to expand its services later. Mary had talked to Sister Agnes, who supported her vision. But the abbess was unable to help with funding, since the abbey itself was struggling. This was a stumbling block, because Mary couldn't set up a tax-exempt charity, hold fundraisers, and so on. It would be too public, too dangerous, and protecting the women from their pimps or abusers was paramount. So how to raise money?

Gradually, a plan dawned on her. Mary asked permission of the abbess to raise tax-free donations for the abbey. Those funds would be earmarked to purchase the house and carry out its ongoing operations. Sister Agnes consulted with their attorney, and the plan was approved. As seed money and a show of good faith, Mary donated $50,000 from what remained of her savings. Afterward, Sister Agnes gave her a receipt that specified what the funds would be used for. That proof was going to be part of Sister Mary's sales pitch.

Intuitively, when Mary escaped LeRoy, she'd kept contact information on her wealthiest johns, the ones with whom she had the best relationships. Mary needed $2 million, and they were all potential donors. She intended to approached twenty of those men, asking each for a $100,000. If they declined, she could simply move down her list. Mary had absolute confidence in her ability to sell the project. *After all*, she silently chuckled, *it shouldn't be any harder than convincing them I loved them.*

The last hurdle was getting into their offices. If she contacted them as their friendly local call girl, they would come running. But that wasn't her playing field anymore. Mary wasn't working for a pimp, and her new Boss deserved respect. She aimed to be professional, so on the first day, Mary put on her habit and set out.

That day she saw two of the three men she'd targeted. The first man recognized her immediately, although he was confused. Finally, Mary figured it out. He thought she was role-playing. Mary assured him that she was a nun. Then he broke into a big smile, came around his desk, and kissed her on the cheek. "So that's what happened to you," he laughed. Mary left a half hour later with a check for $100,000. The man thought her plan was a great idea.

She couldn't see the second john. The third one saw her but didn't recognize her. She had anticipated that this might happen, so she removed her wimple and shook out her hair. That did the trick—another check.

Afterward, she honed her approach to the men's secretaries and saw everyone else on her list. They all contributed, and several asked if they could participate. So she improvised, offering them seats on a board of directors that she concocted on the fly. Mary financed the house in less than a month, and it had been up and running since late 2008, generally with six to ten girls in residence.

***

"It's fascinating how she put the house together," Susan said. "Obviously, the close relationships with her johns were important, and there was a genuine affection between them. But it was more than that. For all intents and purposes, she consulted with them during her move to the hotel. They observed her conceive, develop, and successfully manage her reshaped business. She had a track record, and I don't think her johns foresaw much risk. And putting her money where her mouth was closed the deal. But I'm astonished Sister Mary had that much money."

"I found it hard to believe as well. Apparently, her business was extremely profitable. If LeRoy had had a grain of sense, he would've made her a partner." Joe chuckled. "She relies on a handful of officers like me, a couple of vice cops, as well as Ellen Sandler for her referrals. She also works with clergy in high-prostitution areas."

"Did she ask you to become a board member?"

"Yes, but I declined. I wasn't clear if it was a conflict of interest. Also, I didn't want to request clearance from HQ, because the word would eventually leak out. I prefer to help her on an ad hoc basis."

After the eleven o'clock news, they turned in. But Joe had work on his mind. He'd blocked it out over the weekend, but now as he tried to sleep, it crept back in. He thought about the dead twins and possibly another girl—Sally Thompson. He thought about the battered psyches of Melisa, Janet, Gwen, and Cameron, all struggling to recover. But Cameron was in the worst shape. And finally, as he fell asleep, Joe thought about Zack's letter, a copy of which Janet had sent to Gabi. *It's tantamount to a confession. And an acknowledgment that Zack felt at risk from Rodolphe.*

While Joe was cogitating, Susan mulled over Sister Mary and Joe's abbey interview. She thought about their reactions. Their experience sounded supernatural. Had Joe been a stand-in, absolving Mary? Susan wasn't certain, but she didn't think it was far-fetched. It seemed straightforward and made sense. After all, Mary couldn't fulfill her ministry from jail, and Joe said he didn't have a choice. Then Susan dropped off, thinking how blessed Joe had been.

CHAPTER FOURTEEN

Tuesday, December 18, 2012

The week was shaping up to be irksome. Cameron was being a pain in the ass. This morning, at breakfast, they'd had an annoying argument. Apparently, the clothes washer was giving her trouble. "Fine, just go ahead and buy a new one," Denis said.

"We might as well replace the dryer too; it's just as old," Cameron responded. "Why don't we go to Lowe's or Home Depot, see if they're on sale? Maybe they could be delivered and installed before Kirsten and her husband arrive on Friday. We'll have extra laundry with them here."

Another irritation—Kirsten's dorky husband. And a big-box store—too much trouble. "I don't have time for this. Why don't you get that local guy, Lou? You called him last year to replace the dishwasher."

"Lou would have to order them. I'm afraid the clothes washer won't hold up. So let's do it this week. They'll be cheaper at those stores, and they'll probably have them in stock as well."

"Why the fuck did you wait to the last minute? If it craps out while they're here, go to a Laundromat. It'll be a great sister-to-sister bonding experience."

"Up yours," Cameron snapped, and flounced out of the kitchen.

Cameron could still be intractable. Denis knew these occasional rebellions were attempts to preserve her independence. They were intolerably annoying, though. Always about everyday shit, and that exasperated him. But on the plus side, she was nearly always compliant now. There was only one nagging issue. Despite everything, Cameron still resisted seducing a little girl, but Denis hoped she'd eventually come around.

In a few minutes, Cameron called out, "I'm off shopping," slamming the front door as she left.

Still pissed, I guess.

***

On Wednesday, Denis was up early. Emily, Haniff Seaton's secretary, had called last week to arrange an eleven o'clock meeting while Seaton would be in San Francisco. Although nothing had transpired since their first meeting, Denis thought it was worthwhile to talk again. So he agreed, blowing off classes that morning. Before the meeting would also be an opportune time to shop for Cameron's Christmas gift.

Denis located an upscale jeweler in the Financial District near his lawyer's office and waited for it to open. An attractive college-age woman greeted him. "'Morning," she said with a bright smile. "I'm Jessica. What may I help you with?"

"I'm looking for a Christmas gift for my wife. Perhaps a pendant-type necklace," Denis said, thinking, *Cute figure.*

"We have lovely teardrops in different stones to choose from. What price range were you thinking of?"

"Let's not talk about price yet. Do you have anything with a ruby?"

Jessica selected one from a showcase. "This has a one-and-a-quarter-carat ruby set in yellow gold with an eighteen-inch chain. It's an heirloom-quality stone."

"I like it," Denis replied. He could see the sales clerk calculating her commission. *Let's see where this goes.* "Would you put it on? So I can see how it looks."

Jessica did, chatting and flirting all the while.

"How about opening a few buttons of your cardigan for me? I'd like to see how it looks against your skin."

She played along impishly, hesitating as she finished. "Another one . . . ?"

"Definitely," Denis responded, and Jessica revealed more décolletage.

"Okay, I'll take it. Would you wrap it for me, please?"

He noticed that Jessica hadn't done up her sweater yet. When she handed him his package, Denis traced her cleavage with an unoccupied fingertip. Smiling, he wished her merry Christmas and left.

***

After Denis met with Haniff Seaton, they agreed that no action was required and that they would talk again in ninety days. Denis left his office in twenty minutes and was soon on the way back to the university. On the drive, Denis thought about Kirsten. He looked forward to seeing her again. She was five years younger than Cameron and nearly as hot. Her strawberry-blonde hair was a pleasant contrast to Cameron's brunette. Last year, during a similar Christmas visit, he'd made headway with her, and one morning she'd rubbed him off in the kitchen before Cameron and

Kirsten's husband came down. This year Denis had bigger plans. But Kirsten was going to be a challenge despite his previous success. Cameron was the problem, since screwing your sister's husband was a tricky taboo.

But they already had more of a sexual history, albeit one Kirsten was unaware of. Denis reminisced about the time he and Cameron had visited her parents for a few days. It was shortly after their wedding, and he'd met Kirsten then. She was living at home after graduating from college. The sexual attraction between them was palpable, so unmistakable that Denis was afraid Cameron would notice, but apparently she hadn't. When he and Kirsten were alone, they flirted. He tried to feel her up, but she pushed his hands away. *Well, I'm gonna play with her whether she likes it or not*, he thought. So one night he went to her room. It was moonlit, and Kirsten was atop the covers, sleeping on her back, wearing baby-doll pj's. Denis sat on the edge of the bed before unbuttoning Kirsten's top and softly fondling her. *Jesus . . . I'm an incubus. What a hoot—she has no friggin' idea. Now she's beginning to breathe heavier . . .*

After a little while, when Kirsten began to respond more, Denis buttoned her up and left.

Returning to the present, Denis thought about how spitting mad Kirsten would be when he told her. But watching her would be fun, and his experience with women suggested that once she put this revelation behind her, Kirsten would become more biddable. Their next encounter was key, because Kirsten was the linchpin. *I can't pull off the Cameron– little girl escapade yet. And I don't know about Cameron-Melisa. So why not Cameron-Kirsten? Good lord, a sibling rivalry—yowza!*

***

When Cameron awoke that morning, Denis had already gone. She didn't recall him saying anything about leaving early and figured he must've had an early department meeting or student conference. After breakfast, she gave the appliance guy a call. They arranged for him to come over in the afternoon.

Lou arrived around two o'clock, bringing a selection of product sheets for her to consider while he checked out the basement. After a while, Lou came upstairs. "Are the problems you're having the same as when I was here last?"

"Yes."

"I know you're concerned about the washer dying while you have houseguests, but you should be fine for a little longer. It's a bad week for anything to be delivered. I ought to have everything installed by New Year's Eve, though. Is that all right?" Cameron nodded yes. "Two other things," Lou said. "The gas connection for your dryer isn't up to code any longer. I'm required by law to fix it; I'll just charge you for the parts. Also, I found laundry behind the washer. It must've fallen there, so I put it on top."

Cameron hated to admit it, but Denis was right. It was much easier dealing with Lou.

***

On Thursday the twentieth, Cameron called Joe to wish him a merry Christmas. They talked for a while before Joe said, "There're a couple of recent developments I'd like to tell you about. First, thanks to your tip on Zack, Gabi was able to track down his ex-wife and her daughter, Janet. They're living in San Jose. We obtained Zack's home address in San Juan Bautista from them."

Cameron interjected, "Now that you mention it, that sounds right. Sorry, I couldn't remember."

"No matter, it didn't delay us. We questioned both women. The ex-wife wasn't that cooperative, but her daughter was." Joe filled Cameron in, including the discovery of Zack's body.

"Oh my God. He was murdered, then."

"Yes."

"And you think Denis did it?"

"Yes, but there's no physical evidence."

"That doesn't help you much."

"I know, and if it's your husband, he's blocked us at every step. I'm not convinced we'll ever bring him to justice for the warehouse murders."

"But you were afraid of that already. You've been hanging your hat on Melisa and the rape charge anyway."

"Yes, but there's also bad news on that case. That's the other thing I need to tell you about. Melisa was mugged, badly beaten up, and all her possessions were stolen, including her phone. There were no other copies of the photos except the one of your panties, which doesn't prove anything."

Cameron interrupted. "And you think—"

"Yes. If your husband's capable of murder, arranging a mugging isn't a stretch. Those photos were our last hope of elevating it above a 'he said, she said.' But we're exploring another avenue as well." Joe told Cameron about the research they'd been doing based on Zack's type, and how they'd isolated seven missing girls who might be Denis and Zack's victims.

CHAPTER FIFTEEN

Friday, December 28, 2012

On the drive to the airport, Cameron and Kirsten had been standoffish, making minimal conversation. Now Cameron was on the way home and struggling with two issues. The first was Kirsten. Cameron was glad they wouldn't see each other for a while. She had enjoyed their tryst but needed time to gain perspective. But more important, Cameron was grappling with Denis. She had already recognized that she was a pawn, but the last two nights had brought it home in spades. And now she acknowledged the inordinate amount of manipulation Denis had exerted to bring her and Kirsten onto the same page—at the same time. The good news was that Joe and Sister Mary knew what she was going through, that they would help, and that Cameron wasn't alone or powerless anymore. And she was beginning to grasp the depth of her repressed anger. As a result, Cameron intended to focus on problem-solving.

But first, she needed a time-out from Denis. It wouldn't be possible to sort anything out with him around, since he still held excessive sway over her. And even though she dreaded telling him, Cameron had resolved to do it this afternoon. *Keep strong like Sister Mary* was her mantra as she drove.

Cameron arrived home at four o'clock, but Denis wasn't there. In the kitchen, she saw a note. He was having dinner with the dean. What a break for her, because now she could leave without a donnybrook. Cameron went upstairs, packed for a few days, and called the Kensington Park Hotel, where Joe's friend, the manager, reserved a room for her. Now the hard part: writing Denis a note that he wouldn't overreact to.

Denis:

I'm confused and upset about the last two nights. I need time to think, so give me a few days. I'll be back; please respect my privacy and don't call.

    C.

Cameron drove to the hotel, was checked in by five o'clock, and called Joe. "Hi, you're on speaker—in the car," he said. "Susan's here too."

"Oh, sorry, I didn't mean to interrupt. I'll call tomorrow."

"No, it's okay. We're on the way home. What's up? Do you need to talk?"

"Yes."

"Where are you?"

"At the Kensington Park. I'm checked in."

"I'll drop Susan and be there shortly," Joe responded, and rang off.

"She sounds upset," Susan remarked.

"I know. I'm not certain I want to hear this."

"Just be careful."

At the hotel, John said, "Your friend's in 1011—go on up. I'll let her know you're on the way."

"I'm glad you're here," Cameron said as Joe came in. "I have those panties. I've thought a lot about these, and they scare me."

Joe examined them. "You mean that Denis took them from a little girl who was at your house."

"Yes, and what about the other murders and Melisa? Do you know how this makes me feel? The conclusion is devastating: I've been living with a monster."

"I know."

After a while Cameron settled down, but it took a few false starts before she could tell him about the last two nights. "Damn him—he's plotted this for a long while. You can't see his whole picture or where he's going until bam, it's done." She began ranting. "Denis is insidious. Before I know it, I'm consenting to whatever he wants. For Christ's sake, he trusses me up. What's left—bestiality? I'm glad we don't have a Great Dane! I've reached the end of my tether. I've nearly been there before, but you know that. This is different because Denis is killing whatever remains of me. I feel like I've already bankrupted my soul. You understand . . . don't you?"

Joe nodded, and Cameron told him about her time-out. "That's an excellent idea," he said, "but call Sister Mary first and make certain she has room in case things deteriorate. Then call me after you talk to him, so I know you're safe."

***

It was nearly eight o'clock when Joe left. Cameron hadn't eaten since breakfast, so she took a taxi to a French bistro for dinner. She checked her phone, but there was nothing besides a text from Kirsten, who'd arrived home safely. When she returned to her hotel, she went right to bed.

After breakfast on Saturday, Cameron made two phone calls. The first was to Sister Mary, to whom she reported what was transpiring. Mary assured her there would be room for her if she needed it. The second call was to Melisa. Cameron felt they had a bond, albeit a curious one. She thought Melisa might need support but was apprehensive.

Her worry turned out to be unfounded, since Melisa seemed happy to hear from her. They planned to meet for lunch in Palo Alto on Monday.

The weather was warmer than usual, midsixties and sunny. After her calls, Cameron took a light jacket and walked down to the cable car turntable at Powell and Market Streets. The line was long, so she chose walking instead. She headed down Market to the Financial District, circling around the hills to North Beach, then on to the wharf area before taking a ferry to Sausalito. Cameron went topside and watched the city recede. She was glad to have her jacket, because it was cooler on the bay.

As Alcatraz approached, a young boy and his mom came up beside her. He had a bag of thickly sliced white bread. The boy tore the slices apart and threw the chunks up for the gulls to catch. Looking up, he smiled and handed Cameron a slice.

"Thanks," she said. "Watch this."

Standing still, Cameron stretched out with a piece, holding it away from her body. After a few false starts, a seagull finally came close enough to take it from her hand. The little boy laughed and tried it. He caught on quickly, and they fed the gulls together. When they docked, Cameron thanked him again and ruffled his hair while smiling at his mother.

It was nearly one thirty now, so Cameron walked down Bridgeway to Angelino's, which was beginning to decorate for New Year's Eve. She ordered lunch and bay-watched through the front window. Cameron was glad for the respite feeding the birds had provided, because all morning she had been preoccupied with her problems. One that had just become

clearer to her was that she had been using her successful writing career as a crutch. Apparently, she couldn't rely on that anymore. She'd recently met with her agent to discuss her last novel. It had been commercially successful but had failed to achieve the same critical acclaim as her previous books. Inwardly, Cameron was hurt, although outwardly she accepted her agent's constructive criticism. Her other problems were more complicated than that, causing her emotions to be convoluted and taxing to unravel:

To begin with, she was afraid. Mostly, she feared the uncertainty of what might happen. But a dread that Denis might attack her was also developing. *Joe planted that idea, and it keeps nagging at me.*

She also felt that her self-esteem, self-confidence, and sex appeal were gone. Cameron hated that she'd become dependent on Denis. And she was embarrassed and ashamed, believing that friends and family might blame her for what had happened. *I feel like I'm the root cause of our problems—but that isn't right.*

And finally, she realized she still loved Denis—not the way he was now, but the way he'd been before. It was puzzling that she still hoped he might return to his old self. *But this emotional abuse must stop!*

As she waited for lunch, Cameron began to recognize that if she stopped trying to rationalize her feelings, they were more manageable. It didn't matter how they'd gotten where they were or who had said or done what. The issue was that Denis's conduct had been unpardonable. He had treated her cruelly, and Cameron had every right to be angry and hurt. She was overwhelmed, drained, and had already resolved to see a mental health professional. In any event, it seemed to her there were only two options. She could leave Denis and, at the very least, seek a legal separation, but she wasn't convinced she was ready for that yet. Or she could stay and try to work things out. That would require major changes in their relationship. Denis would either agree or not, and that wasn't within her control. But regardless of what they decided, giving Joe those panties last evening might've removed the future from their hands. *Perhaps it's for the best, because I may be too exhausted to try working through it.*

Her lunch came, and she chose not to think about her problems any longer. Cameron spent the afternoon visiting local shops and people watching. Around four o'clock she took a return ferry, and after docking, she hailed a taxi, stopping at a grocer near her hotel. She picked up snacks and bottled water for dinner. Back in her room, she read for a while. But the fresh air and walking had tired her out, so Cameron was fast asleep by ten o'clock.

On Sunday, Cameron slept in. When she woke up, she decided to unwind and let her mind idle. *I'll process everything subconsciously.* She walked to a coffee shop on Powell for breakfast. Afterward, she strolled around the Union Square area, looking at the Christmas displays in the fashionable stores' windows. Later that afternoon, Cameron returned to the hotel and checked her phone—still nothing from Denis. She rang Melisa and confirmed their lunch for the next day. After that, Cameron ordered a sandwich and soda from room service, read, and turned in.

On Monday, New Year's Eve day, when they met, Melisa said, "I'm glad you rang. I've wanted to call, but I supposed you hated me."

"I'm sorry I left you with that impression. I thought we parted on decent terms?" Cameron responded.

"I know, but I kind of imagined you were making nice."

"No, I wasn't. We have a lot in common, and for better or worse, we're bound together. Denis has caused us a lot of grief. Don't you think it's natural to support each other . . . ?"

"I guess."

Cameron sensed that Melisa was reluctant to talk freely. "Do you know how this new investigation into your allegations began?"

"Gabi told me it came up in an unrelated case. So they chose to take a fresh look."

"That's true as far as it goes. I'll tell you what I know."

When Cameron had finished, Melisa asked, "Do you know about my mugging? You didn't mention it."

"Yes, Joe told me. I felt badly for you. I didn't think a phone call would suffice. That's why I came to visit—provide a bit of moral support."

"Who's Joe?" Melisa asked.

"Joe Cancio. He's the lead detective."

"I don't know him."

"Gabi's his partner, but I've never met her," Cameron answered.

"You know, she thinks Denis may be responsible for my mugging."

"So does Joe. He thinks the motive was to steal your phone and destroy those photographs."

"You know about those?"

Damn, I forgot she isn't aware of my interview or that I saw the photos or heard her recording. "Sorry, I slipped up and shouldn't have mentioned that." Then Cameron told her all about being questioned.

"Oh shit, then you know all about what I said?"

Cameron wasn't sure if Melisa was asking rhetorically.

"Well?"

"Yes, I do." That brought conversation to a halt. In a while, Melisa appeared to calm down. But then a new wave of emotion started.

"And you still wanted to see me?"

"We're not so different, because it seems like Denis has a standard playbook." Cameron went on to share how Denis treated her, including the incident with Kirsten.

"I had no idea. It's worse than what I went through."

"We've been together more than nine years, but he had only begun with you. At least you did something about it. You're my idol. When I grow up, I want to be just like you," Cameron joked. That started Melisa laughing and lightened things up.

"What you've told me does sound like variations on the same theme. It demeans and defiles us," Melisa said.

"You're right. it does. And about Kirsten and me, did he ever push you towards anything similar? I'm asking for a reason—not idle curiosity."

"No, although Denis might've talked about it casually. Not enough that I mentioned it to the police, though. Why?"

"Gabi and Joe have a theory. They think Denis planned to maneuver us into bed with each other. But you short-circuited him, and he shifted to having me seduce a little girl. When that failed, he altered his plan to having me score with a woman. Kirsten was probably a crime of opportunity—too much to resist. It would appeal to Denis: what I deserved for defying him."

"Wouldn't it be ironic if we hooked up? Fitting to have our own inside joke on the prick! Can I ask you something? But you don't have to answer if I'm stepping over a line."

"I think I've moved past keeping secrets from you."

"Well, did you like it—making love to a woman?"

"Yes, but it was complicated, since it wasn't simply lesbian sex. It was also incest. And what about men? It hasn't changed my feelings, because I don't want to be without them. I consider myself straight, so it's confusing."

"I'm not certain how I feel about what you said, but I'm not creeped out, and I don't think it's repugnant. It seems like women are less rigid about their sexuality than men, yet I wouldn't want to be without them either," Melisa admitted. They sat quietly until the check came. After lunch, they walked to their cars, and in parting, Melisa said, "Let's stay in touch."

Talking to Melisa had helped Cameron clarify her feelings about Kirsten. Thus, driving back to San Francisco, Cameron gave her sister a call. "I'm confused and having trouble understanding everything, because I should feel like we did something wrong, but I don't."

"I know," Kirsten replied. "I feel the same way. And I'm upset about cheating."

"So where do we go from here? For one thing, Denis's manipulations have brought everything into focus, and I'll be making big changes."

"I'm glad you brought that up. I'm concerned about you and Denis—about how he treats you. I know it's none of my business—"

Cameron interrupted. "I want to hear what you have to say."

"Your relationship has been deteriorating for a long time. It's hard to pinpoint what's happening, but Denis is weird, and it isn't healthy for you. Should I keep going?"

"Yes."

"At best, Denis is disingenuous, although probably worse. I don't think you've ever caught on, but there's been a great deal of sexual tension between us . . . right from the start."

"I thought it was harmless flirting."

"Well, I've worked to keep my feelings in check—not encourage him. But after what he's done to us, I have no illusions. I saw Denis for what he is, a selfish Svengali. I'll tell you about something he did that time you visited Mom and Dad when I was still living at home. Denis bragged about it last week to me, but I swear, I never knew." Then Kirsten told Cameron about his midnight visit to her bedroom.

"Shit, we were just married . . . how could he do that to me? You must feel awful too."

"There's more." Timidly, Kirsten confessed her kitchen sex with Denis.

"Jesus! What were you thinking? Anything else I need to know about?"

"No . . . sorry."

"Well . . . I'm not as upset as I should be. Probably because of Wednesday and Thursday nights, but we should change the subject."

"Yes," Kirsten agreed. "Tell me what you've decided."

"I'm bringing everything to a head when I return home." Then Cameron explained about her weekend time-out, the police investigations, and Sister Mary Magdalen. "Nevertheless, I still hope this is all a big misunderstanding."

"Cameron, I'm concerned about you. Stay close to that cop and the nun. If you need anything, call. About us, we'll give it a rest. We don't have to decide about hooking up again right away. Is that okay?"

"Yes."

"Call me every couple of days, so I know you're all right . . . please," Kirsten finished.

Cameron returned to her hotel on Monday afternoon and relaxed for the rest of the day. On Tuesday, New Year's Day, she walked and thought. And by evening, Cameron knew that she would make the effort tomorrow, but Denis needed to meet her halfway.

CHAPTER SIXTEEN

Wednesday Morning, January 2, 2013

Cameron left the hotel after breakfast. She thanked John, collected her car, and headed home, but Denis wasn't there. She took her bag upstairs, exchanging the clothes in it for fresh ones in case she had to leave again. Cameron puttered around and was in the living room when Denis arrived. "Where the fuck have you been?" he barked, slamming the door behind him.

He wasn't going to make this easy. "I told you—I left a note."

"Yeah, I saw your note . . . What the fuck? What the hell do you have to think over?"

"We need to talk. You can't believe things are all right between us. They've been going downhill for years. I can't go on this way; Kirsten was the last straw."

"Kirsten . . . what are you talking about? Shit, you had the time of your life with her. I was jealous. You two were out of control. Tell me otherwise."

"Denis, that's not the point. The ends don't justify the means. It's not about how it turned out. It wasn't what I wanted. It wasn't what Kirsten wanted either. You manipulated us, and you've been doing it to me for years. You don't give a shit about how I feel . . . what I want," Cameron snapped.

"Oh, for Christ's sake. What the fuck are you talking about? You love everything we do. You're nothing but an ungrateful whore."

"Calling me names isn't going to solve anything. You're wrong. I may have accommodated you, but in what alternate universe do you live if you think those were my choices? You know goddamned well they weren't. I'm being kind if I only call you an insensitive prick."

"Cameron . . . I'm not listening to this. You need to be punished. Get your box—now. This isn't going any further!"

"No, I'm never doing any of that shit again unless I want to. Get used to it."

"Damn it—do it now," Denis bellowed.

"You're an asshole. This is exactly what I'm talking about. Do you think I enjoy being treated like a dog? You're not fucking normal. I know you're under stress, but you gotta get a grip."

"What the hell are you talking about—stress? You're the only stress in my life."

"Oh, Denis," Cameron yelled. "You can't be that oblivious. Don't you realize the police are still investigating? They like you for the warehouse murders, Zack's murder, and Melisa's mugging. How do you think I feel? Wondering if I'm living with a sicko? Joe Cancio isn't ever giving up until he clears or convicts you."

"What the fuck are you jabbering about? What do you know about any of that? You've been talking to the cops again, haven't you?"

"Yes, a couple of times. I thought that if I cooperated with them, they'd realize they were wrong about you. I want us to move past this. Don't you see? I'm trying to hold us together."

CHAPTER SEVENTEEN

Wednesday Evening, January 2, 2013

It was an old hotel, and Denis chuckled as he approached the reception desk. Hanging on the wall behind the counter, a framed antique sign from the Palace Hotel, Norfolk, Virginia, read:

STREET GIRLS BRINGING

SAILORS INTO HOTEL

MUST PAY FOR ROOM

IN ADVANCE

"Are you Jack?" Denis asked as he entered.

"Yes, everything's ready. What should I call you?"

"Mr. Smith will do."

"Great. The room's two hundred fifty dollars a night, with a minimum of five nights—cash in advance." They settled, and Jack said, "We also have a coffee shop. I'll take your bag up while you park; tell Kenny you're with us."

Afterward, Denis went to his room. It was sizable, with a queen bed in conjunction with a sitting area, couch, and TV. The bathroom was retro, and both rooms looked spick-and-span. He dropped his bag and returned to the coffee shop. It was also well maintained—albeit right out of a film noir—but the menu was sufficient for his needs. Denis ordered coffee and a piece of cherry pie he'd spotted on a cake stand. The waitress told him their hours were six a.m. to eight p.m. After Denis finished, he stopped at reception.

"That's a neat street-girl sign," Denis observed. "Maybe you can help me out. I'd like some company this evening."

"I understand—not a problem. What would you like?'

"A young girl . . . about fourteen. Maybe for the week if she works out."

"Anything else?"

"Well, Caucasian and petite with a cute figure."

"Hair color?"

"You choose."

"Give me a half hour or so." Jack rang back within twenty minutes, saying, "We're in luck. I've located a girl—a strawberry blonde. You'll like her. It'll be a thousand dollars for eight p.m. to eight a.m. Should I go ahead?"

"Let's do it. Does that include something for you?"

"Yes, my contact takes care of me. Just pay Charlene."

***

On Thursday morning the third, when Denis's burner rang, Charlene had already hopped out of bed and was in the bathroom. She'd stuck around for a last romp on her own time.

"'Morning, Haniff."

"Sorry I didn't call back last night."

"No problem, but I may need your help. Yesterday my wife and I had a kerfuffle, and I expect her to file assault charges today. If she does, the cops might try to capitalize on this. So I'm lying low."

"Were there any witnesses?" Seaton asked.

"No."

"Any injuries?"

"She was taken to the hospital. I don't know."

"All right, leave it with me. I'll have Emily find out what Cameron's status is. If she files charges, here's the procedure. I'll negotiate your surrender; the police will book you and deliver you to your bail hearing. After that, you'll post bail and be released. Typically, that all happens on the same day, and you won't spend time in jail. Later, if you're convicted, there'll be a combination of a fine and a suspended sentence, community service, and anger management counseling. It's a first offense, so don't overreact, but continue to stay off the radar."

As Denis was hanging up, Charlene scooted out the door, smiling and waving goodbye. Denis called Jack to confirm that he could have her for the week.

Later that day, Emily called back. She'd learned that Cameron had been kept overnight for observation, then released. "Haniff is going to let things settle down today. Tomorrow he'll see if charges have been filed."

Life in the hotel was boring. Denis had lunch at the coffee shop, then looked through the magazines in the lobby—outdated. Because he was reluctant to go outside, there was no place to buy a book either, so he returned to his room and watched TV. Finally, it was suppertime, so back he went to the coffee shop. Then he took a nap, and around seven, Jack woke him, reporting that Charlene was on the way up. Later, as she lazed in Denis's arms, he said, "I'm happy you came early. I was so bored."

Charlene faked a pout. "Oh, is this all I'm good for?"

"No, that's not what I meant . . . Didn't mean to hurt your feelings."

She laughed. "I'm joking, silly. So you like what I can do?"

"Absolutely."

"You know, I've been a bad girl today. My last appointment canceled, and I didn't tell my boss. Do you think I should be chastised?"

I didn't see this coming. "Well, perhaps," Denis said, playing along. "What do you think is an appropriate punishment for such a serious transgression?"

"It's my first offense," she said, appearing to ponder. "So maybe a spanking . . . until my butt has a pink hue. But I should still feel it tomorrow, because I ought not to forget how naughty I've been. My safe word's *red*." Denis began but didn't hear *red* among her cries of "Ouch!" "Stop it," and "That hurts." So he kept on until her bottom was a deep pink. At length, Charlene asked, "Did you like that?"

"Yes."

"Me too," she giggled, slipping off his lap and scampering to the full-length mirror on the bathroom door. Then, looking over her shoulder, viewing his handiwork, she exclaimed, "Perfect!" before returning to bed. "My cheeks are so warm . . . feel them. Make love to me again . . . please?"

***

Friday morning, she stayed until ten o'clock. When she was gone, Denis anticipated another boring day. Charlene had offered to bring him several mystery novels when she returned that afternoon. Denis was looking forward to them nearly as much as seeing her again. Then around five o'clock, Seaton finally called. Denis had been anxious all day, because he didn't like being in limbo. Haniff had spoken with the prosecutor and reported that Cameron had filed charges on Thursday afternoon. An arrest warrant and a BOLO had been issued, but the prosecutor agreed to accept his surrender on Friday morning, January 11, at ten o'clock. Following that, Denis would be taken into custody awaiting a bail hearing at two thirty the same afternoon. "That sounds fine. So am I free to move around now?" Denis asked.

"Continue lying low, because I don't have an easy feeling about this. I'm coming to San Francisco on Thursday evening. I would prefer to be in court rather than handing this off to a local guy as I'd originally intended."

"Why, what's wrong?"

"I don't know. The prosecutor wanted you to surrender immediately and be incarcerated until your hearing. I told him that was a nonstarter. Next, he wanted you remanded without bail. Both are unheard of on a first offense, especially for someone with your roots and position in the community. Reluctantly, he agreed to your release, but it won't be on your own recognizance. Bail will be steep. I didn't share with him how well-heeled you are. We'll let him think that whatever bail we negotiate is a hardship. I don't know this guy. He's young and may be trying to make his bones at your expense. But I wonder, does someone besides your wife have it in for you? Can you shed any light on that?"

"Well, you know about the statutory rape allegation. The cop handling it, Joe Cancio, is a bulldog. Melisa was mugged, and he thinks I'm behind that also. Obviously, I had nothing to do with it, but Cancio's fixated."

"How did you find that out?"

"Cameron has had several conversations with him, and he shared it with her."

"Oh, for Christ's sake, your wife has to stop talking to him!"

"I know. Part of our dustup was over that."

"Okay, what's done is done. I'll get you out on bail, but it may be contentious. Don't be upset at the hearing. They'll paint the worst possible picture. So in case they're up to mischief, keep doing what you're doing. We'll talk Thursday evening."

A few minutes later, the room's phone rang. It was Jack. "Charlene called and said not to eat supper. She'll bring something when she comes—around five forty-five." Charlene arrived with a bag from a Chinese restaurant and several paperbacks. She kissed him on the cheek and took everything to the coffee table. Then she turned, putting her arms around Denis's neck. "Now . . . for a proper kiss." Afterward, Charlene announced, "Let's eat—I didn't have lunch." She'd brought chicken with broccoli, cold sesame noodles, and shrimp Szechuan style.

"I'm impressed. How much do I owe you?"

"Nothing. My treat."

"That's not right. Let me reimburse you?"

"Oh, you will . . . later."

"Can't wait."

"Well, you'll have to, because I'm famished."

Afterward, dozing, Charlene said, "If you'd like, I can stay till ten tomorrow morning. We can have breakfast together."

"I'd like that." Denis was mystified, because unfamiliar sentiments were emerging. His feelings toward Charlene were changing. Warmth, fondness, affection, perhaps even love, Denis didn't know, but he liked it.

***

At breakfast on Saturday, Denis said, "I've been thinking. You said the other day that you had a few days off next week, right?"

"Yes, that doesn't happen too often. I'm looking forward to it."

"Well, I thought maybe we could do something together. It would be fun, but don't worry, I'll pay for your time."

"I'd love to. But Denis, don't say that about paying—not when I'm off duty. I don't think of you like a john anymore, and I'm worried about your safety. It doesn't take rocket science to figure out that you're avoiding the cops. What can we do that'll be safe?"

"Things are clearing up, but I need to be honest with you." Denis told her about his situation with Cameron. "My lawyer called before you came yesterday. I'm going to surrender on the eleventh. I should have a bail hearing that afternoon, although he still wants me to lie low. I'll figure something out that's safe. It isn't like I don't have plenty of time and money."

"Did you hurt her badly?"

"No, I don't think so. The hospital kept her overnight, then released her. Don't be apprehensive. I've never abused a woman before," Denis lied. "I completely lost it—don't know what came over me."

"I don't think you'd ever hurt me—at least not that way. But I'm afraid I'll never see you again after you return to your real life."

"I was hoping you'd want to keep seeing me, but my life is complicated. I'll tell you, but not now."

"That makes me happy. I won't be a pain in the ass . . . promise. I'll settle for being the other woman."

"We'll figure it out. But there's something I'd like you to know. I'm extremely wealthy—no bullshit—it's family money. If you ever need anything, ask. But more important, I'm concerned about you, because it isn't safe out there. If you want a change, go back to school, anything, I'll make it happen. Up to you."

"You do care," Charlene said, hugging him. "Look, I'm fine for now. I know it's hard to believe, but I like my job—most of the time. I don't work the streets. My boss, Jerome, screens my clients and protects me. He won't let anything happen, since I'm a top earner."

"Okay, but when you change your mind . . ."

"Well, there is something I'd like to ask—and don't laugh. Whatever we do, can I come as me?"

"What?"

Charlene became defensive. "Forget I asked; I'm being silly. You know . . . I'm still only a kid."

200

"It's all right; I understand. You want to come as yourself, correct?"

"Yes, so can I ditch the hooker clothes and makeup?"

"Absolutely."

"You can call me Gracie, then. It's my real name."

"Gracie it is, from now on."

"This'll be great," she exclaimed, after finishing her breakfast. "See you this afternoon, about five thirty."

***

Over the weekend, Denis gave Gracie a burner from his go bag along with his burner's number. Then on Monday morning, he meant to start working on their getaway, but first he phoned Emily. "I called you directly because I need information. Haniff says you're the best at wheedling it out of people."

She laughed. "Well, I try. What's up?"

"I'm meeting Haniff to surrender on Friday, and I'd like to spend Thursday night at the house, because I don't have appropriate clothes for court. But I can't do it if Cameron will be there. Could you find out?"

"Let me see. I should be able to. I'll call you back."

Denis thought the Lodge at Tiburon would be fun. It was a blue-chip hotel with a well-rated restaurant. The lodge was less than a half mile from the ferry landing—easy walking. So he made reservations for Tuesday and Wednesday nights. Then Denis checked the ferry schedule. Tomorrow morning, at eleven o'clock, there was one from San Francisco. Then on Thursday evening, at nine thirty, there was a return to the city.

201

He wished the getaway could be longer, but two and a half days seemed to be all they could fit in.

Emily called before noon. "Here's what I found out. Cameron isn't going to stay there. Apparently, she's at a safe house until there's a temporary restraining order in place. They're going to ask for one at your bail hearing. Haniff has no objection with you staying at home, but he still wants you to keep your head down."

Gracie came early, and he described his plan. She was excited and chatted about what they could do: shopping at little boutiques, reading in the lobby, going for long walks, and so on.

"I'm glad you approve," Denis said. "So tomorrow morning, all you need to do is show up here in a cab by ten thirty. Then we'll head to the ferry."

***

On Tuesday the eighth, Gracie left early to pack for their holiday, after which the morning dragged on. Denis told Jack he would be checking out. "Sorry to see you leave. What about your car?"

"I'll probably pick it up on Friday afternoon."

"All right, I'll tell Kenny."

"Thanks, Jack," Denis said, slipping him $500.

Now all he had to do was wait. But Denis was impatient, so he brought his go bag down and read in the lobby. At length, Gracie's taxi pulled up. She leaned out the window, waved, and declared, "Made it— just on time." As he entered the cab, Denis noticed how cute she looked. Gracie always did, but this morning's light lipstick, jeans, polo shirt, and windbreaker were a great improvement over her working duds. On the ferry, it was pleasant bay-watching as they crossed to Tiburon. After they disembarked, Denis took Gracie's bag and started walking to the hotel. Gracie had already agreed to window shop until Denis texted her the room number, because they didn't want to risk annoying questions about a young girl sleeping in a king-size bed with a middle-aged man. He had arranged an early check-in and within a half hour sent the text. Gracie arrived about twenty minutes later with a shopping bag. "I bought you something. Look."

He opened it, and inside was a navy-blue sweatshirt with a minimalist sketch of a one-masted sailboat heeling to the wind, a few waves, and *Tiburon California USA* encircling the design. "I hope it's the right size. Do you like it?" Puzzlingly, Denis started to tear up. "What?" she asked, but he couldn't say anything. Gracie came over and put her arms around him. "It's okay; I didn't mean to upset you. I'll take it back."

She was confused, but Denis was even more so. He hugged Gracie hard. "You don't understand."

"No, I don't."

"I'm happy and overwhelmed, but this is new territory for me. I love the sweatshirt."

She gently led him to the bed. "Well, since it's all new territory for you, this is the part where you thank me."

Afterward, they walked back to the port, bought sandwiches and sodas from a deli, and ate overlooking the wharf area. Following that, Denis wanted to visit the Railroad & Ferry Depot Museum. When they returned to the inn, they cuddled and napped under the duvet. Later, Gracie roused, saying, "I almost forgot. When I was shopping, I made a dinner reservation for eight thirty at Sam's; we'll have to hurry."

Denis borrowed a flashlight from reception, since it was dark when they began walking down to the restaurant. They were having a wonderful time. Denis felt calm when he was with Gracie and was reluctant to change the mood, so he postponed talking about all the things they ought to. Afterward, over dessert, he suggested taking a long walk tomorrow. *Then I can tell her what she ought to know about: me being a person of interest in four murders and a statutory rape allegation, how dangerous my predicament is, how complicated her life might become, my disappearing into Canada, and my plan for her to follow.*

The next morning, after a light breakfast and looking through brochures, they chose to walk the Tiburon Waterfront Trail to Blackie's Pasture. It was about six miles round trip. Gracie thought it would be fun to have the kitchen fix them sandwiches, fruit, and water for a picnic. Denis was apprehensive when she went to make the arrangements because of her age and their relationship, but Gracie never gave it a second thought. Walking back to the room, she quipped, "Just like normal people." They left the hotel at about eleven thirty, stopping along the way for the views. The weather had cooled, and Denis wore the new sweatshirt under a jacket. Gracie was pleased. "It looks smart, and it's an attractive color on you." When they reached Blackie's Pasture, they stopped for lunch, then Denis told Gracie about his problems with the police.

"I'm scared, because I didn't do those things. But the cops are obsessed with me, so I'm going to have to disappear out of the country."

"Can't you stay and fight? You have the money to put together a dream team."

"If I had my druthers, I would, but I have no idea what evidence they have. And witnesses . . . well, I have a lot of business interests, and I'm certain I've made enemies along the way. Somebody could be out to get me. If I'm arrested and held without bail, I'm stuck. It's a catch-22, because if I go on the lam after Friday's bail hearing, then I become a wanted criminal. But that's what I'm doing, and my plans are already in process."

Gracie started to cry. Through her sniffles, she admitted, "I recognized that our relationship wasn't going to be one of living happily ever after. But I didn't think this was all there was to it—only a few days. I've been afraid to say anything. Afraid of jinxing it because I want to be with you. My feelings changed through the week, and now I can't stand the thought of losing you. It isn't fair. For Christ's sake, I just found you."

"Don't cry; I feel the same way." Saying it felt weird but honest. Denis held Gracie until she calmed down. Finally, he said, "Here's my plan. I didn't want to tell you until I was sure how you felt about us. I've worked it all out." They started to walk back, and Denis continued, "Remember when you said you brought your birth certificate with you from home? Well, with that you can obtain a California ID, Social Security card, and a passport. All in your real name, so you'll be able to follow me. It might take a few months to put everything together, but that's fine, because I want time to elapse between our disappearances. I'll go to Montreal first and arrange everything. After that, you'll follow by bus to Vancouver. Then you can take a five-and-a-half-day train trip to Toronto. You'll spend the night there before boarding another train for a six-hour trip to Montreal's Gare Centrale. Along the way, you'll use cash and won't leave a trail."

"It doesn't sound difficult."

"It isn't," Denis said. "We'll keep using burner phones; I already have a stash. Plus I'm going to open a new safe-deposit box next week with you on as a joint signature. All you'll need is your birth certificate. You'll masquerade as my niece who's living with me because her parents were killed in a car accident. I'll put enough cash in the box for us to disappear on, and I've already transferred over two and a half million out of the country. That'll be sufficient to get started in a new life. So Gracie, what do you think?"

She stopped walking, turned, and put her arms around him. "It's wonderful, and Montreal will be lovely." They returned to the lodge and made a dinner reservation for eight o'clock in the Tiburon Tavern. The rest of their time was unhurried and pleasant, and they arranged with the front desk for a late checkout on Thursday.

When they docked in San Francisco, they took a cab, and Denis dropped Gracie at her rooming house before heading home.

CHAPTER EIGHTEEN

Friday, January 11, 2013

D enis was up early and called the university, leaving the dean a voice mail apologizing for missing days last week. Then he packed enough clothes, toiletries, and so on for a week. He took his go bag and suitcase downstairs, then returned the Beretta and its ammo to the safe. Next, he removed $250,000, adding it to his luggage. Finally, after dressing, he called a cab. Denis went to the Sir Francis Drake Hotel, where he'd previously arranged an early check-in. He dropped off his luggage and took another taxi to police headquarters to meet Haniff Seaton. His booking, fingerprinting, and mug shots took a while. Eventually, Denis was placed in a holding cell, awaiting transfer to court. When he finally arrived there, Denis noticed Cameron in a conference room. He pointed her out to Seaton, who opined that it wasn't unusual for victims to be there in case the judge wanted to hear from them.

They weren't first on the docket, so time moved slowly. After a while, Denis noticed Joe Cancio come in and sit at the back of the courtroom.

The judge seemed fair to Denis; he had a sense of humor and a tendency to think creatively. He frequently challenged the lawyers from both sides. Denis commented about it to Seaton.

"Don't be misled, because he can be tough. I've been before him several times—usually in Superior Court. I wonder what he's doing down here, hearing such perfunctory matters?"

207

Finally, their case was called. After the lawyers introduced themselves, the prosecutor began.

"If it pleases Your Honor—"

The judge held up his hand. "I'd like to get to know the defendant first, if that's okay with y'all?" It was a rhetorical question. Addressing Denis, he said, "I see it's Dr. Rodolphe, correct?"

"Yes, Your Honor. An academic degree."

"Are you at the university?"

"Yes."

"What's your field, and how long have you been there?"

"Literature and creative writing, and I've been there ten years and am a department head."

"Do you own your home?"

"With my wife. About nine years."

"Posh address."

"Yes, Your Honor."

"Please correct any misconceptions I may have about you. This is the first time you've ever been in trouble with the law—parking tickets excluded. You've never done anything like this before, and you don't know what came over you. Frankly, you're horrified at what you've done. It will never happen again, you love your wife, and you want to straighten this out as soon as possible. Is that about it?"

Denis could feel Haniff tensing up, confirming his feeling that he should be cautious. "Yes, Your Honor."

"The medical report I have says your wife was slapped around pretty well. Acknowledging that you're innocent until proven guilty, is that about your take on the situation?"

"Yes, Your Honor."

"Fine. Let the record show that I recognize the defendant's family name. And I'll stipulate to their wealth and prominence in the community. None of it means a damn thing except that the defendant can probably make bail." Then the judge addressed both lawyers. "Have you worked out a suitable arrangement for me to approve?"

The prosecutor hesitated. "Well . . ."

Haniff didn't need a second opportunity to swing into action. "If Your Honor pleases, the defense initiated conversations. But we're far apart on what is appropriate."

The prosecutor started to speak. The judge stopped him once again. "Before we go into all that, I've been rude. How are you, Counselor Seaton? It's been a while."

"It has."

"You're far afield from your home turf."

"I might say the same for Your Honor."

"Well, crime's up and judges are retiring. We all need to do our part. Glad to see you again, Haniff. Before I deal with you, Mr. Prosecutor, some housekeeping. Detective Cancio, I see you lurking in the rear of my court. Do you wish to be heard, or are you observing?"

"Observing, Your Honor."

"Thank you, Detective."

"Next, I assume Ms. Sinclair is here and available if we need her."

"Yes," the prosecutor said.

"All right, let's go," the judge stated, motioning him to begin.

The prosecutor pleaded for remand or a seven-figure bail, surrender of Rodolphe's passport, an ankle bracelet, house arrest, and a restraining order. After that, the judge asked, "Counselor Seaton, is that acceptable?"

"No, Your Honor."

"I didn't think so. Okay, the only thing I heard in the prosecutor's shopping list that I agree with is the restraining order. We need to protect Ms. Sinclair. As to the rest, really—for a first offense? Here's what we're going to do. Bail is set at fifty thousand dollars cash; you'll pay the clerk before you leave. The attorneys will work out the restraining order for my signature." The judge turned his attention to Denis. "Just so we're clear, Doctor. If you go within one hundred yards of your wife before that's signed, I'll throw your butt in jail." He redirected his attention to the court. "Work out supervised access to the house for him until the paperwork is signed. And Mr. Prosecutor, don't feel bad. You got a fifty-thousand-dollar bail. Normally, I would've set twenty-five. Finally, I don't want to see this at trial. Work out a plea. Include Ms. Sinclair or her representative in those discussions. Are we done? Good." The judge rapped his gavel.

Joe had left the court before the judge finished his instructions. He found Cameron in the conference room. Reporting the restriction on her husband until the restraining order was in place, he said, "Call me if your husband violates it."

On the way out of court, Denis said, "Haniff, fine job."

"Don't be overconfident. The judge isn't happy with this case. If the prosecutor hadn't been such a jackass, we might've had more trouble. I don't want this at trial either. And I don't like that Detective Cancio was in court today. He's far too interested for a plain vanilla domestic violence case."

Denis paid his bail and said goodbye to Seaton, who would handle negotiations from New Orleans. His firm's local office could deal with the paperwork, signing, and filing. Denis took a cab to the Hotel Royal, where he picked up his car and returned to the Sir Francis. Once he was in his room, Denis called Gracie.

"Hi, I'm at the hotel. Everything went well."

"I'll come over after work. We ought to celebrate."

***

On Tuesday, January 15, early in the morning, a black-and-white from the Central Division, cruising the Embarcadero near Pier 39, was waved down by a dockworker. He approached the car. "There's a body floating in the water by the pier."

The sun was hardly up, and the officers needed their flashlights to follow the worker along the dock. The body was a large man, facedown, bobbing and bumping into the pilings. "Call it in, Bobby," the ranking officer said, then turned to the dockworker. "Do you have anything to secure him if he starts to drift?"

"No need. What washes in here gets hung up right there. That guy hasn't moved since I found him."

The medical examiner took the body to the morgue, and the dock was back to normal by nine o'clock. There wasn't any other evidence to deal with, but identification was easy. The man's wallet was still in his back pocket, his prints were in the system, and his rap sheet identified him as LeBron Davis, aka Junior. He'd had several arrests for minor felonies and was affiliated with Tyree's crew. The cause of death two bullets to the chest. The entry wounds looked like they were from a .45.

***

Janet called Gabi and said she and Gwen had picked up Zack's ashes from the Marin County medical examiner's office. The San Juan Bautista chief had been helpful. Zack was to be interred at a local cemetery on January 18 at ten in the morning. The chief had arranged for a neighboring priest from the Sacred Heart Catholic Church in Hollister to officiate. Gwen, Janet, and the chief would be there. Janet invited Gabi, who asked for time off. After Joe inquired about the details, he said, "Why don't we both go? We'll make it police business, and I'll drive."

"That would be great."

"I don't know why," Joe commented, "but despite all that Zack did, he seems more like a victim."

"I know, it's confusing. I'll let Janet know."

***

Later, Joe and Gabi briefed captain Weber. They were waiting for the panties' DNA analysis. Joe reported that Rodolphe was staying at the Sir Francis Drake and had resumed his duties at the university. "Everything's back to normal except for a new address, or so Rodolphe would have us believe," Joe quipped.

They'd initiated surveillance on Monday evening, the fourteenth. The captain had approved an overnight stakeout for the next two weeks along with twenty-four-hour surveillance during the upcoming weekend. As they finished, Weber said, "I know you recommended round-the-clock surveillance. But I can't justify the manpower: there are no priors, Rodolphe has roots here, and you have substantial bail. Plus the judge wants a plea deal, and he didn't even bother to confiscate his passport. The only evidence you have is a profile and a hunch. I agree with you, but I need more. So double down on the FBI for that DNA. Then we can bust his ass."

"I'm following up," Gabi replied. "It's taking longer because the sample is degraded."

***

When Tyree arrived at the bar on Wednesday morning, he asked José to bring everyone inside for a quick meeting. He sat at his usual table, placing a semiautomatic in its customary spot.

"A new gun, boss?" one of the thugs asked.

"Yeah. Even though the forty-five has a lot of knockdown power, this ten-millimeter has better penetration and accuracy. I called you in because Junior wasn't here yesterday and I can't locate him. Do you guys know anything?" They shook their heads no. "All right, check your sources, see what you can find out, and let me know. José, hang back a minute." After the others left, Tyree said, "You're in charge for the time being."

"What if he doesn't show up?"

"Well, let's cross that bridge later, but I'm inclined to give you the job."

***

Early the same morning, when Denis had left for work, he spotted a stakeout at the hotel. Thus, he was concerned about surveillance at the university as well. But following several careful look-sees, everything seemed clear. So as they had intended, Denis met Gracie after lunch. They opened a safe-deposit box at a bank on Montgomery Street. Later, driving Gracie to her next appointment, Denis said, "I'm certain the cops are watching the hotel. Do you know of a way in and out besides the lobby?"

"By a side door. It's what I've been using, and most of the girls do also. The concierges close their eyes in exchange for a little TLC." Gracie chuckled. "My account's current."

"Can I go in that way this evening?"

"Sure. It's around the corner on Bush Street. Go to a door marked STAFF. Follow the corridor, and the door on the right at the end is the concierge. Ask for Tom, and tell him you're a friend of Charlene's. He'll point you to the service elevator, then give him a few bucks."

"Great. I'll see you about seven o'clock," Denis said, and Gracie hopped out.

As Denis pulled away from the curb, Tyree texted him that his documents had arrived. When he returned to the university, there was still no surveillance. So Denis went to his office and collected two envelopes before heading to the Tenderloin. Denis didn't see Junior, but José seemed to be in charge. He made a production of patting him down. When Doc entered, Tyree waved him over.

"Here're your two birth certificates, and everything else is in the Toronto mail drop. When do you want to leave?"

"How about this Saturday, the nineteenth?"

"We can do that. I have a truck from one of my legit businesses heading to Vancouver. But it leaves here on Friday afternoon, so you'll arrive on Saturday morning. You can ride up front until you're within a few miles of the border, then move to a cubby in the trailer. Be here at four o'clock Friday afternoon."

"That'll work. How much?"

"I built it into the price."

Denis handed him an envelope containing $10,000. Then he opened the second envelope and removed his car's signed title, handing it to Tyree. "I don't have any further use for this. If you can use it, it's yours. Just call me a cab."

Tyree's mouth dropped open. "Are you shitting me? The S8?"

"None other. The one with the V10 Lamborghini."

"That must've cost a hundred thousand new."

Denis nodded.

"I can't take your money now," Tyree said, returning Denis's ten thousand.

"Fair enough."

"Shit," Tyree exclaimed, running out the front door with Doc in tow. "Look what Doc gave me." He handed José the title. "Ten cylinders—Doc, I love ya! For Christ's sake, José, call the man a taxi . . . and give me back that title."

In the cab, Denis thought about Gracie. The hard part would be telling her he was leaving on Friday. She'd be upset, but Gracie could help misdirect the police over the weekend. It would keep her mind off the rest.

Denis was back at the Sir Francis by four fifteen, making a trial run through the staff entrance. About an hour later, at his regular time, he retraced his steps, then conspicuously entered the hotel through the lobby. The watchdogs were in place, and later, Gracie arrived on time, slipping in through the staff door. They ordered dinner from room service and watched TV, and Gracie spent the night. On Thursday they continued with their deceptive procedures. That evening, Denis finally told Gracie it was their last night together. She cried for a while before Denis calmed her down. Then he engaged her with his plan for Friday and Saturday.

"It should work," Gracie said, "because Tom is on the four-to-midnight shift all weekend. That'll make it easy, but if we want to make certain he's on board, I should go down and see him now. Are you okay with that?"

"Yes, I can't afford any screw-ups." Gracie freshened up and went down the back way. When she returned, Denis asked, "How'd it go?"

"Fine; he's cool with it. Denis, there's something I need to talk to you about."

"That sounds ominous."

"Maybe a little . . . I have a fair idea about your past. You weren't exactly faithful to your wife."

"Gracie, what does that have to do with anything?"

"Well, I won't be around to take care of you. But I don't expect you to be faithful while we're apart. I know any others will just be sex. I mean—look at me. I have sex all the time, but it's only that."

Denis started laughing, and Gracie blurted out, "Don't. I'm serious."

"I know you are. I have no problem with your sex life. Especially if I'm not around. You're right about my past. But I didn't think about this aspect of our separation. Why don't we leave it like this? I'll try to wait. I want to, but if I can't, you'll know it doesn't mean anything. Is that all right?"

She hugged him. "Okay."

"Let's set a date," Denis said. "Plan to arrive in Montreal on Wednesday, April tenth. If you catch a bus for Vancouver on Thursday afternoon the fourth, it should work."

***

On Friday morning, Gabi and Joe left early for Zack's interment. Joe checked in from the car with the crew staking out Rodolphe. Denis hadn't left yet, and Joe reminded them to return to Rodolphe's hotel ahead of schedule that afternoon in case he left work early because of the Martin Luther King long weekend.

After they arrived at the cemetery, Gabi introduced Joe to everyone. At eleven o'clock the chief pulled in along with his friend the priest. The cleric put on his stole and began the rites of commendation and committal to the grave. When he finished, the priest asked if anyone wanted to share a memory. Joe could tell Janet wanted to say something but was hesitant. With all the minefields she'd navigated, he wasn't surprised. But everyone there knew her story and was unlikely to belittle or judge. Gwen reached over and squeezed her hand, and Janet began.

"I loved Zack—Papi, as I called him. He was there for me after my birth father deserted us. He wasn't really my stepfather, but it felt like he was. Papi was a fine stepdad, and we were very close. After he and Mom divorced, I didn't see him for many years, and I missed him terribly. When I was sixteen, I saw Papi one last time, and I'm grateful for that.

"Since then, I learned the rest of his story. By all judgments, Zack was a bad man. I would be deluding myself if I didn't acknowledge it. But I didn't see him like that. He summed up his life in a letter to Mom that was to be opened after his death. It was effectively a will. But more important, Zack revealed how he felt. He had a premonition that he wasn't going to live much longer. He didn't say why except that it wasn't for health reasons. Zack's letter was full of regrets about Mom and him. He also acknowledged his bad judgment and mistakes. And he seemed to be growing remorseful. That's what I focus on. Perhaps there's absolution for him after all. I hope so and pray there is."

Remarkable, Joe thought. *Janet tackled it head on.*

The trip back was quiet. Finally, Gabi looked at Joe. "Go ahead, say it."

"Say what?"

"That notwithstanding what she said, Janet's denying reality."

"Gabi, I don't think that at all. She's an unusually strong young woman. I may not completely agree with her, but I would sure as hell like her in my corner."

***

While Gabi and Joe had been driving to Zack's burial, Gracie and Denis made love a couple of times. Afterward, Denis worked out a simple text code for Gracie: *V* for arrival in Vancouver, *T* for Toronto, and *M* for Montreal. Denis gave her a new burner. As she was leaving, Gracie said, "Before you go, put out the DO NOT DISTURB sign. I don't want anyone in here today."

"Why?"

"Just 'cause," Gracie said. They hugged and kissed goodbye. Gracie looked like she was going to burst into tears as she scurried off. Later, Denis took his briefcase and left through the lobby, where the police were in place. He had breakfast at Sears, then walked toward Union Square, where he hailed a taxi. Denis had the cabby pull up and wait at the staff entrance on Bush, after which he returned to the room, collecting his suitcase and go bag. He hung the sign on the door and then retraced his route to the cab and headed for the university. Later that afternoon, Denis would take a cab to Tyree's and be on the road before Charlene reached the hotel.

As they had connived, Charlene arrived in the lobby about five o'clock Friday afternoon. She had done a great job with her hair, makeup, and outfit. There wasn't any question she was a working girl, but not so tasteless that Charlene would be thrown out before she did her bit with Tom. She spotted the cops and saw they had already zeroed in on her. Charlene went to Tom, who performed excellently. A little too loudly he pretended to call Denis's room and announce his guest. In short order Charlene was waiting for an elevator while muttering the room number as if she couldn't remember it. The cops were taking it all in. Gracie took the sign off the door. The room was as she'd left it. She kicked off her shoes and spotted a note on the desk.

Love you—D.

Gracie started tearing up again. This had been happening all day. She undressed and got into bed, wrapped the sheets around her, and buried her face in Denis's pillow. She wanted him to rub off all over her. Gracie couldn't tell Denis that was why she hadn't wanted housekeeping that morning. *He would've told me I was being silly. Well, maybe I am . . . I'm only fourteen.*

Gracie slept until nine thirty that evening, then ordered room service—two dinners. This was her idea in case the detectives checked.

When the meals came, she picked enough at both to make them look like two people had been eating. Then Gracie put the trays outside the door, went to bed, and slept surprisingly well. When she awoke Saturday morning, her job was nearly done. All she had to do now was leave conspicuously after Denis texted *V*.

Gracie showered, ordered breakfast for two, maintaining the charade, and watched TV. Finally, at ten forty-five, she received Denis's text. A few minutes later she left. The new detectives were easy to spot, and Gracie fought the urge to wave. With any luck, the police wouldn't realize Denis was missing until he didn't leave for work after the weekend. And if the police ever questioned her, Gracie would simply say he'd been in the room when she left on Saturday.

***

On Saturday morning, Denis had been dropped in Vancouver near the Pacific Central Station, and after he texted Gracie, he walked there. He bought a newspaper and sat where he could observe the Rail Canada ticket agents. After a while, Denis selected a young woman, probably in her early twenties. He was in full charm mode before he reached her station, and Denis noted her name, Beverly. But this wasn't about a pickup. This was about buying a ticket with a birth certificate for ID—a little unusual. After Beverly greeted him, his conversation flowed naturally: "I just arrived. Do you know a decent hotel nearby but not too expensive?" He continued conversing with her until he said finally, "Beverly, can you help me buy a ticket on tomorrow's Canadian to Toronto? I lost my wallet, ID, and credit cards, so I feel stupid, but I can pay cash and have a certified copy of my birth certificate."

Beverly looked it over. "No problem."

Denis used the mail drop's address in Toronto, reserving a single bedroom on the train's Sunday afternoon three o'clock departure. Then on Sunday morning, he had a late brunch at a café recommended by the concierge and returned to the hotel. Denis put $100 in US currency in an envelope. At two thirty, he walked to the station. Along the way Denis bought candy bars and mystery paperbacks at a corner store. Next, Denis located Beverly. "Thanks again," he said, and handed her the envelope.

After she looked inside it, Beverly came from behind her station and kissed him on the cheek. "You ought to grab a redcap, because it makes going through security easier." She motioned to one, calling out, "Robby, this is my friend. He's on the Canadian. Can you give him a hand?"

Beverly waved goodbye, and when they came to security, Robby said, "Stay with me," and took him to the head of the line, handing him off to an agent directing traffic there. "I'll meet you on the other side with your luggage."

The agent checked his ticket and waved him through. Robby took him to his railcar, where a porter took over. Denis tipped them generously and settled into his compartment, watching the platform slip by.

CHAPTER NINETEEN

Monday, January 21, 2013

Cameron had been at the safe house with Sister Mary Magdalen for over two weeks. She felt out of harm's way there, even though she was still sore and on the mend. Cameron had a single room on the second floor but shared a communal toilet and shower with three other girls. One of the first things she did was call her sister. Kirsten wanted to drop everything and come west, but Cameron talked her out of it, pointing out the security of the safe house as a concern. They chatted until Kirsten seemingly rebuked Cameron. "Oh lord, you've been sleeping with a monster."

"How do you think I feel? You did as well, you know," Cameron said defensively.

"I know; I can't believe I did him. I feel contaminated. It's all so unthinkable."

"This isn't just about you, Kirsten," Cameron snapped.

"I know . . . sorry. I was thinking of myself. It must be awful for you—all those years."

There wasn't anything else to say. They were both crying and agreed to talk again in a few weeks. *That didn't go well. Damn it, it's not my fault he committed those horrible crimes. And shit, I didn't go to her bed—she came to mine,* Cameron fussed silently.

Sister Mary had spent time with her, and Cameron started to realize that if Sister Mary could reclaim her life, so could she. Cameron was becoming hopeful for the first time in a long while. As their conversations progressed, she began to share the details of Denis's abuses and the things she'd done to please him. Sister Mary wasn't judgmental, and Cameron appreciated how comforting it was to have a woman who knew how she felt. Joe had been wonderful, but there were limits even with him. Cameron realized that Joe had understood this and suggested Sister Mary. *I have a lot to thank Joe for.*

Cameron had no idea what she wanted to do, but Sister Mary had no objection to her staying if she pleased. They were rapidly becoming friends, and it didn't take Cameron long to ascertain the tight budget that the safe house operated on. So when they were finishing one of their "therapy sessions," as Cameron thought of them, she brought up the topic. "Sister Mary, may we talk about more prosaic things?"

"Sure."

"Here's what I've been thinking. I want to reimburse you for my food, utilities, and so on. Would two hundred and fifty dollars a week be enough?"

"That amount's generous—more than enough. It's not necessary, but it would be appreciated. Thanks."

"Fine, then I'll give you a check for four weeks today. I want to make certain you don't throw me out." They both laughed. "Here's another thing. I'm getting to know the girls, but since I wasn't one of them, they were reticent at first. But now they've started coming around, asking my opinion on little things—nothing earth-shattering yet, but . . . well, you know." Mary nodded, and Cameron continued, "Here're my observations. Notwithstanding their lack of education, they're bright. There's no reason they can't make something of their lives with the right help. I know one of your long-term goals is to help them obtain their GEDs, but I don't see you having the funds for that anytime soon. I can help because I can teach remedial English, writing skills, and so forth. I don't know about teaching remedial reading, but I'll find out. Think about it, and if you agree, we'll give it time for me to gain their full confidence, then take it from there. I envision it being a structured program, and we could meet every day for an hour or so."

"That would be wonderful. How can I say no?"

"Great, and if we need supplies, I'll take care of it."

"I'm glad you brought all of this up. I agree; you're winning their trust. I'd like you to consider taking on responsibilities as my assistant, but it won't be paid. Think of it like a part-time volunteer's job, because I can't do it alone anymore. You don't have to reside here either. So give it thought, and we'll talk more another time."

"I'd like that."

***

Gabi and Joe both had Monday off for the Martin Luther King Jr. holiday, so they came in early Tuesday morning. Joe was impatient for the DNA from the panties. They'd been sent to the FBI by overnight courier on the third—over two weeks ago. Joe asked Gabi to follow up while he checked in with the surveillance detail assigned to Rodolphe. They reported that he'd had a call girl come Friday evening who had left Saturday morning around eleven o'clock, and Rodolphe hadn't left the hotel after that.

"What about yesterday?"

"Apparently not, but it was a holiday, so there probably weren't any classes."

"Did you verify that?"

"No."

"What about today? Have you seen him yet?"

"No, but it's still early. Sometimes he doesn't leave until ten thirty."

"Head over to the university and see if he's there. If not, find out about yesterday and have your partner stay at the hotel until we locate Rodolphe. I have a bad feeling about this." Within half an hour, the detective rang back. "There were classes yesterday, but Rodolphe didn't show. He's not here now either."

"All right, go back to the Sir Francis and search the room with your partner. Afterward, start questioning the staff."

Although housekeeping had already cleaned, Joe dispatched a CSU team. Then he went to the hotel and debriefed the detectives. Something was wrong about their Friday afternoon surveillance, because they hadn't seen Rodolphe return from work. The detectives assumed he'd left work earlier because of the holiday weekend. Nonetheless, they weren't concerned, because of the hooker. Joe called the university and established that Rodolphe had in fact left early on Friday. Notwithstanding that, Joe suspected he had never returned to the hotel, because Rodolphe wouldn't risk waiting around for the DNA results. Further interrogation of the detectives revealed the pross's conversation with the concierge about the room number, and that didn't make sense. Thus, he determined, the call girl might have been a ruse.

Joe spoke with the hotel manager and learned that the concierge on duty last Friday afternoon, Tom, was due in today at one p.m. After lunch, Joe interviewed him. He seemed like a sincere kid. "Did you speak to the girl Friday afternoon?"

"Yes, she came to my desk for Rodolphe's room number."

"Didn't you think that was odd? Wouldn't she have already had the room number?"

"Now that you mention it, I guess so. But I didn't give it a second thought."

"Did you know her?"

"No, it was the first time I'd seen her."

"So the hotel tolerates working girls?" Joe observed.

"Well, not officially, but they seem to accept it as part of doing business. Frankly, if the girls use the staff entrance and service elevator and aren't too trashy or loud, they turn a blind eye. If there's ever a problem, we're instructed to call security immediately, but we've never had to. Since this is a high-class hotel, the guests are generally high rollers, and the girls don't want to screw it up."

"But she used the main elevators. Did she tip you?"

"Yeah, she gave me twenty bucks. Don't rat me out," Tom appealed.

Joe wasn't learning anything he hadn't already surmised. "Do you know her name and how to contact her?"

"No."

Joe returned to HQ. This seemed to be a dead end. The more he thought about it, the more he was convinced Rodolphe had been long gone by the time the call girl showed. On a hunch, Joe checked with room service. Two meals had been ordered Friday evening and two breakfasts Saturday morning, all in keeping with the meticulous planning he'd come to expect from Vlad. He also checked with valet parking, and Rodolphe hadn't returned his car after he took it Wednesday morning, the sixteenth.

CHAPTER TWENTY

Thursday, January 24, 2013

Gabi came into Joe's office. "I have news on Rodolphe's disappearance."

Joe looked up. "We haven't seen hide nor hair of him—tell me."

"You remember Danny Wong?"

"Yeah, he's a detective in the Tenderloin."

"That's him. We went through the academy together, and he's a detective sergeant now. Danny called because something rang a bell with him. It's about the first BOLO we put out on Rodolphe."

"We withdrew that after he agreed to come in."

"That's right. It turns out Danny's a car nut, and the description of Rodolphe's S8 ten-cylinder Audi stuck with him. It popped up in a meeting with one of his confidential informants, José."

"How so?"

"It's tangentially connected to a Central Division homicide. They pulled a body out of the bay—down by the piers—Tuesday morning the fifteenth. It had two hollow-point forty-five slugs in the chest. The victim, known as Junior, was a lieutenant in Tyree's crew. Central caught the case and visited Tyree the following day. Nothing much came of it. The investigation is wallowing for lack of information."

"I remember Tyree. How does this tie in with our case?"

"According to José, who is in Tyree's crew, this guy, calls himself Doc, started coming around in early October. Nobody knew him, but he was looking for a gun. He talked his way in to see Tyree, who got him a twenty-two. That's all José knows, since he wasn't involved in the transaction. After that, Doc came around several times and did other business with Tyree. José didn't know what they were up to, but whatever it was, Tyree contacted associates in Palo Alto. Then a week later, a large mailing envelope arrived from those guys. When Doc came in to pick it up, a lot of cash changed hands. Most recently, Tyree arranged a fake ID package for Doc and smuggled him into Vancouver using one of his legit business trucks. They left Friday afternoon the eighteenth around four o'clock. Doc signed his car over to Tyree—maybe a partial payment. José has a memory like mine and saw the title. He recalls the owner's name, the license plate number, and a full description of the vehicle. It was Rodolphe's car."

"How does this tie in to Central's case?"

"Payback. According to Danny, José blames Tyree for Junior's death. They were close, and José's looking to get even." Gabi went on to describe Tyree's berating of Junior in front of the entire crew. "José's convinced it was Tyree, because he replaced his forty-five the day after the killing with a ten-millimeter. You were right. Rodolphe was gone by the time the prostitute showed up at the hotel."

"I knew it. I assume that the CI doesn't know the name on the fake ID package?"

"Not a clue," Gabi replied. "All we know is that he's in Canada."

"He's probably heading for Montreal because of his language proficiency. That's a violation of bail. So put out a BOLO, and Gabi, we need those DNA results."

"I'll follow up again."

Gabi called Quantico. The DNA analysis was finished and awaiting a supervisor's review and sign off. The agent she spoke with said, "It should be in your email tomorrow morning."

***

The Canadian pulled into Toronto's Union Station at two thirty p.m. on Friday, the twenty-fifth. Before he detrained, Denis texted Gracie his arrival. He caught a cab, then on the ride to his mail drop checked the next day's schedule. There was a train at eight thirty in the morning that arrived in Montreal in the early afternoon. Denis collected his new driver's license and so on, then the cabby dropped him at a second-class hotel within walking distance of the train station.

***

Friday morning the DNA email was in Gabi's inbox. There was a ninety-five percent certainty it was Sally Thompson's. Gabi headed to Joe's office, where he scanned the report. "Finally, we've nailed the prick."

"Now all we have to do is catch him," Gabi remarked.

Later that morning, Joe called Cameron. "How are you doing?"

"Better. I'm not too sore anymore. Mary's been wonderful. I can't thank you enough for referring me to her."

"I'm glad. I called to update you. The DNA sample on the panties is back. It matches Sally Thompson, the eleven-year-old who disappeared five years ago when you were on a book-signing tour."

"Oh no, that's horrible. I feel terrible for her family. So this isn't a big misunderstanding. You know, it's hard to explain, but I'm relieved. I think I must have already processed the truth. What happens next?"

"We'll be meeting with the captain this afternoon. I'm positive we'll issue an arrest warrant within the next couple of days. We also know Denis disappeared a week ago today. He's in Canada and probably heading for the French-speaking areas. We'll be getting the Canadian authorities involved now. I think we have a long way to go yet, but we couldn't have come this far without you. I know what it cost."

"Does Melisa know yet?"

"No, I reached out to you first. If you want to call her, it's fine. There's nothing confidential about this now."

"I'd like to . . . I'll do it right after we hang up. Joe, thanks for everything."

Around four o'clock. Gabi and Joe met with Captain Weber. He was pleased that they had solved the case. Joe avoided pointing out that the underlying cases—the warehouse murders and Melisa's statutory rape—remained opened. But Joe knew what the captain meant. He didn't give a damn which crime put Rodolphe away for life, and Joe went home, for the first time in a long while, feeling much better.

***

Denis walked to the station Saturday morning. The train pulled out on time, and after he arrived at Gare Centrale, he texted Gracie an *M*. Then he went to the tourist desk and inquired about hotels. They offered to make reservations, but Denis declined—less of a paper trail. He chose the Hotel Gault on Sainte-Hélène Street, since it was centrally located in the Old City. Using his new ID packet, Denis checked in, booking a corner suite for three weeks. Then he unpacked and began exploring the Old City, had dinner in a small bistro, and was back in the hotel by eight thirty.

On Sunday, Denis had brunch at the hotel and then went shopping. He returned to his suite with his packages, settled in, and called Gracie at four p.m. *If she worked all night, she ought to be up by now.*

"Hi, Gracie, did I wake you?"

"No. How's Montreal?"

"Fine. I went shopping today. Since I brought so few things, I needed to get that out of the way. I forgot to bring a winter jacket too, so I did that first off. This is the new burner number you should use, because I already discarded the other phone."

"Thanks. Where're you staying?"

"It's safer if you don't know. It's in the Old Town, very nice—a small suite. You'll like it."

"Well, I'd feel closer to you if I knew where you were, but I understand. I have a few things to tell you." Gracie reported ordering two dinners and breakfasts to throw the police off.

"Outstanding. Well thought out."

"Also," she continued, "that detective you talked about, the man—"

"Cancio?"

"Yes. He has zeroed in on Tom already. We never coached Tom on how to handle police questioning. I think he did great, but to keep him loyal, I'll need to show him more TLC than I envisioned. Probably at least twice a week. What do you think?"

"I think you're right. Do him as often as necessary, but I hate to ask you to do that."

"It's okay. I don't mind, because he's kind of cute." Gracie giggled.

"Stop that," Denis said, feigning disapproval.

"There's something else you should know. I saw it in the police blotter section of the paper yesterday. There's an arrest warrant out for you for jumping bail, and they think you've fled to Canada, possibly Montreal."

Denis was silent for a bit. "I'm not surprised. I knew they would eventually catch on, although I was hoping for additional time. I'm working on my disguise. I bought nonprescription clear glasses yesterday afternoon, and I've already started growing a beard."

"A stubble beard will make you look cute."

"All right, that's what I'll do. Overall, I think everything's going fine. I mean it when I say you've been a tremendous help. We make a great team."

"Bonnie and Clyde."

"Absolutely. I'll call within the next ten days. Don't call unless it's an emergency."

"Talk to you then. Love you."

"Me too."

***

On Monday the twenty-eighth, Joe and Gabi met with Dr. Sandler. "Ellen, we would've never located Sally Thompson if it hadn't been for your conviction that the warehouse murders weren't Rodolphe's first kill," Joe began.

"I'm glad it's working out," Ellen said. "I agree with your focus on Montreal, because it will be easier for him to blend in with his language skills. I have another thought for you. Remember my friend from Paris, Bridgette Dubois? She's at the Sûreté du Québec in Montreal for a training program. While you deal with your official liaison, I could talk to her. She might be a back-channel resource for us. What do you think?"

"Let's do that."

Back in the office, Gabi and Joe brainstormed what was next. Gabi would question Tyree with Danny Wong, reinterview Tom, apprise the Gilroy chief of police of what they knew about Sally Thompson, talk to Melisa about Rodolphe's disappearance, and contact the Vice Squad for the names of pimps running girls in the Union Square area. While she was doing that, Joe would deal with the captain and the press conference, liaise with the Sûreté du Québec, and talk to Cameron about her husband's disappearance.

CHAPTER TWENTY-ONE

Monday, February 4, 2013

When Gabi and Joe came in, they continued working on their to-do lists they'd begun the prior week. And Gabi reminded Joe, "I'm following up with Danny Wong on the information we received from his CI. We're going to Tyree's this morning."

"All right, but go cautiously. We don't want to blow José's cover."

Arriving at Tyree's headquarters, Gabi and Danny flashed their badges to the group hanging around outside. One of them—Gabi assumed it was José—said, "Wait here," and went inside. He returned, held the door open, and pointed to Tyree, who was sitting at a table in a rear corner. They asked him about his relationship with Doc and so on, pretending that when he transferred the title of the Audi to his name, the DMV had notified the SFPD because of the BOLO. Tyree was cordial but not forthcoming; he claimed to be a simple importer/exporter who knew nothing about fake IDs.

"You don't know anything about Doc's disappearance? What name he's using? Where he's living? Anything that could help us?" Gabi probed.

"No, my connection with Doc was only because of the car." Then Tyree told a nonsensical story about helping an associate. "My friend lent Doc fifty grand but was having trouble collecting. So I purchased Doc's debt to help my colleague, who had his own cash flow problems. Eventually, Doc offered me his car in settlement, and we met two or three times to finalize the transaction."

237

"You don't know why the original loan was made?" Danny queried.

"No, nada." Tyree wouldn't disclose his associate's name. "Discretion is the stock-in-trade of my business." Then, turning his palms up, making an empty gesture, he finished, "That's all I have, Detectives."

"Total bullshit. He knows a lot more," Gabi said when they were back in the car, and Danny nodded in agreement.

***

On Tuesday afternoon, Gabi reported to Joe on her and Danny's interview with Tyree. Afterward, she said, "I've reviewed everything regarding Rodolphe's getaway. I don't mean to give him too much credit, but he's been two steps ahead of us. I'm wondering, what if he staged the call girl to mislead us?"

"Well, Rodolphe certainly staged it, but I'm not with you."

"I mean, if it was a deception, we could be chasing our tails looking for a nonexistent call girl. Maybe she's a lover, a mistress, or a friend simply masquerading as a prostitute."

"Let's assume you're right. How do we proceed?"

"I think we ought to question any women who have more than a casual relationship with him. Cameron, Melisa, faculty, students, and so on. Also, we'll ask everyone we talk to if there's someone else we should chat with. I'll prioritize Tom, but we ought to pursue this line as well."

"Let's see where it goes."

***

Gabi called Tom, and early Wednesday afternoon, February 6, he came in before his three o'clock shift. She greeted him in reception and showed him a draft of an upcoming press release about Rodolphe. "I'm on a conference call; I'll be with you shortly," Gabi said, stalling to give him time with the release. When she returned, Gabi led Tom to an interview room. "I'm Detective Cancio's partner; he spoke with you before. Frankly, I don't believe a bit of the bullshit you gave him. I think you can tell us a great deal more. I showed you the press release so you can see what we're dealing with. We need to talk to the prostitute who arrived Friday afternoon. And if anyone else stayed with Rodolphe besides her, we need to talk to them as well. But you know all about this. You need to come clean." *Might as well be aggressive—rattle his cage.*

"Detective, I don't know what I can tell you that I haven't already. I saw Rodolphe going in and out of the hotel a couple of times that week. I don't know if he had any other visitors before Friday afternoon. You can check all that with the reception desk if you haven't already. As far as girls go, it's hard to say. I told your partner that they mainly use the staff entrance and service elevator. I stand by what I already said about the one who arrived on Friday. From what you've told me, either one or both were gone by the time I came on duty Saturday. I'm sorry if you don't believe me, but that's the best I can do. I'd like to leave now. If that's a problem, I'll call my father for him to arrange a lawyer."

He's savvier than his golly-gee-shucks demeanor implies, and he's not being truthful. Maybe she's rewarding him in kind. "No, Tom, you don't need a lawyer. But if anything comes to mind, please let me know." Gabi handed him her card. "Before you go, I want to tell you something else. If a young girl is involved with him, you may not be doing her a favor by covering for her. You saw the press release. He's a person of interest in five crimes, including three murders of young women. Keep that in mind."

Tom left, but he didn't look any more disturbed than when he'd walked in, meaning he didn't look disturbed at all.

***

On Thursday, Gabi visited the administrative offices at the university. The staff had been concerned when Dr. Rodolphe didn't come in. Apparently, he was popular, especially among the women. *Wait until the news breaks about an arrest warrant being issued for murder*, Gabi thought. No one had any suggestions about whom Rodolphe might be dating besides Melisa. One woman, who worked part-time as a secretary in the English department, said she'd been checking his voice mail and there were two calls the police might be interested in. Both were from the week of January 21 and were from the same woman, Jessica, who sounded like a student. The university checked enrollments, and there had been no Jessicas this year or the previous one. The messages were similar. "Please, give me a ring—I'd like to see you."

Gabi returned to the office and called Jessica. There was no answer, so on Friday, Gabi tried again. This time Jessica picked up.

"This is Detective Sergeant Gabi Müller of the SFPD. I left you a message yesterday."

"Yes, Detective, I have it. I was going to call you today. I'm a little nervous."

"That's normal, but don't worry; you're not in any trouble. This is only an inquiry. I have your name and phone number from Dr. Denis Rodolphe's voice mail at the university. All I have is your first name. Could you identify yourself? Then I'll tell you why I'm calling." Jessica provided her full name and said she was a sophomore boarding at Stanford. Gabi continued, "I need to talk to you, because Dr. Rodolphe is a fugitive. He skipped bail on a domestic violence charge for which he

240

"Tom knows you're leaving eventually, right?"

"Yes, but he thinks it's much further in the future than it is. He might be daydreaming that I'll change my mind and stay. I'm showing him the time of his life!"

"He'll get over it. Anything else I need to know?"

"Yes, the police held a press conference yesterday. They distributed releases with your picture. It's been all over TV, and you're becoming a household name."

"I saw it in the paper but nothing on TV yet. I'm concerned about all the notoriety—it's stressful. But I'm staying in the Old Town—blending in with my glasses, and my beard's coming in nicely. I've let my hair grow longer too."

"You'll be as adorable as before. Denis, don't get pissed, but I need to know you didn't do what they're alleging. You didn't kill that little girl?"

"Gracie, don't worry. I didn't do it, and I've racked my brains trying to understand why Cancio is fixated on me. Here's what I think. Zack had a key and stayed with us when he was working at the house. When that girl was abducted, he was there, working on a rose garden for Cameron. She was away on a book tour, and I wasn't interested in the project. So I left Zack to his task and took off for Vegas with a new instructor I'd hired. She was hot and sick and tired of her husband. We hooked up for four or five days. Later, I discovered that Zack's divorce was caused because he'd abused his stepdaughter. She was only nine or ten. Obviously, he had a thing for little girls. He must've abducted Sally while I was away. Zack discarded her body afterwards but overlooked those panties when he cleaned up. Cameron told me that a serviceman found them behind our washing machine. It's causing me problems because Zack is dead, and the cops think I'm responsible for that to boot.

Then the woman I took to Vegas won't alibi me, because it would ruin her marriage. It was over five years ago, and I paid cash for everything involved with that trip. I have no receipts, so it's a mess. You believe me, don't you?"

"Of course I do."

Denis changed the subject. "I have a new best friend, by the way. Jacques."

"Who's Jacques?"

"Well, he's a chocolate Lab. I walk to the Old Port almost every day and amble along the Promenade du Vieux-Port and the Rue du Quai King-Edward. There's this kindly looking old man wearing a fire-engine-red parka. When I arrive, he's either sitting on a bench or throwing a ball for his dog, and sometimes I throw the ball too. Then, when the old man's ready to go, he calls Jacques, who always obeys, but reluctantly. I think he prefers my throwing arm to the old man's. Then as they leave, we wave."

"Why don't you talk to him, make friends? I know you're lonely."

"I don't know; I kind of like it the way it is."

***

Joe had called Cameron on the fourteenth. They'd agreed to meet on Friday, and she'd invited him to the house for lunch at noon. When he arrived, she said, "Let's sit at the kitchen table. How about a glass of wine, or are you still on duty?"

"Still on duty." She poured a white wine for herself and a glass of iced tea for Joe. He watched Cameron and noticed she was moving normally, without any signs of Denis's beating. "You look like your old self," he remarked.

"Thanks. I feel much better."

"I know you have a shopping list of items to talk about, but I have a couple of police matters. Let's do them first, all right?" Cameron nodded yes. "Is there anything you can tell us about his disappearance? I gave you the broad strokes when we spoke last," Joe continued. "But is there anything you can add?"

"No, although I think you're onto something about the French-speaking area of Canada. If he's acquired another ID, Canada might well be a temporary stop; however, Denis could be anywhere, since his family has vast business holdings all over the world. Also, he's an organizer and has probably been planning all along."

"Yes, he has acquired another ID, but we don't know the name he's using. We know who made the arrangements for him, but he's a seasoned criminal and isn't cooperating. We're also convinced that your husband had an accomplice, a young woman, possibly a prostitute. She bamboozled our surveillance team into thinking he was still at the hotel when he'd already left for Canada. That's the most important thing I want to ask you about. Would you have any idea who that woman could be? We need to talk to her. Plus we know how your husband likes to tidy up loose ends, so she may not be safe."

"I have no idea," Cameron replied. "The only woman I know of is Melisa, and I assume she's out of the question?"

"Yes, yet we did uncover another woman he met right before disappearing. Gabi interviewed her, but I don't think she had anything to do with it."

"Who was this other woman?" When Joe was finished telling her about Jessica, Cameron said, "So even though they never got together, he was picking her up while buying my Christmas gift?" Joe nodded, and Cameron shook her head. "How old was she?"

"Nineteen."

"But nothing happened other than Denis touched her, right?"

"Right."

"Well, I don't have any idea who it could be, but on another subject, you might investigate his family money. He has accounts and investments in his own name. According to him, they're substantial. They weren't a secret, but I don't know anything about them. All that mail goes to his office. You might track down those accounts, because it's conceivable Denis has already been moving funds around."

"I wasn't aware of his separate finances. How about your joint accounts? Any unusual activity there the last couple of weeks?"

"Nothing out of the ordinary."

"Fine. I'll have Gabi check with the university and see if they're holding any mail. If they're reluctant to release it, would you see if they'll give it to you? That's a lot easier than the route of a court order."

"Sure, I know the dean. It shouldn't be a problem."

"While we've been talking about family money, it occurs to me that we haven't reached out to his parents. Do you have phone numbers or addresses for them?"

"That's a problem; it might not be worthwhile. I met them once in 2003 at our wedding. They flew in from Russia for a couple of days.

They're both in the diplomatic service, but I don't know if they're still posted there. I don't think Denis has spoken to them since then. To say the least, it's a peculiar relationship."

"They sound estranged. What were they like?"

"I scarcely knew them. His father was charming and his mother gracious. When I met her, she was nearly sixty and attractive for her age. Denis's mother was affectionate and seemed genuinely glad to see him. But he didn't respond; I don't think Denis likes her. She was welcoming to me and gave me a beautiful heirloom ring as a wedding present. It was in a Tiffany box, but even that turned out to be bizarre. I took it to them for an insurance appraisal, but they said it wasn't one of their rings and thought it was an antique. Tiffany's believed it was worth millions. When I took it to a museum for an evaluation, I found out that it was made in France by a court-appointed jeweler prior to the French Revolution. The cost to insure it was astronomical, so it's in our safe-deposit box. Frankly, I'm scared to wear it. Later, Denis told me the ring had been worn by his mother, grandmother, and so forth going back to before the family emigrated here, but he didn't know for how many generations. I couldn't help but think his mother was passing on a matriarchy to me, which made no sense, and I still don't understand it. It's an odd family—that's the only word I can use."

"You're right; it's strange. I'll see if Gabi can track them down. That's all I need to go over. What did you want to talk about?"

"I've been splitting my time between the safe house and here. I think I'll be here full-time shortly. That will free up another bed for Mary. Mary and I have talked about me becoming her assistant, maybe running the day-to-day operations. Also, I started working with the girls, giving them remedial writing and reading help. It fits in with Mary's long-term goals. That brings me to a plan I've been thinking about, but I'd like your opinion.

"It's about my finances. On my own, I've made excellent money. There are the ongoing royalties from books, and my agent is negotiating a couple of film deals. I don't have to worry about a thing for the rest of my life. Denis was never involved with that, never a signer on any of my accounts. He was fine with that because of his wealth. Additionally, we have substantial joint accounts requiring one signature. Denis did me a favor by disappearing, because I can keep managing them. And I have no intention of seeking a divorce or having him declared dead. It doesn't make sense, because those actions would tie up those joint assets. So I'll start moving those into my name, and if anyone asks, Denis is traveling the world over, indulging his midlife crises. And fittingly, I'll use some of what I liquidate to help Mary achieve her long-term goals. I haven't said anything to her yet. What do you think?"

"I think it's a great idea, and I know Mary would be forever grateful. But what about your writing?"

"I had a brainchild that I've started working on. The book will be an exposé on the sex trade, rape, underage prostitution, trafficking, and so on. It'll be a collection of fictionalized interviews with the girls I've met at Mary's. It's well underway already."

"That's a great idea. I'll help you in any way I can, and I can direct you to other sources inside the PD."

"Thanks. I was counting on that."

"How are things going with your sister?" They had finished lunch, and Cameron started clearing the table and tidying up, but it seemed to him like she was stalling after he brought up Kirsten.

"Where to start . . . it's complicated. Kirsten says she feels corrupted, violated, and unclean—join the club. She hasn't focused on us at all but rather on what Denis did to her and keeps telling me it's not my fault. But Kirsten brings it up so often that it's tantamount to an accusation. And it hurts me, because it isn't my doing that Denis turned out the way he did. Plus, she disclosed she'd fooled around with him a few times before the three of us made it . . . but nothing serious. Anyway—we can't resolve our intimacy issues until we settle everything."

"You two will work through this."

"It isn't clear, because we're estranged now. Then there's Melisa. That's a complication for me as well."

This is probably what Cameron wants to talk about, Joe surmised.

"Okay, so you know about me. I mean about my appetite. Even with our problems, I never stopped having sex with Denis. The last time was the Wednesday night through Friday morning with Kirsten and him, and that was nearly seven weeks ago. Are you following me?"

"I think so."

"This is where Melisa comes in. When we had lunch, we talked about everything, and I mean everything. It's confusing because we don't want to live without men, but we're wary of them now. Melisa probed my feelings vis-à-vis doing it with Kirsten, then hinted about us hooking up because we would feel safer."

"That's normal with what you've been through. It'll work out."

As Cameron walked him to the door, she paused. "You know, I feel safe with you." Then she stood close and gently coaxed, "Just whistle."

***

In bed that evening, Susan snuggled. "Tell me."

"How did you know?"

"Just did. I knew you were meeting Cameron today. I'm guessing it's what I've been afraid of since last September when I saw you two in the window of the Kensington Park. Am I wrong?"

"You're right." Then Joe told Susan everything about their meeting.

"I'm not trying to be unkind, Joe, but do you think you're in control?"

"Yes, she didn't pressure me."

"Well, the way I see it, there wasn't anything left for her to do but a striptease."

"I'm not certain what you're driving at."

"You don't see that she's been giving you a sales pitch all along? A features-and-benefits statement about her sexual prowess. She's revealed her most intimate thoughts and actions. Don't you see she's letting you know what's on the menu?"

"No."

"Well, I think so. It may have been instinctive at first—a tactic for control. But it's been more than that for a while."

"You're portraying her like a manipulative bitch, Susan."

"That's why I worry so much, since you don't. I concede she cares for you. You've been her rock. But Cameron is out from under her husband's thumb now. She's selfish, and all it took was six weeks or so without sex to show her colors."

who is later identified as Zack Wheeler, is Rodolphe's accomplice. Next, on November 21, lawyer Steinberg is retained. He has a boutique firm specializing in international law and global funds movement.

- *On December 14, the Marin County ME established the middle of October as the date of Zack's death. Then on December 28, Rodolphe sells $12.5 million in securities from a third brokerage account. Next, on December 31, he sells a like amount from a fourth brokerage account. These funds, totaling $25 million, end up in Janes Steinberg's escrow account.*

- *On January 2, 2013, he learns about the panties and assaults Cameron. On the same day, Rodolphe visits Tyree and disappears until his bail hearing. On January 7, $25 million in securities were sold from the brokerage accounts previously mentioned. The funds end up in Steinberg's escrow account as before. Rodolphe's total liquidated funds, September 2012 through January 2013, now total $52.5 million.*

"Good lord." Joe looked up. "How much friggin' money does this guy have?"

"It seems like there's still another fifty million left in the accounts we've discovered here, but I won't commit that we've found everything," Gabi said.

"Shit, and that doesn't count his joint assets with Cameron."

"Then," Gabi continued, "on January eleventh, he makes bail and checks into the Sir Francis. He resumes his normal work schedule. On January sixteenth, Rodolphe visits Tyree and transfers his car. Then on the afternoon of January eighteenth, he takes a cab from the university to Tyree's and leaves for Canada by truck. Later that day, as a deception, a prostitute-friend goes to his room at the Sir Francis. That's it so far."

"How did you piece together the information about his visits to Tyree?"

"Intel from Danny Wong's CI."

"What's Steinberg up to with Rodolphe's money? For all we know, it's still sitting in a San Francisco bank."

"I have calls in to both him and Seaton," Gabi said. "I checked Steinberg out. He's low profile, powerful, and well connected in the old-monied San Franciscan community. He's Harvard educated with no scandal or ethics charges, but he's a bit of an enigma."

***

On Monday, Joe spoke with Ellen Sandler and briefed her on the case.

"You're kidding me?" she said. "That much money?"

"Yes, and Gabi's researching how to access records from the foreign countries now. Most are members of the Hague Service Convention, which complicates things. Also, those countries have blocking statutes, which do what the name implies. Our underlying reason for requesting his records is a bit shaky, because his funds have been legally acquired. We would be better off if we were searching for funds laundered from drugs, sex or human trafficking, illegal arms sales, and so forth. Next, we're continuing to track down the prostitute who helped him as well as see if lawyers Seaton and Steinberg can provide any information. Additionally, Gabi will try to locate his parents. They're a lower priority, because according to Cameron, they're estranged. Do you have any thoughts on his blowup with Cameron and his mental state?"

"I've thought about it. There's no doubt Rodolphe was pushed to the limit. Obviously, he released a lot of pressure. I'm not certain it was a psychotic break, though. Those breaks can last for months. They're challenging to diagnose because, in no order, there're a wide range of symptoms, such as strong or no emotions, withdrawal, delusions or hallucinations, decline in self-care, persistent unusual thoughts, and unclear thinking. I don't have enough information, but I'm leaning towards no. Why? Because within hours, Rodolphe successfully goes to ground. That's impressive on-the-fly organizing. So there's no doubt he's still under control. If there's anything else I can do, let me know."

"There is something, but it involves Susan. She's the woman I've been seeing for the last five months."

"It's about time. I was wondering if you were ever going to tell me about her."

"How did you know?"

"Joe, I'm a shrink. Didn't you think I might notice a change in your behavior? You haven't been this happy since before Laura died. It wasn't rocket science."

"I'm sorry. I wasn't excluding you. You know I don't bring my personal life to work."

"That's why I never asked. How can I help?"

Joe reviewed his conversation with Cameron concerning the business aspects of the case.

"I think she's doing remarkably well in a short period of time. But she's not strong enough yet to stand alone. Sister Mary's filling the void left by her husband's departure. But that's not what you want to talk about, is it?"

261

"No, it's personal." And then Joe told Ellen about how close he'd become to Cameron, how they'd parted, the *just whistle* line, and Susan's apprehension over Cameron being a threat.

Ellen thought for a bit and finally joked, "Would Susan like a job working for me? Seriously, though, I'm not trivializing your situation. I would listen to Susan. She may be paranoid, but that doesn't mean she's wrong. Have you decided about Cameron?"

"Really, Ellen, I thought it went without saying that I would turn Cameron down. If she calls again, Gabi's going to run with it."

"I'm glad, because Susan makes you happy. Why would you jeopardize that? Cameron will cause you nothing but heartache. And eventually, when she doesn't need a security blanket anymore, she'll simply move on."

CHAPTER TWENTY-THREE

Thursday, February 28, 2013

Haniff Seaton returned Gabi's call. He was cooperative within the bounds of not breaching his client's confidentiality. He explained that the possible statutory rape charge and the domestic assault case were the extent of his engagements. "How did you become involved with the assault case?" Gabi inquired.

"It was because he'd already consulted with me on the rape case. But then he called on January third regarding the assault. At first, I thought the case could be handled by our SF office. But Rodolphe was concerned that one of your detectives was gunning for him. I thought he was overreacting until I talked to the prosecutor who wanted remand. Following that, I became convinced Rodolphe might've been correct when I saw Detective Cancio in court."

"Did you have any other meetings or conversations regarding the assault case?"

"No, the prosecutor and I were charged with working out a plea deal. But nothing was done before all hell broke loose."

"Can you share what happened after that?"

"Not much; technically, we still represent him. But I can't reach Rodolphe, because the two phone numbers I have are out of service. We're under instructions to use his office address for mail. But I don't think he's employed any longer. Eventually, we'll send a letter there, withdrawing and requesting instructions about what to do with the balance of his retainer. If we can't reach him, we'll put it in an interest-bearing account."

"Then you didn't have any contact with him after the bail hearing?"

"No."

"Do you have any idea where he was between January third and tenth?"

"I spoke to him twice, once each on January third and fourth, and my secretary spoke to him on the seventh as well. We used one of the phone numbers that are now out of service. Rodolphe said he was lying low, since he didn't trust the police. He told my secretary he intended to go away for a few days. That would be the eighth through the tenth, and she thinks he mentioned Tiburon."

"Do you have any information that would help us locate him now?"

"No, I have no idea. If Rodolphe ever ends up in the judicial system, our firm has some soul searching to do. What's been in the news is beyond the pale."

Gabi also spoke with James Steinberg that day. "I've been expecting a call from the police."

"We discovered your name through a canceled check Rodolphe wrote to you on November 21, 2012," Gabi said.

"That's correct—a retainer. How may I help you?"

"I'd like any information you can give us about Rodolphe's whereabouts and the fifty million dollars he has wired to your escrow account."

"Detective, you've been thorough in a short time. I've followed the exploits of my client through the news and your press conference. I knew nothing about any of that when he retained me. I intend to cooperate if you cover my ass. Which means a comprehensive court order. Here's what I can tell you now. Although we'd never met, we both knew of each other because of the circles in which we move. It seemed natural Rodolphe would reach out to me. He sought help in facilitating several international transactions. I can assure you everything was legal. My engagement with him is complete now."

"Does that mean the funds are gone?"

"Use your own judgment. With that court order, I can confirm everything. I'm certain you've checked me out. I know I have a bit of a reputation—a man of mystery. It helps business, but I run a scrupulously honest practice. Think of me as the international equivalent of a tax lawyer who knows all the loopholes. I don't knowingly work for crooks. As an officer of the court, I presume my former client is innocent until proven otherwise. But should he be found guilty, Rodolphe deserves to rot in hell."

And lawyer Steinberg won't mind punching his ticket there if I cover his ass, Gabi thought. The next morning, March 1, she told Joe about her conversations with the two attorneys. There wasn't anything of note to report from Seaton. "Steinberg will need a court order but assures me he'll help in any way he can. I'd like to have that as soon as possible. Do you think we ought to contact the captain?"

"Yes." Several hours later, Weber called Gabi and told her to have the order delivered to Judge Greiner's chambers. Later, after it had been signed, Gabi called Steinberg.

"Glad you're so prompt," he said. "I already have a package prepared; however, fax the order for my review. If you're free for lunch Monday, I can see you then. Why don't you come to my office? I'll order sandwiches or salads, and we can go over everything. I think reviewing it in person will make your job easier."

***

Gabi enjoyed her relationship with Melisa but hadn't spoken to her since Christmastime, so she gave her a call.

"I'm glad you rang," Melisa said. "I've got lots to tell you."

"You sound up. What's happening?"

"Well, I moved in with Cameron. We're a couple now."

Gabi wasn't flabbergasted, because Joe had told her about Cameron and Kirsten's tryst and Cameron and Melisa's exploration of a relationship when they'd had lunch. Notwithstanding her reservations, Gabi said, "I hope you'll be happy."

"It gets better. I'm returning to university this fall, and Cameron's picking up my tuition and expenses."

"Wow!"

"I'm not a total freeloader, though." Melisa laughed. "I've already started helping Cameron research her new book, organize her notes, and so on. It gives her time to think and write. It's fun, and I'll help at Sister Mary's sometimes as well."

"It sounds great. Let's have lunch?"

"I can do it here or Palo Alto since I'm back and forth, keeping an eye on Dad. I'll call you."

When Gabi told Joe, he chuckled. "Kudos to her." On the way home that night, he thought, *I can't wait to tell Susan. Her fears of Cameron manipulating Melisa may have been premature.*

***

Monday afternoon, Gabi and Steinberg met at twelve thirty. Later, when Gabi returned to the office, she reported, "Steinberg is an interesting character. He's soft-spoken and short—maybe five six—but not inconsequential. He had a complete package prepared, and I'll spend further time with it. Here're the highlights. Steinberg said he was aware of the Swiss bank account, although he wasn't involved in any transactions regarding it. Rodolphe retained him to facilitate several international transactions. Steinberg characterized these matters as investments in four different EU companies through the acquisition of restricted, non-dividend-paying, and nonvoting capital stock. The term *restricted* here means that the investments could not be sold without the consent of the company and were not tradable on any exchange. I asked Steinberg if these purchases were in effect money laundering, but he had no opinion. So I asked him if he objected to me characterizing them as such, and he simply smiled. We need to read between the lines, because Steinberg wants to help. He said there were four investments identical in nature. Rodolphe supplied him with the details of the transaction and the companies, then Steinberg prepared the contracts accordingly, issuing opinion letters as to their legality. The signed documents were held in escrow until the funds were transferred. 'It was all straightforward, albeit unusual. Obviously, Rodolphe knew these people well and trusted them,' Steinberg opined. I asked if he had any idea how the companies would use the funds. Then Steinberg asked me, 'Are you inquiring if the funds could be paid back to Rodolphe, say as an annuity? Probably through a maze of other entities?' When I said yes, he responded, 'I don't see why not.'"

"And we would have no way of tracking any such payments, because the foreign entities aren't subject to our jurisdiction?" Joe asked.

"That's right, and because the countries involved are all members of the Hague Service Convention."

Gabi had discovered that of the four companies, two were in France and one each in Germany and Italy. The companies weren't affiliated with each other, but she assumed that an in-depth search would eventually uncover a connection to the Rodolphe family's businesses. The purchases had been closed on January 14, and everything had been released from escrow.

"Let's not waste time on further searches; we may not be successful, and I'm not sure what value they would add," Joe concluded. "Jesus, it's a friggin' never-ending game!"

CHAPTER TWENTY-FOUR

Tuesday, March 5, 2013

Cameron was putting her life back together. She had returned to the house and continued transferring joint assets to her name. Mary had appointed her as assistant manager; Cameron taught the remedial classes, and money for the safe house had become less of a problem thanks to her generosity. And Mary continued to raise money for the new programs she envisioned. Cameron accompanied her on calls to her ex-johns, and between the two of them, the men didn't stand a chance. They increased their support, and the safe house's future seemed secure.

Cameron worked hard on her new book, and since Melisa had moved in, she progressed rapidly. The book was scheduled for publication in May, and her PR agent had already booked her in advance on morning and late-night talk shows.

***

Sam was glad to be inside the warm, crowded bar. Friday, March 8, was a bitterly cold evening in Montreal. Average nighttime temperatures were still below freezing. It was nearly eight o'clock, but Denis wasn't there yet. She ordered a drink that she couldn't afford. *Today's lunch and this drink have already used up half the fifty dollars I made last night. I never seem to make any headway,* she bellyached silently. Sam declined the bartender's offer of a refill, and when he looked annoyed, she gave up her stool and stood. Waiting another hour or so, she fended off a couple of guys. They seemed all right, but Sam was still hopeful. And while she waited, Sam justified what she'd done last night. *It wasn't that bad. That guy was cute—gentle too. If he'd bought me dinner, I would've gone with him anyway. But that's like bartering. Last night felt different . . . seamy.* Then, grudgingly accepting what would probably happen again this evening, Sam continued to fuss silently. *I hope tonight's guy will be nice too. With another fifty dollars, I'll make it to payday—if I skip a few meals.*

When he didn't show, she imagined he wasn't feeling well. Sam decided to walk to his hotel and see if everything was okay. As she entered and passed reception, the regular evening clerk said, "He isn't here. He checked out."

"I was supposed to meet him. Do you know where he went?"

"No, but he said that if you came in, I should give you the room key. It's paid through tonight, and you can use it if you want."

"I don't need it," was her first reaction. "Is there any way I could have a refund? How much is it, anyway?"

"It's a hundred dollars, but I can't give you one. The payment's already processed. Would you like the key?" he asked sympathetically. "You don't have to take it."

Sam gathered he was catching on to what was happening and blushed. "Let me check and make certain I didn't leave anything upstairs," she said, accepting the key.

Riding the elevator, it struck her. *If I go ahead, he won't be here to screen them, but I should be able to keep myself safe. After all, I've been doing it all along—never had a problem.* Other thoughts ran through her mind. *I'll have to finance the room, but I can keep the rest. I could do it just when I need money. It isn't like it's my day job.* She went inside. *Did he leave anything? A note?*

As she was leaving, Sam noticed that the drawer of the bedside table was ajar. Opening it, she saw a three-pack of condoms and a one-hundred-dollar bill. Riding down on the elevator, Sam started crying because Denis had known what she would do.

In the lobby, between her snivels, Sam waved to the clerk.

"See you later."

***

When Denis left for Toronto on March 12, he took fifty thousand dollars in cash, hoping that a sizable deposit would allow him to open an account without any hassle. The trip had taken about five hours, and when he arrived, Denis called Gracie before setting out.

"I'm at Union Station. I'll be seeing about the trade name certificate and opening an account. So I may be here a couple of days, but when I return to Montreal, I'll start looking for an apartment."

"I'm excited. I've never had a place of my own. You can hardly count a boardinghouse."

"Yours isn't so bad."

"You know what I mean. And I'd like a shower, with a great big tub. Can we do that?"

"Big enough for two?" Denis asked.

"You're reading my mind." Gracie giggled. "A king-size bed too?"

"Of course. Anything else?"

"No, not for the time being. What else have you been doing?"

"I did further research on my paper at the Grande Bibliothèque. I don't think it's going to end up where I was hoping. It may be an exercise in futility, but I'll finish it."

"You ought to, because it's important to you. Have you been playing with Jacques?"

"Yes, every day that I go to the Old Port. We're truly buds now."

"That's wonderful. You're in better spirits after you play with him."

"I never thought about it, but you're right. That's about the only time I'm happy besides when I'm talking to you."

"Are you still upset?"

"Yes."

"You know what I think you ought to do."

"Yes, but I've just been to the port a couple of times since our last call."

"All right, I won't nag. Do you want me to come earlier? I can leave on the twenty-first."

"No, I'll make it through. Let's stick to the original plan. Is there anything else we need to talk about?"

"That's about it. Love you," Gracie closed.

"Great. I love you too."

At the tourist desk, Denis arranged a hotel within walking distance. It was a different one than where he had stayed in January, since he was still being careful. Denis talked to the concierge and obtained directions to a money exchange and remittance office nearby where the owner was a commissioner of oaths. Denis found it easily and was greeted by a young woman.

"What can I do for you?"

After Denis told her, she said, "Well, I can't help you today, but my mother can tomorrow; she'll be in then. I'm a student—just covering for her. I'm Annabella, by the way."

"What are you studying?" Denis asked, slipping into charm mode.

"Accounting."

"Excellent choice. I think the arts are overrated. Unless you teach or write, it's a useless degree. Vocationally oriented ones like accounting, business, engineering, and law are better."

The more they talked, the more interested Denis became. Annabella was average looking but had attractive eyes and a dimpled smile. It was hard to judge her figure under the baggy sweatshirt that hung below her ass, but her personality was pleasant, and she was bright. He wondered, *Should my ministrations be better employed on mom? But then, mom isn't here. If I play it right with Annabella, maybe she'll simply slip the docs under her mother's nose for signing.* So they chatted on. When he left, they had a date for dinner.

That evening, Annabella arrived at the hotel early, wheedled his room number from the clerk, and went up instead of waiting in the lobby as they'd agreed. When Denis answered the door, he was just out of the shower, wearing only a towel. He noticed she was still wearing jeans but had changed into a crew-neck sweater. *Fills it out attractively. Cute ass too.* Annabella walked over to a chair and dropped her backpack.

"We don't have to rush off to dinner right away, do we?" she asked. Then, not waiting for his response, she continued, "Why don't you lose that towel?"

After dinner, Annabella decided to stay the night. The next morning she was up before Denis and, after showering, said, "Hurry up. You can walk me back to the office." Her mom had an early dentist's appointment, so Annabella was opening.

While she did that, Denis bought bagels and accompaniments across the street. After breakfast, he got a haircut and beard trim at a nearby unisex salon. When he returned to Annabella's office, her mother took care of his trade name certificate. Annabella left for a class, and once she was gone, her mom introduced Denis to the manager at the Bank of Montreal branch around the corner. He opened a trade-style checking account in the name of Phoenix Consultants. Neither Annabella's mother nor the banker picked up on the slight inconsistencies between his driver's license and Social Insurance card and his trade name certificate.

Annabella spent another night, and Denis was on the eleven-thirty Thursday-morning train to Montreal.

As they pulled out of the station, Denis began thinking about Gracie. He couldn't wait until she arrived. He felt so much better about everything when he was with her—especially about himself. It struck Denis that he wasn't thinking about the sex. Which was great, and he missed it terribly, but it was all the other things. Denis simply loved the way she loved him. Gracie made him feel happy. He didn't understand why he felt that way, but he liked it. He had tried to be as faithful as possible. Denis believed Gracie understood his needs—*well, most of them*—and was all right with his occasional dalliance. He'd had four hookups since arriving in Montreal. Four women in about eight weeks—not bad. Although he probably shouldn't count Annabella, because she was business.

Denis kept reflecting on the women. Before the middle of February, he'd had his first French Canadian girl, Janelle. She'd waited on him when he bought a shirt in a men's store. She was freckle faced and plump. Not his type, but he couldn't resist her smile and vivacity. Plus, she was making all the moves. Janelle spent the night at the Gault and was a little miracle, taking his mind off Gracie's recent bad news: an arrest warrant and the police suspecting that he was in Montreal.

Denis had spotted the second woman in a bar after Valentine's Day. The pressure was building because of Gracie's news about the press conference. He needed relief, and this broad was drop-dead gorgeous. No one was hitting on her, probably because she was too intimidating—*easy pickings*. He bought her a drink and chatted her up. *Jesus, she's boring.* So Denis rushed her into a nearby no-tell hotel. *Don't need her showing up at the Gault when I'm done.* Although he wasn't disappointed with her body, she was tedious in bed. *Used to being toadied to. Thinks all she needs to do is lie here, looking beautiful.*

Denis toyed with her, taking his time. Eventually, she whined, "Stop messing around," but he rolled off.

Then the woman grumbled, "Bastard," and headed to the bathroom. In a bit, Denis followed, and when she saw him enter, she turned away, exasperated, caterwauling, "Get out of here!" started trembling, and got off.

Once she returned to the room, Denis said, "I called a cab."

She dressed and wandered about before exclaiming, "Screw you."

I think she expected me to pay for the taxi. But treating her like crap hasn't provided much relief, Denis fretted.

Number three was Sam. She was different, and he'd met her on March 4, before Annabella. By the time Denis picked her up, his wrath was nearly all-consuming—beginning to feed on itself. His anger had always been directed at women, and now his rage was intensifying. Gracie was his deliverance, but she was in San Francisco and he was stuck in Canada. And notwithstanding Gracie's influence nipping at the edge of his rage, Denis needed to act. That's when he spotted Sam at an after-work bar.

Instinctively, Denis knew how exploitable Sam could be. *She'll do. A cute little brunette. Shit, she's flirting and teasing a kinky streak. A perfect surrogate for Cameron.* The first night he'd learned that Sam and her girlfriend lived paycheck to paycheck, struggling to pay the rent. Three squares a day was out of the question. They dated guys for dinner. All this played into his plan, since it couldn't have worked if Sam was flush. *I'll take my pound of flesh out of this one.* When he'd taken her to bed that night at a no-tell hotel, it wasn't hard to push her to the edge of her comfort zone, but Sam kept up.

They continued to meet at the same bar each evening. On the second and third nights, notwithstanding a few instances of temporary hesitation, he pushed her well past her prior boundaries, and she was hooked. *So tonight, I'll go for the gold.* When she came in, she was cheerful and upbeat, but he acted quiet and withdrawn. After nearly an hour and a couple of drinks, Sam said, "Are you all right? You look down."

That was his cue. "Well, I wasn't going to bring it up. But since you mention it, I'm upset with you."

"Why, what'd I do? I thought we were having fun. Is it the sex? Haven't I been doing it the way you like? Tell me."

"Well, it's not the sex, because you're great in the sack. The truth is that you're costing me a lot of friggin' money. My business isn't doing well. I hate to admit it, but that's where I'm at. You're too expensive: the nightly hotel room, dinner, and drinks—too much. And you haven't offered to help."

"I told you; I'm always broke because of the rent situation. I literally don't have lunch money until I'm paid again. My roommate's always hanging around the apartment, so we can't go there. Can't we go to your place, save money?"

"That's not going to work. Figure it out for yourself."

"Oh . . ."

"I have an idea, but you'd never go along with it."

"Tell me. What is it?"

"No, it wouldn't work."

"Please, let me be the judge."

"Here goes, then. You're an incredible piece of ass, but you're giving it away."

Sam got it but played for time. "Do you mean what I think?"

"There're a lot of clean-cut affluent types at the bar. Just sit here looking adorable. I'll take care of the rest. We could get a hundred bucks. That'd be a big help with tonight's expenses." *She'll be hurt because I'm selling her short. It's half the battle if she starts negotiating her value.*

"So you think I'd let you peddle my ass. Sitting here while those guys ogle me. Would I even have a say? And I suppose you'll keep the money. And for a hundred dollars—really!"

Negotiating! "If you knocked him dead, I'll bet you'd land a big tip. We could split it—lunch money solved."

"I'm so fuckin' angry, I don't know what to say."

He changed his tenor. "You're right, of course. I have no frame of reference. How about one hundred fifty? It'll be easy, and I'll give you my room key. There're lubed rubbers in the bedside table. Come back when you're finished, and we'll have something to eat."

"That isn't what I meant." Sam sat for a while, snuffling. "I care for you . . . I thought you cared too. Please, don't make me." Denis sat, and Sam was scared he would walk out. At length, she sighed. "Fine."

Then he walked to the bar and came back in a few minutes with her first client. Later, Sam returned alone, looking disheartened.

"How'd you make out?"

"Okay."

"Did he tip you?" Sam reached into her purse and passed him a fifty-dollar bill. "It looks like you blew his top—you keep it. Did you make it, or were you just along for the ride?"

Sam studied the table. "Please . . . you're humiliating me."

"Well?"

"Yes! Are you satisfied now?"

* * *

Back in the hotel before midnight, they showered together, and afterward in bed, Denis gentled her. Lying in his arms, she murmured, "Why . . . what did I do? I feel worthless."

He didn't respond, and soon Sam was asleep, lying on her side with her back to him. He'd heard her almost imperceptibly sobbing before she dozed off. Eventually, she'd get it. He'd done it simply because he could. They'd agreed to meet tomorrow, Friday, March 8, same time, same place. But he wouldn't show. His mind was racing. Denis felt exhilarated. *Jesus, I never made it this far with Cameron.*

It was late now, but Denis was still awake. He finally dozed off and slept lightly, restlessly. Chaotic, anxiety-peppered dreams swirled. Caricatures paraded through them: Cameron, his mother, his mother's friend, and the little girl buried in the rose garden. Then Zack, that detective, Kirsten, the twins, and even Melisa meandered past. All reached out—at his clothes, at him.

Denis was awake with a start.

"Are you all right?" Sam asked softly. "You woke up with a shudder and a gasp."

"I'm fine . . . one of those times when all your muscles relax suddenly. Sorry I woke you." She was still on her side, facing away from him. He reached over and patted her hip. All the angst associated with the parodies from his sleep continued bothering him. *What's going on?* He'd never had a dream like this before.

Finally, Denis was asleep again. Then suddenly he was shivering, freezing. Denis woke with a jolt—or had he? He raised himself and looked past Sam to the clock on the bedside table. One o'clock. Then all went dark.

The air was heavy. Denis looked over at the window: no light coming in there. Next, he looked toward the hall door's transom: no light coming in there either. *Must be a power failure. Or maybe I'm asleep but dreaming I'm awake.*

Denis needed a glass of water, but he couldn't get up. His arms and legs couldn't move. Denis felt trapped, like in a coffin. Then there were darker shades of dark, melding into the heart of darkness. The air was heavier now, damp, palpable, clinging to him like a shroud. His breath labored, and it was becoming colder and colder. The air was motionless, and the room was silent.

Slowly, the atmosphere changed. Now it was living, breathing, its weight moving over his body. Denis tried to understand. *It's like a child's night terror. Everything will be all right in the morning.*

The atmosphere changed yet again. Still no light, still no warmth, but something was leaving. Then he heard a tormented voice.

"A cry that was no more than a breath—The horror! The horror!"[3]

"What the fuck?" Denis cried, sitting upright. He knew those words but was having trouble dragging them up from the depths. Then it came to him—

"Kurtz! Oh my God, fucking Kurtz."

It was three o'clock. Sam slept on, and Denis finally did too. When he awoke, she had already left, and there weren't any signs of Kurtz. But Denis remembered him. Cynically he wondered, *Was there actually a visitation? Probably not—it was probably merely "an undigested bit of . . . cheese."*[4]

The train would be back in Montreal in less than an hour, but Denis continued reflecting. His dream still perturbed him. Then there was Sam. She'd taken an emotionally devastating body blow. Bad feelings were developing about what he'd done to her. And where was the release he'd expected?

Enough!

***

Denis walked to the Vieux-Port the following Monday. The old man in the red parka sat in his usual spot, and Jacques dashed toward him, carrying his ball. But when the dog spotted Denis, he changed course, dropped the ball at Denis's feet, and wagged his tail eagerly. The old man laughed, thinking, *Maybe he'll talk today? Let's see.* "Well, I guess I know who rates."

"I think Jacques simply likes a change of pace."

"Probably, and you can throw his ball a lot farther than me."

Denis hesitated to respond further.

The old man sensed this but kept trying. "The weather seems a little warmer today."

"Yes, perhaps we'll have an early spring." Denis hurled the ball and continued toward the river, where he called Gracie.

"Hi, Denis."

"I'm impatient!"

"Me too. How'd it go in Toronto?"

"I took care of everything."

"Do you feel better?"

"No, rotten."

"Denis, I'll be there in less than three weeks. Hold on for me, please."

CHAPTER TWENTY-FIVE

Tuesday, March 19, 2013

San Francisco

G abi stopped by Joe's office, reporting that the Vice Squad had questioned the half dozen pimps plying the Sir Francis area. Nada on the prostitute, so they put the search on hold. Before Gabi left, she added, "You know that inquiry you asked me to make about Rodolphe's parents? It's odd. I called State, and they have no record that either of them worked for the Department of State or its diplomatic corps. Then on a hunch, I rang a CIA operations officer who owes me. He's at their SF office. I filled him in on the murders, and he checked out Rodolphe's parents. He called back but couldn't confirm or deny that the CIA had employed them. It was classified. My acquaintance isn't the type to make such an unforced error. If they hadn't worked for the CIA, how could it be classified?"

"You're right," Joe commented. "It sounds like CIA speak."

"Exactly, so I invited him for drinks this Friday. I Googled Rodolphe's parents. There were a fair number of hits, mostly at society dos in Europe, but not too many after 2005. They're usually represented as wealthy philanthropists. But his father is also reported as being on the boards of family-owned businesses. I couldn't locate an address here or elsewhere. Their physical descriptions tally with Cameron's. Also, on another hunch, I called James Steinberg. He said he'd met Rodolphe's parents years ago at a fundraiser. Steinberg is shrewd and thought there was more to Henri and Margaux Rodolphe than their public personas. He especially didn't buy Mrs. Rodolphe's charade of social butterfly.

Steinberg had no idea how to reach them. Honestly, I'm confused. I think we're being stonewalled."

"Curious. Let's see what CIA actually has to say."

Gabi met with CIA at Scala's Bistro on the twenty-second. After their drinks arrived, her contact said, "This is an excellent idea. I didn't want to talk on the phone, because something is strange. So I poked around a bit more after we made this date."

"I thought so when you answered me in CIA speak."

"I didn't think you'd miss that.," he laughed. "I can't give you all the machinations of how I got this information, because I've been told to stand down by the Director of National Intelligence. But I got more info than he imagined through a Langley analyst I'm friends with. This guy's a hacking savant."

"I hope you didn't get in trouble."

"No, it's cool. Just keep me out of it, okay? This is the big picture: their antecedents are public. They were recruited at university and joined the company after they were married. Because of their blue-blood lineage, wealth, and contacts, we set them up with a diplomatic cover. You've seen their photos. They posed as bright, young, beautiful people and were soon A-listed all over Europe. They were excellent sources of information and by 2005 were top-secret deep-cover agents, reporting to our director with their files classified accordingly."

"Interesting."

"There's more. It seems to be tied in to the 2005 reorganization of all our clandestine services. That was because of nine-eleven. The Office of the Director of National Intelligence is now in charge. I can't tell you how we unearthed this, but they now report only to the ODNI's director, their current files are classified accordingly, and all their CIA and State files have been scrubbed. The scuttlebutt is that they're deeper than deep-cover, that Mrs. Rodolphe is the lead, and that she's well connected at the highest levels of the FSB."

"Russia?"

"Yes. The ODNI was tipped off about my inquiry almost instantaneously, hence my warning."

When Gabi returned to the office, she informed Joe. He concluded, "It's bizarre, but it's tangential to our investigation, and it doesn't seem like there has been any contact in years. Let's sit on it for the time being."

"Agreed. I'll reach out to Ellen's friend Bridgette and see if she has thoughts on how to track the Rodolphes."

***

In Montreal on Friday, March 29, it was nearly time—only a couple weeks and Gracie would be here. Denis had been making progress on his remaining items. First, he'd located a prewar apartment in the Old City. It was on the fifth floor, with views of the Basilica of Notre-Dame on one side and the Old Port on another. There was a fireplace and parquet floors throughout. The rooms were large and included a master bedroom and bath with a huge tub. Gracie would be happy, so he signed a one-year lease. Next, he changed his address using his fake IDs, applied for a passport, and opened a personal bank account. Finally, he contacted the CEOs of the four EU companies where he had invested. He intended to move $750,000 a year. Every month, they would send funds to Toronto. Each transfer would be for a different amount, routed through the company's accounts payable, and then on to a second company. Following that, the money would be wired to Phoenix Consultants.

And even though Denis was busy, he struggled with the dream. He had never been introspective; he didn't ask why he was the way he was, he just accepted it. But his mother and her friend's cameo appearances the other night had started him thinking, recalling memories from Paris. His mother had abused him, and therein may have been the genesis of his anger toward women. Denis didn't think his memories had been repressed, since he remembered them easily. Nonetheless, this was an aha moment.

It had started before high school when Denis was twelve, and Mother wasn't around much during the day. That's when one of her friends (he couldn't remember the woman's name) seduced him. She came around one afternoon and did him in his mother's bed. It was his first time. But the friend was odd, because she wouldn't let Denis touch her breasts or pudenda. All they did was screw, with her on top. It struck him now that it was a control-denial ploy. The affair, or whatever it was, went on for several months until one afternoon when his mother walked in on them. She had a conniption, and the 'lovers' jumped out of bed. Denis was confused and stood there while his femme fatale shouted, "Denis made me do it!"

Mother grabbed her friend's clothes and threw them at her, yelling, "Go!" The seductress ran downstairs. They could hear her crying, cursing, and struggling to dress before slamming out the door. Then Denis's mother stared at him. Finally, she snapped, "You need to be castigated. Lie down—finish it yourself." Then she sat on the edge of the bed, watching.

Denis recalled how humiliated he felt. "I can't believe you did that to my friend," she said. "Did her in my bed! So this is how I'll discipline you. Maybe if you're a good boy, I'll take care of you someday."

Later, she taught him what to do for her. This continued for nearly two years until they moved to Moscow, but it always ended the same way.

***

Even though he'd spoken to Gracie about a week ago, Denis gave her another call. Gracie was surprised but happy. He familiarized her with the banking transactions. Denis could tell she was bored, but she perked up when he shared the details of their apartment. Nevertheless, he intended to surprise her with the big tub.

He was feeling better now. They chatted for a while. Finally, Denis said, "Before you leave, I'll call you on Tuesday the second."

"Fine. Is there anything I need to do?"

"Yes. On Monday, go to the safe-deposit box and remove all the cash. How much do you think is left?"

"At least ten thousand dollars. I haven't spent much."

"All right. Keep four thousand aside for your trip." Then Denis explained the expenses he'd incurred. "You ought to have money left over. Are you comfortable with that amount?"

"Yes."

"Okay. If you think you need more, take it, and tell me what's left on Tuesday. Afterward, go to the post office and send it—priority mail— as follows." Denis gave her the Toronto mail drop address. "Let's change burners too."

"I'll be glad when all this cloak-and-dagger stuff is over."

"Me too."

"Denis, I feel like it's happening—it's so close. All the waiting's over."

287

***

April 2 was their last phone call. Denis was at the Old Port playing fetch with Jacques. "How'd you make out at the bank?" he asked.

"Fine. There was two hundred dollars more than I thought. I kept that too and put six thousand in the mail. It has already gone."

"Great. After you text me the code on Thursday, don't forget to discard that phone."

"I won't." Finally, Gracie said, "I'm meeting a client. I gotta go— sorry."

"Okay, love you." That was it. Nothing left to do. Nonetheless, Denis didn't want to hang up. Gracie felt his mood.

"Denis, I'll always love you—no matter what. Just love me back. That's all you need to do."

***

On Wednesday, April 3, Gracie went to the Hotel Royal, because she wanted to say goodbye to Jack. Even though he'd never said anything, she knew he kept an eye on her.

"*¿Qué pasa?*" he said. "I haven't seen you in a while. Need a room?"

"No, I'm stopping in to say goodbye. I'm leaving tomorrow, permanently."

"Oh no, Charlene, I'll miss you. Is it for the best?"

"Yes, but will you call me Gracie? That's my real name."

"That's an excellent name—much better than Charlene. Is it Mr. Smith?"

"Yes—Denis."

"I kind of thought you two had something going. Gracie, are you certain? You know he's wanted by the police?"

"I know. Denis told me everything. I can't tell you where I'm going, but I don't think I'll ever be back. I'm excited."

"Well then, I'm happy for you."

Gracie had hardly slept and was up early on the fourth. All her Charlene outfits were hanging in the closet, and she'd laid out what she was going to travel in. The rest of her Gracie clothes were already packed. For the third time, she counted her money and verified she had burners, her passport, California ID, and Social Security and credit cards. Finally, she threw on jeans and a T-shirt and went to her usual coffee shop for breakfast. While she ate, she thought about Tom. He was upset, and yesterday morning when she'd been with him, she'd thought he was going to cry. Gracie was glad he hadn't, because she would've blubbered too. She already had her ticket to Vancouver on a Greyhound, leaving at four fifteen p.m. today, and Tom was seeing her off at the bus terminal.

Gracie ate a big breakfast, said goodbye at the coffee shop, and returned to her room. Her business mobile was ringing. "Charlene, I have a great job for you. A new client—a high roller. He's a doctor and is paying top dollar. One of our regulars referred him." Jerome started in without saying hello.

"When?"

"Today."

"I told you. I'm going away for a long weekend. I can't, because I have people waiting on me. Remember? You said it would be okay."

"What time do you have to be done by?"

"One p.m., but I don't want to. Can't you find another girl?"

"You know I like to start new clients off with the best."

"Oh, bullshit," Gracie said, while thinking, *But if I keep refusing, he's gonna show up here to pressure me. One look and he'll know I'm leaving.*

"Please?"

"Oh, all right, but I mean one o'clock—no *ifs*, *ands*, or *buts*."

"Let me see. I appreciate this, and I'll call you back." He called back in fifteen minutes. "The doctor's fine with that. I told him eleven o'clock at the Hotel Royal. He'll pay for the room and give you cash. I said you need to be done by one because you're booked across town."

"All right, but you owe me!" *It's crazy to do this job. But I have plenty of time to return here and get ready for the trip. Jack's gonna be surprised to see me again.*

Gracie changed into Charlene. Next, she texted Denis with their prearranged code. Then she disposed of the burner and arrived at the hotel before eleven o'clock. Jack wasn't on duty, but the part-time clerk, Brud, recognized her.

"Hi, Charlene. Working today?"

"Yes, I'm expecting someone in a few minutes. He'll pay for the room. Can I have the key now?"

"Sure."

"Give me a heads-up when he's on the way up, please."

Gracie was barely in the room when the phone rang.

He turned out to be handsome, neatly dressed in a suit, and carried a briefcase. She undressed the doctor, then led him toward the bed. *He's hard already . . . This is gonna be quick!* After about forty-five minutes, the doctor said, "How about we take a break; I need to recharge." *Okay, so maybe not so quick.*

He left the bed and went to his attaché case. "I brought bottled water, because I wasn't certain if there'd be a minibar." He removed two bottles, unscrewed a cap, and handed the bottle to Gracie. "I gotta take a leak. Be right back." Gracie hadn't finished her water when he returned. "Drink up. I wanna watch you pee." She laughed and finished her water. "Let's give it a few minutes so your bladder fills up."

Gracie felt warm and relaxed. *This is pleasant.* The doctor walked to his case, taking it into the bathroom with him. *Groggy now.* After a while, he returned. "Showtime. Let's take you for that piss." He laughed and helped her into the bathroom. Then he closed the door and slammed Gracie's back against it.

"What the fuck," she mumbled.

"Don't pass out on me, bitch." He was pressing her into the door with his hands under her armpits, and she was becoming limp. The doctor drove his knee into her crotch, grabbed a forearm, and hauled her arm up, affixing a wrist to an over-the-door clothes hook. Gracie hung there, lopsided. He backhanded her hard before securing the other wrist to a second hook, and she sagged with her tippy-toes scarcely touching the floor. The doctor harshly scrabbled at Gracie's breasts, chortling, "Perfect!"

Gracie still had enough mindfulness to grasp what was happening. *He's gonna beat the shit out of me. Oh, I'll be a sight for Denis!*

***

By seven thirty that evening, in Montreal, Denis had left the Gault and was walking to one of his favorite bistros. He was relaxed and felt cheerful. Gracie's text had come at one thirty that afternoon, earlier than expected. But she was probably running last-minute errands and was afraid of forgetting. He was pleased with how well she'd handled everything. And soon Gracie would be here. He'd celebrate with a glass of wine.

But at the same time in San Francisco, in the Hotel Royal, on the back of a bathroom door, Gracie hung—dead. Simultaneously, the doctor arrived home relaxed and happy. "We'll go out to dinner," he told his wife. She was glad, since she wanted to try a new bistro in the French Quarter. "Do you mind driving? I feel like a couple of glasses of wine tonight," he said.

"Not at all."

"If you ply me with liquor, you might have your way later."

"Is that a promise?" she joked. But then his mood seem to change. "What's the matter? You're acting bummed out."

"I don't like bringing my problems home."

"Tell me."

"We lost one today."

She knew what he meant: a patient had died during an operation. He was a top-flight, experienced anesthesiologist, but when these things happened, he always got down on himself, wondering what he could've done differently. And she knew this was her cue to perform like a jezebel. "Why don't we skip after-dinner coffee and head home?" she said, then cooed, "I'll kiss it and make it better."

CHAPTER TWENTY-SIX

Friday, April 5, 2013

Yesterday at the bus station, Tom had called and texted Charlene—nada. The driver waited an extra fifteen minutes in case his girl was running late. At length, Tom walked home but had continued trying all evening as well as this morning. And he didn't know where she lived, either. So at ten thirty, Tom came to the Hotel Royal. He and Jack had never met but were aware of each other through Charlene. Maybe Jack knew something.

When he arrived, Jack was just coming on duty. Tom cornered him right away. Responding to his questions, Jack said, "I don't know. She stopped in to say goodbye on Wednesday. That's the last I saw of her. Charlene was taking a bus to Canada yesterday afternoon."

"I know. I was there to see her off, but she never showed. I can't reach her either."

"Let me square things away here first, then we'll try to figure this out." In a few minutes, Jack called, "Tom, come over here. I found this note on the computer from the guy who was on days yesterday."

Jack:

Charlene took a room around 11 a.m. today—she had a john. It's paid through Friday at checkout. When I left, they were still at it—a DO NOT DISTURB sign on the door.

Brud

"What time does Brud leave?" Tom asked.

"About six. This doesn't make sense," Jack said. "I'll grab a passkey." The elevator crawled to the third floor. "I'll go first," Jack continued. When he opened the door, Jack saw Charlene's clothes draped neatly over a chair. "Stay here; let me check it out."

Everything appeared normal, although the bathroom door was ajar. Jack began opening it, feeling its weight, then glimpsed her in the mirror and saw the blood. He called out, "Tom, stay back. We need to call the cops."

"No way, man!" Tom said, elbowing his way past Jack. "I need to see."

"Don't! We can't touch anything!"

"Oh my God," Tom howled, and almost reached the bedroom's wastebasket before hurling. Jack put his arm around him.

"Come on. We need to leave. There's nothing we can do for Charlene anymore."

Both were badly shaken, and Tom cleaned up while Jack called the police. In a few minutes a black-and-white arrived: they cordoned off the far end of the third-floor corridor, verified that Charlene was dead, reported back to HQ in the Tenderloin District, called the crime scene unit and the medical examiner, took initial incident reports from Tom and Jack, and waited for the detectives to arrive. Detective Sergeant Danny Wong caught the call and headed to the hotel.

After finishing Tom's incident report and getting his contact details, the first responders had released him for his one o'clock shift. The officers informed Danny that the men's statements had been filled out separately but agreed in all material respects. Danny spoke to Jack. "I'm going to the room now. I'll talk to you when I come down."

When Danny arrived at the room, he went to the bathroom, where the medical examiner was still working. Danny had seen a lot of brutal killings, but this was bad.

"Oh Christ, it looks like the lingchi."[5]

"Well, maybe not a thousand slices, but I'll count them during the autopsy," the medical examiner said. "The slash to her femoral artery in the upper thigh killed her. After that, she bled out almost instantaneously. That's what most of the blood is from. Looks like she was slapped around before he started cutting. The killer probably had some medical training. Can't tell about sexual activity until later. There were no reports of any noise, so I'm guessing she was drugged . . . thank God. I'll check that out. Time of death between noon and three p.m. yesterday. That's about it for now. After you've looked things over, I'll take her to the morgue."

Danny released the body, placed her personal belongings in an evidence bag, and left the CSU to process the room. Then he went downstairs to talk with Jack, who seemed more composed now.

"Charlene was barely fourteen. I liked her; she was nice, caring. It's sad, because things were starting to work out for her," Jack offered.

Danny removed the girl's clutch from the evidence bag and spread its contents on the reception counter: lipstick, unopened three-pack of rubbers, mobile phone, room keys, California ID that had recently been issued, about twenty dollars in mixed bills and change, and an illegal gravity knife with a five-inch blade. *A lot of help that was.* Then Danny glanced through Jack's incident report.

"Jack, you called her Charlene, but her ID says Gracie?"

"That was her real name. Charlene was a street one."

"Tell me about the part where 'things were starting to work out for her.' From the beginning—don't leave anything out."

"She stopped by Wednesday afternoon to say goodbye because she was leaving for good. Going to Canada to meet a guy she'd met here in January. He's the one who has been in the papers. The one the police had a press conference about concerning the little girl who'd been abducted and killed five years ago. I warned Gracie, but she said it wasn't him. It was a guy who'd worked for him."

"Do you know the dates he was here in January?"

"No, it was a cash transaction—no check-in. He was here about five days, and it was at the beginning of the month. Then they went away for a few days, and he left afterwards."

"Do you know his name?"

"She called him Denis."

"How does Tom fit into all this?"

"He was shacking up with her. Tom's a concierge at the Sir Francis and knew her from there. Denis stayed there after he left here in January. I don't know how Tom and Charlene became involved. Tom was supposed to see her off at the bus station yesterday afternoon. She never showed, and he couldn't reach her, so he showed up here this morning."

"How did he know you?"

"Gracie must've mentioned my name—never met him before."

"Did Gracie have a pimp?"

"Jerome. I don't know his last name." Jack gave Danny the pimp's number, and the rest of the interview agreed with his statement. When Danny finished, Jack said, "I've been aboveboard with you. Can you give me a pass on the no-registration cash transaction? I need this job."

"I'm not from Vice or the Department of Buildings. I don't care what you tell your boss if you're straight with me. You'll need to come to HQ for a formal statement," Danny finished.

Next, Danny left for Gracie's boardinghouse. The neighborhood was an assortment of small retailers—a dry cleaner, coffee shop, corner tavern—and older houses. It was a big old Victorian, reasonably well maintained. He met the owner, who was about eighty and had been a widow for years. Her boarders were her only income besides Social Security. She was upset when she heard about Gracie. "She was so gentle. No noise, always polite."

"It's sad. Did she pay her rent on time?"

"Always, but her boss, Mr. Jerome, paid. He pays the rent for several of my girls."

"You know what Gracie did and what Jerome is?"

The widow averted his eyes. "Yes, it's a tough life for a young girl out there . . . on her own . . . with no family to help. I was fortunate to have this house when my husband died young. I don't know what I might've done without it. I don't judge, Detective."

"Neither do I. How was Jerome's relationship with his girls?"

"He seemed to treat them well. I think Mr. Jerome had a special spot for Gracie, though. He always asked, 'How is she really doing?' He keeps an eye on me as well. Takes care of any little repairs and such. Mr. Jerome teases me that he wants simply the best for his girls."

The landlady showed Danny to Gracie's room but seemed reluctant to leave . . . reluctant to close the door on Gracie's life.

Gracie had been packed for her trip. The clothes in her suitcase appeared to be new and were regular street clothes—no hooker duds. Those were hanging in a closet. Danny found her regular purse. A quick look showed over four thousand dollars in cash, a bus ticket to Vancouver for the four-fifteen bus the day before, two burner phones (not activated), her passport, a Social Security card, and her birth certificate. No IN CASE OF AN EMERGENCY card. Danny put her purse and its contents in an evidence bag, sealed the room, and told the landlady not to let anyone in except the police. "I'll probably be back on Monday with the CSU. This doesn't appear to be part of the crime scene. There's no rush."

"I won't let anyone in until then. How did she die?"

"Can't say."

"Can't or won't?"

"Both."

"That bad? Was she in pain?"

It was Danny's turn now to avert eyes, and he didn't reply. The widow was tearing up as he thanked her and left.

***

On Monday, April 8, when Joe came in, Gabi was already on the phone. It looked like she was deeply focused on something. About fifteen minutes later, Gabi knocked on his door. "I was on the phone with Danny Wong. You know the prostitute who was murdered in the Hotel Royal at the end of last week? He caught the case. He's working it alone because his partner's on vacation." Gabi described what Danny had told her about the crime scene and how the guys who found her were badly shaken.

"Jesus," Joe said, "and they just walked in on her."

"Danny's looking for help. He'd like a second set of eyes when he visits her room with the CSU. I'm certain she was our prostitute from Rodolphe's disappearance. It all fits, if Tom was her lover. That's why he was covering for her. Danny will turn the case over to us if it should be ours."

"All right, give Danny a hand," Joe said, and returned to his paperwork.

Gabi was back shortly. "I was on the way out. Guess who's here? Tom, and he wants to see us. I put him in the interrogation room."

"I'll take this. Go catch up with Danny." Joe went down the hall and stuck his head into the room. "Tom, I'm getting coffee. Do you want one?"

"Yes, please—light and sweet."

"What can I do for you?" Joe asked when he returned.

"Do you know what happened at the Hotel Royal? I was there— saw it. It was awful—"

Joe stopped him. "I'm up to speed; you don't have to go over it again. Detective Müller is on her way to meet with Detective Wong now."

"Detective Wong wants me to give him a formal statement in addition to the incident report I already provided. Today is my first opportunity to do so, because I was in Bakersfield all weekend with my parents. I'll do it later. Look, I know you're familiar with the underlying case. I just want to make certain that you catch this bastard. Can you take her case over?"

"We're looking into that now. But if we don't, it's in safe hands with Danny Wong. He's a top-flight detective. But Tom, we need to clear the air before we go further. You haven't been forthcoming with us."

"I know. I was covering for Charlene." Then Tom told Joe all he knew, concluding with, "I knew Rodolphe was skipping bail, but believe me, nothing about the little girl until your partner showed me a draft press release. I didn't know for quite a while either that Charlene was in touch with him all along. She finally told me everything. I warned her that he was bad news, but she didn't care."

"What was your relationship with her?"

"Charlene took care of me, at first as a thank-you for helping them. I understood, but then our relationship seemed to develop. I loved her and tried to talk her into staying with me. I was willing to wait. In four years, I'll be twenty-three. Charlene would've been eighteen—all legit; no one would've given it a second thought. But in the end, she was following him to Canada. So I went to see her off. You know the rest."

"All right, I believe you. Before you go, write out and sign a statement for me. I'll call Detective Wong and tell him you've already made one. It'll take a few days for us to take over the case, after which I'll keep you up to speed."

***

Gabi returned to the office in the afternoon and reported to Joe. Charlene's room hadn't revealed anything new except a birth certificate, which confirmed her name was Gracie and might help in tracking down family. Then Gabi had gone to the Tenderloin District's HQ. She and Danny met with his captain, who had already begun transferring the case. The evidence collected by Danny had been sent to the crime lab—except her phone. Gabi and Danny were able to listen to all of Tom's messages and read his texts. It verified his story. There were two texts from Jerome, the first saying he was leaving on Friday morning for LA, as his mother was in the ICU with a heart condition. Then there was another message on Sunday, saying he was back.

Late Monday afternoon, Gabi and Joe reviewed Charlene's messages and sent her phone to the lab for analysis.

"It's sad," Gabi commented.

"I know," Joe replied. "You and Danny are doing an excellent job, and I had a positive meeting with Tom; he's telling us the truth now, but unfortunately, nothing of much help. I'd like you to locate Gracie's family so we can plan for them to claim her body. I'll follow up with Jerome."

Later, Joe reached Jerome, who agreed to stop by on Thursday morning, April 11.

***

Tuesday morning, April 9, it turned warmer in Montreal, sunny and around fifty degrees. Denis strolled to the Vieux-Port. He saw Jacques and the old man and waved. Jacques raced over, and Denis played with him a long time. He threw the ball farther and higher than usual. Jacques was ecstatic, making Denis laugh. Finally, the old man clapped for Jacques and waved goodbye.

Denis walked a while longer. He was happy, because Gracie's train arrived tomorrow afternoon at one forty-five. *Everything's going well.* On the way back to the Gault, Denis shopped for a small gift, finally settling on a simple gold necklace. He paid extra for wrapping, picked up flowers for the room, and bought a card in the hotel's lobby.

CHAPTER TWENTY-SEVEN

Wednesday, April 10, 2013

Eleven thirty a.m. in Montreal, and the warmer weather had held. Denis walked to the Old Port. Before he left his suite, he'd put the flowers, card, and jewelry on a table, where Gracie would see them when she walked in.

Denis was happy but impatient. The old man and Jacques weren't there yet, so he paced and planned the rest of the day. He'd grab a cab at one fifteen—plenty of time to get to the station. Following that, they'd have a late lunch before going to the Gault.

Finally, about noon, Jacques and the old man arrived. Jacques wagged his tail, and when the man released him, he raced over. Denis played with the dog for the better part of an hour. At length, Denis walked him back to the old man. "I'm leaving early today—meeting a friend at Gare Centrale at one forty-five."

The man smiled. "Have fun. Don't be late."

The cab arrived in plenty of time, and Denis was on the platform at about one thirty. Then, with several horn blasts, the train arrived a couple of minutes early. Passengers started disembarking. The train had been crowded, but now the platform was empty, and there was no Gracie.

The engineer made two blasts, and the train started to move away to the yard. Denis grabbed a conductor on the platform. "I'm meeting a friend, but I think she's still on the train. Can you stop it?"

"I'm sorry, sir. I walked the entire train before it left—checked all the restrooms too. There's no one on board."

"Are you positive?"

"Absolutely, sir. Sorry. Maybe she missed her train?"

***

On Thursday morning, Joe was in early. He called Sister Mary for background on Jerome, because he hadn't run into him before. Joe briefed her on Gracie's death. "It's terrible. All the girls are nervous. It's hard to keep something like this quiet."

"I need information on Jerome—her pimp. He's due here in a few minutes. Do you know anything about him?"

"A bit. Jerome arrived on the scene about fifteen years ago. He was probably in his late teens. He became an enforcer for one of the gangs— a killer. He was bad tempered and brutal, and even hardened crooks walked on eggshells around him. Jerome made decent money but ultimately figured out there was a better way. So over time, he built up a first-string stable, targeting the high end like me. Jerome's bright. One of those people who, if he had applied his talents to legitimate business, would've been successful. And because of his reputation, nobody crossed him or gave his girls shit. That's about it, and I think he's a square shooter if you play nice."

Jerome was polite, in his midthirties, and well dressed, with neatly trimmed hair. "Are you up to speed with what happened to Gracie?" Joe asked.

"Yes. Monday morning the eighth, when I couldn't reach her, I went to the Hotel Royal. I thought Jack might know something, since she'd

306

been working there on the fourth. He filled me in, and then you called that afternoon, so here I am."

"What was your relationship with Gracie?"

"We're off the record and I'm not being recorded, correct?"

"Correct. As I see it, you're the sole link to the killer, and I need your help."

"And I need yours as well, Detective."

"How so?"

"As far as I know, she had no family, or at least none that gave a fuck about her. I want you to release her body to me. Charlene isn't going in any pauper's grave if I can help it."

"I don't know if I can do that yet. My sergeant is trying to locate her family. Their rights come first."

"Okay, but if they don't step up, do we have a deal?"

"Yes, with conditions. I checked you out. You're not to take this into your own hands, and you'll cooperate fully, understand?"

"You're asking a lot, because I gotta protect my girls—send a message."

"I know but don't."

"Fine."

"So tell me."

"Businesswise, she was my best. But this is personal. I was closer to Gracie than any of my other girls, and I probably loved her. It bothers me that she never told me her real name—foolish, I guess. What that man did to her was barbaric. And for no fuckin' reason." Jerome was choking up now. "You gotta catch this prick. I'll honor our deal, at least for a time, but I won't wait forever."

"No time limits."

"Live with it. It's up to you," Jerome answered.

"Can you give me the killer's name, address, and/or phone number?"

"No. Another client referred him, calling him 'the doctor.' That's all I know, but I'll find him."

"And then stand down unless I ask for help."

Jerome smiled. "I'll be in touch."

***

That afternoon, Gabi came by Joe's office. She was upset. "I tracked down Gracie's family in a small town near Buffalo, New York. I put a call in to the local PD and then spoke with her mother. She doesn't want the body." Gabi stopped, tearing up. "What a fucking bitch. Her mother said, 'I don't give a rat's ass. Not after what she did—good riddance!' Then she went on a rant about how Gracie had ruined their family. I told her that Gracie had died an awful death, but she didn't bend."

Joe was pissed. "It's her goddamn daughter. He mutilated Gracie while she was still alive. No one deserves that. I have a mind to unload on her. Christ, Gracie's pimp cares more about her than mom does."

"Let it sit a bit, Joe. Maybe she'll reconsider."

***

When Joe arrived home that evening, he was still upset. After Susan asked, he said, "A bad day. I inherited the murder of that prostitute in the Hotel Royal last week. It's one of the worst and tangentially related to the warehouse murders."

"Oh no, is he at it again?" Susan asked.

"No, nothing like that. This is a tough one. But here's what bothers me the most." Joe went on to describe Gabi's conversation with Gracie's mother. "I have a mind to call her tomorrow and rip her a new one. What could Gracie have done that was so terrible? She was only eleven when she ran away."

"I think Gabi's right. Give it a while before you call her," Susan said.

"Gracie reminds me a lot of Sister Mary," Joe continued. "She nearly escaped the life, even though it was with the wrong guy. And apparently, she knew all about Rodolphe. I don't understand what happened between them, but it was out of the ordinary—perhaps even transcendent."

***

By April 15, Susan had settled into doing the books and paying the bills at the gallery. This turned out to be a big relief for Linda, since it was the part of the business she hated. Susan was reluctant to take a salary, so Linda had made her a ten percent owner like Derrick. Susan and Joe had been keeping enough clothes, toiletries, and such at both houses, so they slept wherever they were when it was time to turn in. Linda seemed satisfied with the arrangement. Nonetheless, she was the only one who was inconvenienced.

Talking in bed that night, Susan said, "How would you feel about letting Linda use your small guest room? That way she wouldn't need to traipse back and forth."

"Why not give her the bigger one? I can't remember the last time I've had overnight guests besides you."

"Awesome. I'll suggest it to her. And by the way, is that all I am, a guest . . . ?"

"No! I didn't mean that."

"I know," Susan said, laughing. "I'm just pulling your leg. So I guess you won't mind if I change my mailing address to here?"

"Does that mean you're moving in?"

"Well, haven't I already? This is my home now. Let's make it official."

"Okay, so does that mean you'll marry me?"

"Absolutely!" And they nestled closer.

The next day, when they were having dinner at Linda's, they discussed her using Joe's guest room. "I'd like that," she said. "It'll make life easier."

"There's something else we ought to talk about," Susan said. "Linda, how would you feel about being my maid of honor?"

"What . . . ? Oh my gosh, congratulations—of course! I'm happy for both of you. But do you still want me to set up a room at your house, Joe?"

"We're a family already. We simply move around between houses. We'd like it to stay that way."

Later, in bed, Susan said, "You said exactly the right thing. Linda's pleased. I'm glad it's all resolved."

"Me too."

***

On Wednesday morning, April 17, the crime scene photos were in the interdepartmental mail. The pictures were worse than Joe had envisioned. When he called Gabi in, she gasped, because it was her first look at the crime scene as well. "I know," Joe said. "I'd like to mail these to Gracie's mother."

"Don't!"

Instead, a short time later, Joe reached out to Gracie's mom, who responded aggressively. "I told the other officer who called that I don't care. I don't want anything to do with my daughter. Good riddance to—"

"Bad rubbish—really? Is that what you're calling your daughter? Do you know how Gracie died?" Then Joe told her, finishing with, "He sliced her over a hundred times before he slashed her femoral artery. I can't believe that no matter what she did, you don't care . . . don't care if Gracie's buried in a pauper's grave!"

"Don't lecture me, Detective," she snapped. "You have no idea. Goodbye."

Gabi had walked in. "I told you mom was a bitch."

"Bitch is too kind!"

The next day, Joe received a call from Gracie's mother. He'd had time to think and realized he'd been rough on her. "I'm sorry. I was out of order—"

"Detective, stop; let me speak. I need to get this out. It's me that owes you an apology. Gracie as well . . . God rest her soul. After I hung up, I was furious. Well, you know that. I started railing about you and Gracie to my husband. And then it all came out. You see . . . I caught them. You know what I mean, right? I don't have to explain, do I?"

"No, I understand."

"He told me that Gracie had started it by parading around naked. And after it had begun, when he tried to stop, she blackmailed him into keeping on. After it blew up, Gracie ran into her room, crying. I went in to confront her, but when she didn't say anything in her defense, I believed my husband. Later, Gracie stormed out with a small suitcase. I figured she'd be back after a night or two on her own. I notified the police after three or four days. They never turned up anything. I was so embarrassed, and my husband was so scared that we didn't pressure them. We never heard from Gracie again, and you know the rest. What I didn't know, but found out last night, was that my husband lied. Gracie never did anything wrong. It was all bullshit: all him taking advantage of her. I can't believe I was so gullible: I know better! That's why she ran away. I killed my little girl. When he heard I was going to let her be buried in a pauper's grave, he said, 'We can't do that,' and told me the truth. What should I do?"

After they were silent for a bit, Joe said, "I have a suggestion," and went on to tell her about Jerome's offer to provide a service and a proper burial, about her landlady, and about her friends Jack and Tom.

"Was Jerome her pimp?"

"Yes, it may be hard for you to believe, but he treated Gracie well. Jerome cared a great deal for her."

"Great . . . her pimp treated her better than her mother. I don't know what I want to do yet. But my first reaction is that she should be near the

312

few people who cared for her, not with those who abandoned her. I'll call you Monday. If I go along with Jerome, I won't cause trouble."

Later, Gabi stuck her head into Joe's office, reporting that the PD in Gracie's hometown had returned her call. "The chief apologized and reported that it had been a perfectly botched investigation. They never even put her fingerprints, DNA, or photo into the National Center for Missing and Exploited Children!"

***

It was midday on April 18, and the old man walked the short distance down the Rue Sulpice, the Rue de la Commune, and into Montreal's Vieux-Port with Jacques. He had started visiting the Old Port near the end of January, wearing his bright-red parka, the warmest one L.L.Bean made. And even though it was mid-April now, he continued to wear it because of the wind chill off the river. Arriving around noon, he had a routine. The old man played fetch with Jacques. The dog's obsession was tirelessly chasing his ball. Following that, the old man would sit, watching the St. Lawrence River or holding his face up to the sun, eyes closed, catching the warmth. Sometimes he'd read the paper, but the old man was always waiting.

Finally, at the beginning of February, Denis had shown up. He had his routine too: walking, sitting on a bench, or occasionally making a phone call. Whenever he did that, he seemed happy but never talked long. One day Jacques altered his retrieval route and dropped the ball at Denis's feet. They played for quite a while until the old man clapped his hands, and Jacques reluctantly returned to his master. The younger man had a big smile on his face and gave his new acquaintances a wave as they left. There was no question Jacques preferred his new friend's throwing arm.

After that, the men nodded to each other whenever Denis entered the park. They settled into a routine, and the only time it varied was when

313

Denis made a phone call. Then the old man called Jacques back so he wouldn't interfere.

About two weeks ago, Denis's routine had changed. He'd seemed elated, playing harder with Jacques and staying longer. Then one day— the old man thought it was the tenth—the younger man was already there when they arrived. But he cut his visit short, saying he was meeting a friend at Gare Centrale. Then the next time Denis came to the park, his routine had changed once again. After that, he was always there when the old man and Jacques arrived and played distractedly with the dog. He frequently attempted unanswered phone calls. seemed worried, and left around one fifteen in the afternoon.

But today was different. Denis had checked his watch several times and at one o'clock made a phone call, which was answered. But it wasn't a happy conversation; it was serious, and Denis's demeanor became businesslike, persistent. The old man could read his lips.

"Jack, please. Tell me!"

Jacques was impatient to play, so the old man attached his leash.

Denis looked grim, and at length, his voice became terse and loud. "What! . . . I don't understand. That can't be right . . . How? . . . What do you mean, I don't want to know? No, damn it . . . tell me!"

The old man watched; he thought he'd never seen such a terrible expression. Denis was frozen, but then dropped his phone, clenched his fists, and howled in an anguished voice.

"No . . . no!"

Finally, Denis collapsed to his knees, burying his face in his hands, his body racked with sobs. The old man released Jacques. "Go."

It had finally happened—no more waiting. Jacques raced to Denis and began nudging him, licking his face. Then the old man stood and walked over to them.

"Let me help."

After Denis stood up, the old man leashed Jacques.

"Here, you take him." He handed over the leash and slipped his arm through Denis's.

They walked slowly, talking for a long time. Denis began to calm down little by little, saying, "I've been going to the station every day to see if Gracie's on a later train—nothing. She hasn't been answering her phone either. So today I called Jack and found out why." Then he told the old man about Gracie's death and most of the rest, avoiding the mugging and murders, concluding with, "I've done terrible things."

"Have you told me everything? If not, now's an excellent time. I keep secrets well."

Denis studied his face. The old man's eyes were coaxing but insistent. *Why does he ask? He seems to know everything already.* "No, I haven't," Denis said. "I can't bring myself to say those things aloud, and I'd be putting my life in your hands."

"But you can do that—put your life in my hands."

Denis evaded the old man's invitation and talked about Gracie instead.

"She was becoming my hope. I thought I saw a path forward with her. I felt encouraged and better about myself. She loved me unconditionally, and it was changing me. Now that's all gone."

"Unconditional love is a special thing—rare. Perhaps Gracie was your guide? Think about it."

But Denis was confused.

"I know you're in terrible pain. Unfortunately, that won't go away for a long time. It's not just about Gracie, because you haven't taken responsibility for everything yet. Walk me home while we talk. As time goes by, those unshared and unspoken horrors will become increasingly painful. But if you're truly penitent, then they slowly, almost imperceptibly, will lessen. Then one morning, you'll wake up and realize they're gone. Fond memories of Gracie will reemerge. It's the way it works . . . honest."

"I wish I could believe you."

"You can."

They strolled up Notre-Dame Street West until the old man said, "This is me," and pointed to the doors of Montreal's Basilica of Notre-Dame.

"You're a priest!"

"Yes," the old man replied. "I thought you knew." Then he realized his zipped-up red parka had concealed his clergy collar. "I wasn't incognito on purpose," he said unzipping his coat. "You must've thought me quite the prig." They both started laughing. "Actually, I'm the monsignor here."

"What do I do?"

As the monsignor entered, he turned. "If you're sincere, you'll find a way. 'There will be more joy in heaven over one sinner who repents than over ninety-nine righteous persons who need no repentance.'[6] And not to overstate the obvious, but this is an excellent first step. This door will always be open to you. You only need to walk through it; that's all there is to it. It's up to you," the old priest finished.

"Yes, but I may need to follow up when you're back in San Francisco."

"Okay, let's do it now. I have a half hour before my next meeting."

Joe had Googled him before the call: midfifties, married with two teenage daughters, and Ivy League educated. When Joe finished reviewing, the hedge fund manager said, "I first met the doctor at college, and later we reconnected at a West Coast alum event. After that, we occasionally golfed or had dinner with our wives. I invest a portion of their portfolio now. I consider him an associate but not a friend." They talked for a while. Joe thought he seemed like a straight shooter, albeit addicted to underage call girls.

"Would you give me a physical description, then tell me about the man?"

After providing a description, Jerome's client said, "He's a successful anesthesiologist and department head. He also teaches, lectures, and is published. He appears to be a pillar of the community, socially active, and philanthropic. His wife's fifteen years younger—a knockout. They've been married about eight years, seem to be happy, and have two kids."

"And you referred him to Jerome?"

"Yes."

"Any other bad habits? Drugs? Alcohol?"

"No, I don't think so. This whole matter is confusing. It's hard to accept the awful things Jerome ascribes to him. He's a doctor, for Christ's sake. What about his friggin' Hippocratic oath?" Before they hung up, Jerome's client reminded Joe, "I won't testify—you need to keep me out of this."

"Agreed; your morals aren't my concern. And you couldn't have anticipated or prevented any of it. I'll call you an anonymous tipster."

***

Gabi went to the Hotel Royal on Friday morning, May 10, with a photo array. Brud identified the doctor, and the physical description he provided matched the one Joe had obtained. Brud also confirmed the arrival times of Gracie and the doctor, adding that he'd been carrying a briefcase. When he left for the evening, Brud thought they were both still in the room because of the DO NOT DISTURB sign. "Charlene was a kind, softhearted kid. It bothered me what she had to do to get by."

Later, Gabi contacted the hospital and confirmed that on the day of the murder, the doctor had had two back-to-back surgeries. They'd begun at five o'clock in the morning, and he'd left the hospital at ten fifteen.

Gabi updated Joe, and they reviewed the file. The CSU report had revealed no usable prints. The killer had worn gloves or wiped down the rooms. The medical examiner's report disclosed that Gracie's vagina had shown signs of recent normal sexual activity, but no usable fluids for DNA analysis were present. Gabi had also discovered that the clothes hooks Gracie was hung from were readily available.

"But on balance, I think we have enough evidence for an arrest warrant now," Gabi concluded. "Brud's ID is solid. Jerome can confirm the doctor's appointment, and we have Jerome's voice ID if needed. Then there's the doctor's profession and the timeline, so we've established means and opportunity. I'd like to do it ASAP, before the hospital tips the doctor off that I called."

Joe and Captain Weber agreed, and an arrest warrant for murder was requested.

***

On Tuesday, May 14, the warrant came through. and Gabi asked Joe if she could execute it. "Sure. Do you need me to come along?"

"No, I have it covered." Gabi had been doing a slow burn over Gracie's murder, so she arranged a special arrest for the doctor. She called the hospital and got his schedule. Then Gabi contacted the SWAT commander, cashing in a favor. When she finished explaining her plan, she said, "Commander, this is window dressing. There's no chance of a shootout."

"Is this about the pross at the Hotel Royal?"

"Yes."

"Okay, I'll give you five guys. I assume you want full riot gear?"

"Yes."

"Have fun!"

Gabi and the SWAT team waited until the doctor had time to get into surgery. Then they entered the hospital and made their way to an anteroom outside the operating room in which the doctor was working. The press had been covering a multicar pileup on the Bay Bridge but had gradually realized something was up. Gabi deployed a SWAT officer to keep them in line. She began to worry that she'd overdone it, but then it was time to rock 'n' roll. The surgery team began exiting the operating room, and the doctor emerged with a mask dangling from his neck. Flanked by four officers, Gabi stepped forward. "Doctor, you're under arrest on suspicion of murder." She spun him around and slapped cuffs on his wrists. He looked dazed as the police perp-walked him to the elevator, then through the main lobby.

That evening Joe, Susan, and Linda were watching TV, but Susan was perusing a magazine as well. When Joe saw the film clip, he muttered, "Son of a bitch!" Susan looked up, catching enough to see what was going on.

"Did you orchestrate that?"

Joe broke into a grin. "No, that was pure Gabi."

Then Linda exclaimed, "You go, girl!" accompanied by a fist pump.

The next morning the department, including the captain, gave Gabi a standing O when she arrived. The news story went viral on all outlets, including social media. In no time it took on a life of its own—a cautionary tale about everything from child abuse, runaways, and improved parenting to underage prostitution. In Montreal, Denis handwrote a note:

Gabi:

Thank you!

Rodolphe

It looked like hotel stationery with the name trimmed off. Joe was shocked—no attempt at deception. As expected, the lab confirmed Rodolphe's fingerprints.

***

After Gracie's service and the doctor's arrest, Joe and Gabi felt the letdown as they coasted into the three-day Memorial Day holiday. Joe reflected on the cases. It had been a year since they'd begun investigating them. As far as he was concerned, he and Gabi had solved all the murders—Sally Thompson, the Rowe twins, Zack, and Gracie—not to mention Melisa's mugging. There were two arrest warrants out for Denis Rodolphe: one for flight to avoid prosecution and the other for the murder of Sally Thompson. Next, the doctor had been remanded without bail. And because the California Department of Corrections and Rehabilitation had determined it was too dangerous for him to be housed in the general population, he was awaiting trial in solitary confinement at San Quentin State Prison. These were reasons to feel successful, but there were also reasons for disappointment. They had no idea where Sally Thompson's body was; all they had was her DNA. And then there was Rodolphe. Joe doubted they would ever apprehend him unless he made a catastrophic error. The van was gone, Zack was dead, Melisa was a reluctant witness, and they had no idea of Rodolphe's false identity. Other than a picture of Cameron's panties and a strong suspicion that he was in Montreal, they had nothing. And the handwritten note wasn't much of a breakthrough, because they'd already assumed Rodolphe was there.

Sunday evening, while Linda was at friends, Susan and Joe watched TV. A breaking-news alert interrupted them. That morning, the doctor had been murdered in San Quentin. Apparently, reduced staff over the Memorial Day weekend had led to a major screw-up. The general population had been released into the yard fifteen minutes before the doctor completed his solitary exercise. By the time that was discovered, the doctor was sitting propped against a wall with a shiv through his heart. No one had any idea how the slipup had occurred.

When Joe arrived at work Tuesday morning, Gabi came in and asked, "Did you hear?"

"Yes."

"Do you think Jerome had anything to do with it?"

"I wouldn't be surprised. But you could argue that he lived up to the terms of our agreement."

"Should we contact the Bureau of Prisons?"

"Why, to assert jurisdiction? No, let them handle it. We'll cooperate if they ask."

***

During the following week, Gabi and Joe met with Ellen Sandler. Regarding the handwritten note, fingerprints, and signature, she said, "It could mean a change in his mental state, i.e., not caring. That's one symptom of a psychotic break, or Rodolphe might not have perceived any additional risk. And the note sounded sincere, none of which helps us. I'm still bothered by the number of killings we've turned up. It simply isn't possible that there are only three women. There must be more. I'd also like to know why his mother got him out of France when she approached the Lawrenceville school."

"Well, we've searched thoroughly," Gabi commented.

"I know. But it's the lack of an MO that's stymieing us. And further, about his mother, I wish we could confirm my notion that she was his abuser, the underlying cause for his behavior. There must be a reason for their dysfunctional relationship."

Then on June 7, Danny Wong reported to Gabi that Tyree had been gunned down near Union Square. It had been a drive-by shooting using a semiautomatic rifle. There were no other injuries.

"Who's responsible?"

"My money's on José. He's never forgotten the murder of his buddy Junior and has harbored a grudge against Tyree ever since. It'll be interesting now. If he succeeds in holding on as Tyree's successor, José will be invaluable as both a crew boss and a CI. The bad news is that José can't help us with any additional information about Rodolphe," Danny replied.

***

On June 14, Gabi and Joe met with the captain. They summarized their investigation, particularly the international aspects:

- A Red Notice (a request through Interpol to locate and provisionally arrest a person pending extradition or surrender) had been issued. Bridgette Dubois was back in Paris now. Because her official inquiry in October 2012 had been unsuccessful, she was calling an acquaintance, Moscow's chief of police.

- They continued to liaise with the Canadians.

After they finished, Weber said, "Joe, it's been over a year. I know you're both invested in this case, but don't you think it ought to be classified as inactive now?"

"I hate to admit defeat, but honestly, I've run out of ideas."

The captain said, "Gabi?"

"I feel like Joe does. But I hate to think of Rodolphe getting away with it."

"Okay, let's do this. Reclassify it as inactive but review it every six months. I know how you both feel. We haven't given the Rowes the closure they deserve. Try to focus on the fact that you've solved it and that if he ever resurfaces in the US, Rodolphe's going to jail for the rest of his life."

CHAPTER TWENTY-NINE

Wednesday, June 19, 2013

Chief Gleb Balabanov of the Moscow Police was at his desk, having arrived at his usual time, seven o'clock, after picking up a triple espresso. He'd already begun his routine of reviewing last night's reports and was making progress when his phone rang an hour later. Caller ID displayed *Police Nationale, Paris. What the hell does the Sûreté want this early?* he thought. He took a sip of coffee and picked up.

"Gleb, it's Bridgette in Paris."

"You're in early. How long has it been since we talked?"

"The law enforcement symposium in Munich several years ago."

"Right—hope this is personal?"

"Afraid not. I need some help." Bridgette described how she was working with the SFPD.

"Sneaky bastards—don't trust us to cooperate." He laughed.

"You're so cynical, Gleb."

"I'm Russian. Okay, I'll run the files for Denis Rodolphe, check immigration, and ask around—give me a week."

Balabanov got off the phone and reflected. He recognized the name because there'd been Interpol inquiries about Denis Rodolphe in October 2012 and Henri and Margaux Rodolphe in the middle of March 2013, and finally a Red Notice earlier this month on Denis Rodolphe again. Arseny Draco had chosen not to acknowledge any of them. *I'd better check with Draco before I upset the apple cart.* Fifteen minutes later he had his answer. "Cooperate fully, but don't mention Henri or Margaux Rodolphe. They didn't ask this time, so let's keep it to ourselves. And Gleb? Keep me posted."

Less than a mile away on Ulitsa Kuznetskiy Most, Arseny Draco sat in his FSB office. It was his turn to think. He'd known the Rodolphes for years and even remembered Denis as a baby. Back in the day, they'd worked the same turf—Europe. That was before the KGB had been succeeded in 1995 by the FSB. Officially, he'd been a colonel in the KGB then, but today he no longer had a title. His business card simply had his name, the Kremlin's address, and a phone number. Nevertheless, he ruled all of Russia's clandestine services, reporting only to the president, and was the second most powerful person in the country. *I'll sit on this until Gleb reports back. Then I'll decide if I ought to call Margaux.*

A week later, Balabanov called Bridgette, reporting that nothing had shown up on Denis Rodolphe, after which she passed that information on to Gabi.

***

In Montreal, time dragged, and without Gracie it was depressing. So Denis had buried himself in Raskolnikov's Conundrum. The Grande Bibliothèque, combined with the internet, provided ample research material. But his research didn't pan out the way he'd hoped, so Denis didn't publish it or send it to Joe Cancio.

And then Denis thought about the old monsignor often. He convinced himself that the priest hadn't been what he appeared to be. Was the old man offering a road map to salvation and forgiveness? That led to inferences that scared Denis. Occasionally, he walked past the basilica, hoping to see the monsignor or Jacques. Finally, one day he entered and sat for a while before a middle-aged priest approached. "May I sit with you?"

Denis slid over in the pew.

"I don't mean to interrupt your prayers, but do you need to talk?"

"Oh, I wasn't praying."

"You fooled me." The priest chuckled.

"But I'd like to talk to the monsignor."

The priest looked confused. "I'm the monsignor—Father Matt."

"No, I mean the old priest. The one with the red parka. I met him and Jacques down at the Vieux-Port last winter. I walked him home once—here to the basilica."

"Well, that does sound like my predecessor. Are you sure? Because he passed away two years ago, and I replaced him. Your description doesn't sound like any priest who's assigned here now."

"I'm positive." Then he told Father Matt about the old man being unintentionally incognito.

"Monsignor was a bit absent-minded." Father Matt chuckled. They sat for a while. Finally, the priest said, "I have a meeting now, but if you'd like to stop by and talk, I'm here most mornings. I'll walk you out?"

On the steps, Denis said, "I'm sorry, Father. Maybe I imagined or dreamed it."

They shook hands, and as Denis turned to leave, he saw Jacques tearing toward him with a stick in his mouth. Jacques dropped it at Denis's feet and started jumping. "Hey, Jacques!" Denis exclaimed, kneeling and hugging his friend. Jacques licked his face before Denis stood and hurled the stick. The dog was off in a flash. "I didn't imagine that," he said, looking at the priest.

The men parted, and Father Matt went inside. Jacques followed Denis to the edge of the basilica's property. As he walked down Notre-Dame Street West, he turned and waved, then Jacques barked a few times. Denis was confused and didn't return. And Father Matt was disquieted for several days, feeling that he ought to have done something for the man. *Maybe he'll come back. I hope so.*

Then everything got worse for Denis. *That fucking book! And those interviews with her talking about me, my murders, my escape to Canada. Cameron just sits there, innocently gibbering. With her skirt a half inch too short. Christ, there'll probably be a docudrama. And shit, overnight my name's become a household word again, and my picture's all over the US and Canada as well.* Denis was furious.

Time continued to march on, and Denis lost interest in everything. He didn't even think about women, nor did he want to talk to anyone. The only feelings Denis had now didn't rise above being pissy. He didn't bother to get his hair and beard trimmed and started drinking. And if you believed Father Matt, he'd done some hallucinating.

Denis missed San Francisco as well and occasionally picked up the Sunday *Chronicle* from the Gare Centrale's international newsstand. When he was there, he walked to the platform where Gracie should have arrived. Once, Denis thought he'd seen her and startled a detraining woman. After that, he stopped looking for Gracie.

And then it worsened again. There it was in the ART & EXHIBITS section of the San Francisco paper. The photo burst like a thunderclap. The June 16 edition ran a black-and-white of Cameron and Melisa entering a gala fundraiser the prior evening at the Mark Hopkins. The San Francisco Women Against Rape's coalition had honored Cameron for her best seller's contribution to heightening awareness of the pervasiveness of rape. The caption read: MS. CAMERON SINCLAIR, HONOREE (LEFT), ACCOMPANIED BY HER GUEST, MS. MELISA WILLIAMS. It was an incredible photo; Annie Leibovitz[7] couldn't have done better. Cameron and Melisa were holding hands. Both women were dressed in long, silky, tight-fitting evening gowns. They were climbing the entrance steps, nearly side by side. Mirror images, each with a left foot above the right, legs fully exposed through the slits in their gowns. He couldn't stop looking. Then it hit him. *They're lovers! I can see it in their body language. Fuck, that was my idea. I'll bet those bitches are laughing at me.*

Denis had begun frequenting strip clubs, hoping that might spark an interest in women again. One night during the week after Cameron's photo appeared, he went to a club he occasionally visited. Ginger was dancing on the bar, waving a scarf that she tied around her waist when she wasn't performing. She came right over and after a few gyrations said, "Are you ever taking me to a VIP room?" When Ginger finished her set, she collected Denis, leading him to one of several little rooms across the bar. After Denis paid, she said, "Now we can do whatever we'd like." Ginger settled on his lap, moving seductively, and handed him a rubber. Denis was surprised because she was getting a reaction. Not easy, considering how much he'd drunk tonight and his state of mind these days. He reached around for her breasts and began clutching them. Denis lost himself until Ginger said, "Not so hard."

338

"What—?"

When he didn't stop, she twisted free, saying, "You're hurting me," and got up.

Denis flared. His old ally—hate—was back. They were both standing, facing each other. Denis began shaking Ginger by her shoulders, yelling, "Don't pull away from me, bitch. Don't you dare!"

A pain exploded in his groin, then Denis was on his knees, trying not to puke. Ginger hit a panic button, lights came on, an alarm beeped, and two bouncers entered. They hauled him to his feet as he shouted, "I wanna see the manager. That bitch kneed me."

They manhandled Denis through the club and tossed him onto the sidewalk. One of the bouncers snapped, "You're not seeing anybody. And don't fuckin' come back!"

Denis stumbled to his feet and tottered on until he hailed a cab.

When Denis awoke the next morning, his balls and head were still sore. *That's it*, he thought. *If I'm going to be miserable, I might as well go where it truly is! Not to mention a place that won't extradite to the US. Moscow.*

Over the next week, he visited the basilica several times. He wanted to see Jacques once more. Finally, the dog appeared. Denis bent down and hugged him again. They played fetch with a stick for a half hour. When Denis left, he looked over his shoulder and waved, and Jacques barked.

By the end of the first week in August, Denis was in Moscow. He'd traveled using his Canadian fake ID, but once he landed, Denis switched to his real name. He didn't want the Moscow flight linked to him. Denis had brought plenty of cash and took a small suite at the Four

Seasons Hotel near Red Square. Then he opened a bank account using its address, contacted the EU companies to reroute his income stream there, and instructed his Swiss account to transfer $250,000 to his new Russian one.

***

Back in San Francisco, as summer wound down, Joe and Gabi met with Captain Weber. They hoped that Cameron's notoriety from her talk show appearances might shake something loose. But all they could do was wait.

***

In September, Susan decided it was time to tell her family about their engagement. It wasn't for lack of commitment that she'd waited; it just seemed so vague, since they hadn't set a date yet. *Mom will be full of a thousand questions*, Susan fretted. *And she's not going to be happy about Linda.* But finally she called, and that evening she said to Joe, "I rang Mom today and told her we were engaged."

"I know you've been avoiding it. I'll bet it wasn't as easy as telling my parents."

"Not too bad, but she wants a commitment about when we'll come east so they can meet you and start planning. I told her we were thinking of between Thanksgiving and Christmas next year for our wedding, so there was no rush. But I suggested we could spend Christmas with them this year. We could fly out on the twenty-second and return on the twenty-sixth. Are you okay with that?"

"Works for me. How about Linda?"

"I was surprised; my mom didn't object to her as maid of honor."

They left as planned, flying to JFK, then driving in a rental car to Susan's hometown, Wappingers Falls, New York, a small bedroom community near Poughkeepsie. They all got along, and Susan and her mother made progress with the wedding plans.

***

On Friday, December 27, when Joe returned from New York, he received a letter from Denis Rodolphe that had been postmarked in Moscow:

December 19, 2013

Joe:

I haven't written in a while. I thought it was time to wrap things up. Here's a tally:

- *Fleur Petit—Saint-Tropez, 1986, my first. We were on holiday.*

- *A couple at Oxford—don't remember their names.*

- *A hooker in Marseille before I left the Sorbonne—just assault, 1995. How'd my mother ever find out? She screwed up everything in France for me.*

- *Tippy at Lawrenceville—the bitch got away and complained. The administration covered it up—a he said, she said—but they asked me to resign, 2001.*

- *Cassie Dunne—Palo Alto, 2002*

- *Sally Thompson—with Zack, 2005*

- *The twins—with Zack, 2012*

- *Zack Wheeler, 2012*

- *Melisa Williams—mugging, 2012*

- *Then during March 2013 in Montreal—a last one, Sam. I didn't kill her, but I'm still haunted by what I did.*

I'm sure you've asked why. I think it all started because my mother began abusing me when I was about twelve. I know it sounds commonplace, but I was revolted. A harsh verdict, but I don't understand how she could do it. So I hate women and want to punish them. That's the only answer I have.

After you reopened Melisa's statutory rape allegation, I began planning to disappear as a precaution. But after the panties surfaced and I assaulted Cameron, I was convinced you'd eventually nab me for Sally Thompson. She's buried in the center of Cameron's rose garden, by the way. So I was off to Canada, but you don't need to know the details. Before I left, I hid out at the Hotel Royal. I hired Gracie for a week. She was special, we fell in love, and she wanted to come with me. But we agreed Gracie would follow later, so as not to be associated with me. You know the rest.

It's an understatement to say I was devastated when I found out she'd been murdered. Gracie was a gift. She loved me unconditionally and was becoming my salvation. I even started to feel better about myself. Then suddenly, she was gone. Nonetheless, I thought I'd discovered another way forward. I'm talking about the old priest with the bright red parka at the Vieux-Port. He was the monsignor from the Basilica of Notre-Dame. He helped me up the day I learned Gracie died. We talked for a long time, and I walked him back to the basilica. When we parted, he told me the door would always be open—all I had to do was ask. Later, I knew I needed help, so I went to the basilica to see him. Instead, I saw the current monsignor, Father Matt, who told me the old priest had died over two years before. He implied I was hallucinating. Father Matt was no help at all. But when I left, we saw Jacques, the old priest's dog, outside the basilica. And he wasn't a hallucination, so how could the old monsignor have been one?

I still don't know what was going on. But my way forward wasn't going to be with Father Matt, because he wasn't curious enough to explore this mystery with me. Since then I've been depressed. I started drinking and don't care anymore. I'm in pain every day. You know what I mean, Joe, because you felt the same way about Laura. Then in August, I came to Moscow—misery loves company. But it has only gotten worse, so it's time to go.

Rodolphe

PS: I finished my paper on Dostoevsky. I didn't send it to you, because it didn't work out.

After reading the letter, Joe was convinced it was genuine. He scanned it and emailed a copy to the captain. Joe's phone rang in a few minutes.

"'Mornin', Captain."

"Son of a bitch . . . after all this time. Finally, some answers. Do you buy it?"

"I think so, but I want to talk to Ellen."

"About that. Who knows besides you and me?"

"No one."

"All right, keep it that way. I want to think about this. Is Gabi working Monday?"

"Yes."

"Excellent. The two of you come to my office first thing—seven thirty."

Joe walked over to Gabi's desk and told her about the meeting.

"Anything wrong?" she asked.

"No."

"Well, so much for my beauty sleep."

***

Monday morning, after they were seated, the captain began. "Has Gabi seen the letter?"

"No, as you requested, I kept it to myself. I have a copy for her." Ben Weber nodded, and Joe handed it over.

After Gabi read it, she said, "Do we think this is truthful?"

344

"We're operating on that premise," Captain Weber said. "You two are wondering why the secrecy. Since the warehouse murders case is classified as inactive, I want to be cautious and make certain this is for real before reactivating it. If we go public prematurely and we've been hoodwinked, it'll look terrible."

"How do you want us to proceed, then?" Joe asked.

"The three of us know. Let's include Dr. Sandler and leave it at that for the time being. Also, keep a lid on his relocation to Moscow. As far as we're concerned, he's still in Montreal."

"Forensics?" Gabi asked.

"Not yet. I'm willing to gamble that if the letter's a fake, the sender was smart enough to cover their tracks. And if it's real, forensic confirmation doesn't add anything. I want you and Joe to handle all aspects of the investigation."

"Do you want to sit on Sally Thompson too?" Joe asked.

"At least until we've verified Fleur Petit and Cassie Dunne."

"How do you want the international inquiries handled?" Joe continued.

"Let's not worry about Oxford or Marseille for now. There's too little to go on. Handle Saint-Tropez and Russia through official channels."

"What about Bridgette?" Gabi asked.

"Not yet. We can call her later if it makes sense."

As they left, Gabi asked, "Why's Weber so paranoid?"

"He's not," Joe joked. "He's just a politician—doesn't want the press to catch on until we're satisfied."

***

Joe called Dr. Sandler, emailed her a copy of the letter, and got her up to speed with Captain Weber's instructions. Then on Tuesday, December 31, Gabi and Joe met with her.

"Working through the letter," Ellen started, "the list of killings seems straightforward. He's not bragging. It's a confession with a hint of remorse. I'm sorry I was right about there being more killings. We'll probably never know what the stressors were for Fleur Petit, Tippy, Cassie Dunne, and the unknowns. All we know about Sally Thompson is that it was all tangled up with Zack. And as far as Sam is concerned, I haven't a clue. The rest is how Rodolphe feels and a suicide note.

"Let's explore the subjective areas. We'll never know what his mother did to him. It doesn't matter, because it's how he felt that counts. He tells us he was revolted. I think Rodolphe correctly diagnoses himself when he writes, 'I hate women and want to punish them.' He has been able to keep it under control, at times for long periods, until enough stressors build up. The next part about Sally's burial place is straightforward. It's not clear why Rodolphe's telling us—perhaps remorse.

"Now we come to Gracie. She's a prostitute like Sonja in *Crime and Punishment*. I don't know what to say about this. Gracie's name means gift from God, God's grace, or unconditional love. We're starting to move into a spiritual rather than a psychological realm. Something is going on here, and I don't think it's in his imagination. He's beginning to struggle with remorse and salvation. Now the old priest, the red parka, and Jacques appear. The old man is talking about repentance and forgiveness. More spirituality, and something's happening here as well.

I've been practicing psychology long enough to know that everything can't be explained in an earthly way. I'd be interested in Sister Mary's take when you can share this with her. So what are your next steps?"

"Gabi's going to follow up on Tippy and Cassie Dunne. I'll do the international queries. We'll cite anonymous tips or sources as our justification. Then if that pans out enough for the captain, we'll contact Cameron for permission to dig up the rose garden. If we find remains, we'll run their DNA. Hopefully, we can give Sally's family closure. Then I'll call the Rowes. But I don't see Weber going public with this until he finds a way to make it work for him." Joe chuckled.

CHAPTER THIRTY

Thursday, January 2, 2014
Moscow

Gleb Balabanov needed to call Arseny Draco. He should have already. The problem was that the case had been screwed up from the outset; add in the holidays, the vacations, and there you had it. Despite Arseny's suave veneer, he was Jesuitical and dangerous, so Gleb was apprehensive.

The facts were that:

- On December 24, 2013, a body had been fished out of the Moskva River in the late afternoon and taken to the morgue. It was identified as Denis Rodolphe, an American living at the Four Seasons Hotel. He was presumed to have gone into the river earlier that day and drowned.

- On the third day, December 26, the coroner discovered that Rodolphe wasn't dead but unconscious and in deep hypothermia. He was immediately transported to the Central Clinical Hospital.

- On December 27, Rodolphe regained consciousness but refused to answer questions.

- On December 29, the reports finally reach Balabanov's desk, and he dispatched an investigator to Rodolphe's hotel suite. The investigator brought back a laptop, and forensics found a file therein containing what Balabanov believed was a suicide note addressed to Detective Lieutenant Joe Cancio, San Francisco PD. The note included other shocking revelations. Balabanov opened an investigation to see if there was foul play.

And of course, Gleb recognized the name and recalled Draco's instructions. *Fuck!*

Several hours later, the message Balabanov had left with Draco's FSB office was answered. "What's up, Gleb? You caught me at my dacha."

"Sorry to disturb you on your holidays, but I think you ought to know about this." Balabanov explained what had happened.

"Shit. Post a round-the-clock guard at the hospital. Next, suspend your investigation for the time being. I'll be in my office on Ulitsa Kuznetskiy Most tomorrow. Come over at seven thirty and bring the laptop."

***

Friday's meeting wasn't going the way Gleb had expected. There was no criticism of the police delay in discovering that Rodolphe was still alive. Instead, Draco was focused on other issues.

"Gleb, why did you instigate an inquiry? It seems straightforward to me. He writes a suicide note, throws himself in the Moskva, but survives."

"It's standard procedure. What if there's foul play?"

"How so?"

"You read the letter. What about enemies?"

"In Russia? How would they know about all that shit?"

"Sir, it's just good police work."

"Well, I think you're wasting time. All right, continue your investigation, but limit it. Check immigration and find out when he arrived. Review your files for any assaults, rapes, murders that could be attributed to him. Then find out if Rodolphe's employed and how he occupies his time otherwise. But keep this low-key. And I don't want any of my departments involved until I see where this is going."

"What if he signs himself out of hospital?"

"No—place him under house arrest, protective custody, whatever. Don't release him without my say-so and keep a guard on his room. I want time to think."

***

On Monday the sixth, Gabi phoned the Palo Alto PD and was transferred to Captain Hernandez.

"It's a cold case, but we still review it every six months. I can help because I have direct knowledge. My partner and I were the first responders. Cassie lived at home and was a senior at Palo Alto High School. Her parents had gone away for a weekend in October. When they returned Sunday evening, they found her dead in the main bathroom's tub. She was naked, bound, and gagged. The autopsy revealed multiple stab wounds, mainly in her breasts and groin area. Those weren't the cause of death, though. Cassie was eviscerated while she was still alive and bled out."

"It sounds terrible," Gabi responded.

"It was one of the worst crime scenes I've encountered," Hernandez said, and continued, "Cassie went out drinking on Friday night with a girlfriend, Jane. Jane told us they were both high when a cute older guy started hitting on Cassie. In the ladies' room, Cassie raved about how hot he was, saying, 'I'm taking him home to bed.' Jane cautioned, but Cassie ignored her and left with him. Her time of death was around noon on Sunday."

"Then he had all weekend."

"Yes. Her parents' bed showed signs of sexual activity—plenty of Cassie's DNA but nothing from the murderer. A weekend to remember that went horribly wrong."

"Captain, could I come down and review the file?"

"Sure, I'll give you access to all our records. Jane still lives locally. I'm certain she'll talk to you—bring pictures along. Who knows; you might get lucky with an ID. I'll coordinate everything. I'd love to see this one solved."

Later, Gabi went to Palo Alto. She reviewed the file, and the crime scene photos' were as gruesome as she'd imagined. Following that, the captain drove her to Jane's. Jane repeated what had happened, and it was consistent with the police report. Then from a photo array, Jane picked Rodolphe, saying, "I'm pretty sure that's the guy."

Gabi thanked them and headed back to the office with a copy of Palo Alto's file.

***

Arseny Draco called Margaux Rodolphe on Wednesday the eighth. "It's been so long. How are you, Draco?"

"At least two or three years. I'm well, and you?"

"Getting old."

"Join the club. We need to meet."

"Business or pleasure?"

"Both. How about drinks at Bosco Mishka's—six o'clock?"

Wednesday night, after meeting with Draco, Margaux was sleepless. And the next morning, she continued absorbing everything he had told her about Denis—his attempted suicide, the hospital, and the note, which Draco had given her a copy of. She wasn't looking forward to calling Henri in London, where he was on assignment.

When she reached him, Margaux spoke for a long time and read him Denis's note. Finally, Henri spoke. "Your chickens have come home to roost this time."

"Must you be that way? Please . . . don't let's go over it again. Can't you ever forgive me for what I did to Denis?"

"I do, but it's not my forgiveness you need."

"I know."

"What are you going to do?"

"I'm mulling over a plan now, and tomorrow I'll go to the hospital. Arseny promised help: Russian diplomatic passports, a jet, anything. I must get Denis out of here, because if the wrong people find out, we won't be safe. They'll use him to get to us."

"Agreed. Give Denis my best. And let me know where you are. I'm sorry, but I just can't come home right now."

***

On Thursday, Joe initiated another inquiry with the Russians through Interpol. Hopefully, they could confirm Rodolphe's suicide. Then Joe contacted the National Police Force in Saint-Tropez about Fleur Petit. It took several days to retrieve the cold-case file. An *inspecteur* called back, reporting that over a weekend in mid-August 1986, the eighteen-year-old had been reported missing by her parents. The family was on holiday from Paris. Fleur was later found cudgeled to death in a Vieux-Port alley. Her clothes were torn, and there were signs of rape. Rodolphe's name didn't arise in their investigation. The police were able to locate her parents, who had retired to Tanneron, a small village in the south of France.

***

Joe called Captain Weber on January 15. "I'd like to show Sister Mary the letter and get her take on it. There's a lot going on with Gracie and the old priest that I don't understand. Ellen thinks her input could be valuable too. She'll be discreet."

"Okay, if you think it's important."

Joe had a copy of the letter delivered to Mary, and after she'd spent time with it, she asked if they could meet at the abbey. When he arrived, they went to her cell.

"I hope you don't mind meeting here. I talked to Father Matt at the basilica in Montreal. I'll tell you what I think happened. But I want to clear the air about something we haven't talked about completely. I thought we should meet here, since it's where it all started for me."

"I don't understand—"

Mary stopped Joe with her hand. "I'll be direct. What I told you about our last meeting in here wasn't the whole story. When I returned, I was out of control. I couldn't stop crying."

"I know."

"Let me get this out . . . please. Sister Agnes came in, and she understood immediately. She held me and finally said, 'It's terrifying but wonderful when you've seen the face of God.' She was talking about you. I've thought about it a lot. I concluded that if all religions are replete with tales of exorcism and demonic possession, why couldn't it work the other way around? What if the Lord deems a situation so serious that it requires direct intercession? Couldn't God step in and become you? I'm convinced that's what happened, and I was in the Lord's living presence. But why Joe Cancio? The answer made sense as well. It was simple. You see, you have free will and could've short-circuited God's plan by arresting me. So the Almighty simply took charge."

"I told Susan, and she understood right away. But Susan thought I was the Lord's surrogate. It still mystifies me, but I know something special happened that day."

"I needed to tell you, and I hope you're not embarrassed."

"I'm not, because our relationship is one of a kind."

"All right, so here's what I learned. Father Matt remembers meeting with Rodolphe. Afterward, he concluded that the man needed a priest, but Father Matt had dismissed him as being a little nutty. As we talked, I realized Father Matt was troubled by the way he handled their meeting and thinks he dropped the ball. But he had no way of contacting Rodolphe. Then I told him Rodolphe's story. His reaction was predictable. 'Oh my Lord, that man was in desperate need of help!'

"I had read the letter a couple of times before I called. Where Rodolphe writes about the old priest, he says, 'He helped me up,' and I was reminded of 'Footprints in the Sand.'[8] I started looking at the letter differently, especially the parts about Gracie and the old monsignor. I talked to Father Matt about this for a long time. He was skeptical at first, because as clerics, we're reluctant to attribute supernatural qualities to events until all other explanations fail. Reluctantly, he thought I might be onto something. Father Matt was also confused about Rodolphe's relationship with Jacques. They were obviously acquainted. Jacques is still at the basilica, by the way.

"Here's what I think. The Lord created humans, making them more intelligent than animals. But then something else was added—free will. The Almighty doesn't make us do anything but sets guidelines for our conduct—the ten commandments, for example. As a result, unexpected decisions are made. Most aren't bad. They're just different, having no injurious consequences. But sometimes a rogue decision is so bad, with unintended consequences, that God must do something about it. And it takes a while to put things back on course. This is a plausible explanation for why bad things happen to good people.

"Here's how I think this applies to Rodolphe. Early on, a bad decision was made. His mother abuses him. I think the Almighty has been working to fix that mess ever since—but what to do? To begin with, God blesses Rodolphe with extraordinary intelligence. He'll figure it out and get help—that should solve the problem. But as time goes by, it becomes apparent that Rodolphe is headed in the wrong direction—Fleur Petit.

"Then the Lord removes him from his mother's influence— Princeton, England, and France. But it's still not working—a couple at Oxford and a hooker in Marseille.

"Following that, employment nearly six thousand miles away from his mother. Next, God nudges Rodolphe towards scholarship, wherein he becomes fascinated with Raskolnikov and Dracula, one a story of redemption, the other of blood lust. That should do it. But Rodolphe still doesn't understand and continues to deteriorate—Tippy, Cassie, Sally, the twins, Melisa, and Zack.

"But the Lord is still giving it time. Why wait so long to introduce Gracie is a mystery, or maybe it's just the way it is. The Second Epistle of Peter covers it: 'With the Lord one day is like a thousand years, and a thousand years are like one day.' Eventually, Gracie appears. She represents unconditional love, God's grace, and redemption. Even if Rodolphe doesn't recognize it, he's subliminally processing the parallel story of Raskolnikov and Sonja. My sense is that this solution was finally taking hold, Rodolphe was beginning to change under Gracie's guidance, and he was becoming aware.

"Then where the hell does the doctor come from?" Mary asked rhetorically. "Who knows? Now Rodolphe continues to spiral down. It's more confusing, because the old monsignor is in place before Gracie is killed. So the Lord has no time left for another indirect approach.

"Who is the old man, then?" Joe asked.

"It seems to me the Trinity is the last resort. All different—all separate—but all the same. I think it's the Holy Ghost who helps Rodolphe up and guides him to the open door of the basilica. It can't be any clearer that redemption is his if he only walks through that door. But the Holy Ghost can't make it happen—that's free will again. I think Rodolphe finally understands, but by that time the Lord has moved on. And Father Matt, who was left to finish the task, didn't get the memo.

"I'm leaning towards the old priest being the Holy Ghost because of his bright-red parka: it's the Holy Ghost's color. Also, this all takes place in the period leading up to Pentecost in early June. That commemorates the descent of the Holy Ghost, breathing life into the Apostles, and church altars are draped in bright red then."

"What if he'd walked through the door with the old monsignor, or if Father Matt hadn't dropped the ball?" Joe asked.

"We'll never know."

"And Jacques . . . I still don't understand that."

"I don't know either. Perhaps a loving, temporal message reminding Rodolphe not to give up, and that the old man in red hasn't forgotten him."

***

In Moscow on the seventeenth, Gleb Balabanov rang Arseny Draco. "We need to talk about a few things. I checked with immigration. They have no record of Rodolphe entering the country."

"He probably used a fake ID to throw off US or Canadian authorities," Draco commented.

"Yes, that adds credibility to his letter. Why would Rodolphe use a fake ID if he weren't a fugitive? I also did some investigating of high school records, because his family lived here then. He graduated in 1986 and entered Princeton that fall. That's all—no criminal record."

"What else?"

"Rodolphe doesn't have any employment but hangs out at the university, picking up tutoring jobs. He has native proficiency in Russian and French."

"Probably doesn't have any trouble getting jobs. Did you check for any recent unsolved crimes that might fit?"

"Yes, and back in the day as well."

"Fine. Discontinue your investigation."

"Plus, I received another Interpol inquiry about him on behalf of San Francisco's PD—a detective, Joe Cancio."

"Are they looking for anything specific?"

"Yes, if we can confirm his death."

"Stall them," Draco said. "I'm still not sure what course of action is best for us. I'll call you back."

"He can be released from the hospital now," Gleb continued, "and his mother has been visiting him every day. What do you want to do?"

"He's free to go, but give me a couple of hours."

"Do you want us to tail him?"

"No, I'll take care of it. That's why I need time."

So much for keeping your departments out of this, Gleb thought as they rang off.

***

In San Francisco, Gabi and Joe met with Captain Weber on the twenty-fourth. "Run down where we are," he began.

Gabi went first. "I met with Captain Hernandez in Palo Alto about Cassie Dunn. We were in luck, since he was one of the first responders. I also got a solid ID on Rodolphe from the girl Cassie went drinking with that night. I don't think there's anything left to do."

"Is Hernandez notifying her parents?"

"Yes. All he knows is that we received an anonymous tip."

"And Tippy?"

"I have another call in to the Lawrenceville school."

"Joe?" Weber asked.

"I contacted Moscow through Interpol on the ninth; no response yet. I'll follow up if we don't hear from them. Then I spoke with Saint-Tropez. It took them a few days to locate their cold-case file. It checks out. Fleur was found raped and beaten to death in an alley, but Rodolphe was never on their radar. Their PD located her parents using the same story as with Cassie—an anonymous tip."

"Tell me how you made out with Dr. Sandler and Sister Mary."

"Ellen buys the note as legitimate," Joe began. "She also thinks some inexplicable things were going on." Then Joe continued with Sister Mary's observations, leaving out the part about his prior meeting in her cell.

"Interesting, and Mary confirms Rodolphe's take on Father Matt. I don't know what to make of the rest. If there's any truth to it, it begs the question: why would our Maker put such time and effort into salvaging such a bad apple?"

"I have no idea," Joe opined.

"Should we talk to Cameron and Chief Evans now?" Gabi asked.

"No—once we go down that path, the exhumation will generate activity. Wait for Moscow. But check with me first."

***

When Gabi came in on February 7, Joe greeted her with, "I had an odd phone call this morning when I came in. Moscow's chief of police, Gleb Balabanov, called me, responding to our recent inquiry through Interpol."

"Anything interesting?"

"All the usual apologies—they're backed up, computer problems, and so on. Here's what he said: 'I put one of my guys on it. Rodolphe lived here with his parents during high school and then returned to the States for university—nothing since. No unidentified bodies—suicide or otherwise.' But when Balabanov rang off, he said, 'If Rodolphe went into the Moskva this time of year, it's tricky. The water temperature is only a few degrees above freezing. He wouldn't survive more than fifteen or twenty minutes and could be swept downstream to the Volga, or he might wash up on our banks.'"

"We didn't mention anything about rivers," Gabi observed.

"Exactly. Are you hearing what I'm hearing?"

"CIA speak. I think Moscow was investigating already. And Rodolphe went into the river, washing up on their banks. But we don't know if he's alive or dead," Gabi inferred.

"I don't think we'll ever find out. It seems like Balabanov isn't on board with what the Kremlin's up to and is giving us as much information as he can."

"I wonder why the Kremlin cares?" Gabi thought out loud

CHAPTER THIRTY-ONE

Wednesday, February 12, 2014

Gabi updated Joe on the Lawrenceville school. "On Monday, I followed up my call of September twenty-first. I spoke with the same woman in personnel. First, I asked her if she could recall any more about Rodolphe's mother's involvement. She said no. Then I told her about Tippy, and that Rodolphe had been asked to resign prior to end of term in June 2001. The woman said she had no recollection but would ring me back. She called today. They don't keep records of nicknames, but she searched using it as a first name—no luck. Then she went back to the school's yearbooks. The lady could locate books for the first two years Rodolphe was there. She read through them—no Tippy. That means Tippy would've had to be a postgraduate student during Rodolphe's last year—it's a long shot. Following that, the woman spoke with the head of school, but he won't allow us access to the disciplinary committee's records without a court order. Plus I'm not certain Rodolphe's dustup even reached the committee. I think this is a dead end."

"All right, I agree. Let's call Weber and see if he'll authorize us to talk to Cameron about digging up her rose garden. I think we have as much as we're going to get." They briefed the captain on Tippy and the peculiar call from Gleb Balabanov.

"I think you're correct about Tippy," Weber offered. "Let's put it aside for the time being. We can always revisit it if we think it's necessary. I also think you're correct on the call from the Russian. He knows more than he's saying. Odd—why do they care, and why does Balabanov want to help, albeit in a vague sort of way? Something's going on, but whatever it is, it isn't in our bailiwick. We don't need to stumble into some clandestine op originating in Moscow. The good news is, he's confirmed Rodolphe is there—dead or alive. It's a shame we'll never be able to use it; too much conjecture. Let's do this: First, send the letter to forensics. Then continue to use the anonymous-tip cover, and see if Cameron will let us exhume. If there are remains in the garden and the DNA checks out, call Chief Evans."

***

On February 20, the forensics lab returned the results from Rodolphe's note. The envelope had dozens of prints; however, the letter had only Rodolphe's. The lab also reported that the paper used was A4, which was a standard European letter size. DNA wasn't available, because the stamp and envelope flap were self-sticking. The postmark and stamps were authentic.

***

Cameron had been away on a book-signing tour, so Gabi wasn't able to catch up with her until the week of the twenty-fourth. "Cameron, it's Sergeant Müller."

"Hi, Gabi, how are you?"

"Fine. I saw the article in the paper about your award—congrats."

"It was a surprise. Melisa was a big help in getting the book out so fast. You know she's living with me now and went back to university last fall?"

"Yes, I keep in touch with her. I need to ask you something." Gabi told her about their anonymous tips. "This guy has already given us information on the warehouse murders' case, but I can't share it with you. He has always been accurate and now claims that Sally Thompson's body is buried in the center of your rose garden,"

364

"Oh my Lord, I never would've guessed. How the hell could Denis do that? Do you want to exhume her?"

"That's why I'm calling. We'll be careful to restore your garden."

"Okay, just give me a heads-up."

"Thanks. Will you send me an email, giving us permission?"

"Sure."

That evening, talking in bed, Joe told Susan about Gabi's call. "Did Cameron ask after you?"

"No."

"I'm sorry."

"I'm not."

"That makes me happy. Let's not talk anymore," Susan said, nestling closer.

***

By the middle of March, remains had been unearthed in Cameron's garden, right where Rodolphe's letter had asserted they'd be. Gabi and Joe were now waiting for the DNA analysis.

On March 26, Gabi stopped by Joe's office. "The DNA is back. It's Sally's."

They phoned the captain, who said, "All right, call Chief Evans. Notwithstanding the ambiguity from Russia, I think the evidence is considerable that Rodolphe's letter is accurate."

"Are you thinking of going public, then?"

"No, I'm still not sure what course of action is best."

Gabi rang Robert Evans, updated him on the anonymous tipster, and said they had located Sally's remains.

"After all this time," the chief said. "Are you certain?"

"Yes, we have a DNA confirmation."

"Was it a peaceful place?"

"Yes, in a lovely rose garden. Please tell her parents, and we'll arrange for her remains to be returned."

***

On April 11, Ben Weber asked Joe to lunch and suggested TIS. That had never happened before, so Joe was intrigued. "I'm going to have an IPA. How about you, Joe?" They both ordered one, then chatted casually for a while. "I want to go over a few things with you. First, review the warehouse murders."

I wonder why he wants to go over this again? Joe thought, but said, "It's still a cold case. Our efforts to locate Rodolphe in Montreal haven't produced anything. We've spent our time verifying his letter. We've confirmed the Cassie Dunne and Sally Thompson murders and located Sally's remains. Sister Mary confirms the old priest/Father Matt scenario as well. Thus, I'd suggest that we have a high probability he went to Moscow. But we don't know if he's alive or dead, because the Russians aren't cooperating. For lack of information on his alleged crimes at Oxford or Marseille, we haven't pursued them. Tippy at Lawrenceville was a dead end also. We have no idea what Rodolphe's talking about with his reference to Sam. I don't think there's anything more to do unless you decide to go public."

"You're satisfied that Dr. Sandler's analysis fits, and that her and Sister Mary's otherworldly analysis, while interesting, is anecdotal?"

"Yes."

"And Gabi agrees?"

"Yes."

"Excellent. Then we're all in agreement. Here's what I've decided to do: I'm not going public. The press didn't seem to pick up on the exhumation, so we don't have to do anything. Here's why: We've solved everything that we can. We've brought closure to the victims' families where we could. How would we benefit from releasing the information that we have a high probability that Rodolphe escaped to Russia and committed suicide? It only highlights our inability to arrest him, and God help us if he pops up somewhere later sipping piña coladas. We'd look like utter fools."

Predictable, Joe thought, but said, "I accept that, unhappily."

Weber chuckled. "No one said you had to be happy. Here's what we'll do: Keep reviewing the case every six months, and if it makes sense, I'll reconsider my decision."

"I should tell the Rowes."

"Yes, brief them fully, sticking to the anonymous-tip scenario, and that we still think he's in Montreal." Ben Weber looked at his watch. "I guess we've killed enough time. So, now to more pressing matters. The commissioner announced at noon that the chief of detectives is taking early retirement. His wife has been fighting cancer for several years, and he's her primary caregiver. The chief of DS finally had to throw in the towel; he can't do both anymore. We're sad to see him go."

"He has been a fine chief of DS."

"I agree. I hope I can do as well."

"Congratulations, sir. I'm confident you'll do us all proud,"

"Thanks . . . but I thought you would be curious who my replacement is."

"Well, of course I am."

The new chief of DS put out his hand. "Then congratulations to you as well, Captain Cancio."

Joe was flabbergasted. "I didn't see that coming—thank you! I thought you were going to tell me who you were bringing in over my head."

"Why would you think that?"

"Well, I'm still smarting over not corralling Rodolphe."

"Oh, don't talk piffle. You and Gabi got excellent grades on that case. Plus, I'm selfish. Do you think I want to break up the politician, the strategist, and the tactician? Which brings me to two other things. It's your shop now, so the decisions are yours. But I would be pleased if you'd promote Gabi to your spot. She passed the lieutenant's exam and is number one in seniority. I've already cleared it. If you want to, you can do it."

"Gabi never told me she took the exam."

"Quite a while ago. Also, bring Danny Wong over."

"No problems with either. Can I tell her?"

"If I were you, I'd do it as soon as you return. The word's probably making the rounds already. Put her out of her misery." Weber laughed.

"Thank you again, sir."

When Joe returned, he called Gabi to his office, shutting the door. The bullpen was nervous but shortly heard a gleeful whoop. Then Joe came out with Gabi and made the announcements. The new chief of DS had been hanging at the back of the office. *Plenty of time to grab the spotlight in the future. This is their moment*, he thought as he left, waving to Gabi.

***

Later that afternoon, Joe called Susan and told her about the promotions. "I'm proud of you. It's well deserved."

"I couldn't do it without your support."

"Well, I don't know about that. Congratulate Gabi for me. How do you feel about the captain's new position?"

"He's ideally suited. It won't be much of a day-to-day change in routine." Then Joe started to laugh. "He said he didn't want to split up 'the politician, strategist, and tactician.' We had no idea he was aware of our nickname."

"I think he's craftier than he's given credit for."

"Yes. I'll tell you more tonight—not on the phone."

That evening in bed, Susan slid over. "Tell me." Joe went through Captain Weber's reasons for keeping the case inactive and not going public. Susan nuzzled closer and murmured, "Just be happy. Enjoy your promotion." Then, dozing, she said, "You never know. This might not be over yet."

EPILOGUE

Tuesday, May 27, 2014
Zurich

My son, Denis, is sitting across from me. After we took off, I tried to read, but my mind keeps wandering. Now I'm mulling over a gallimaufry of past episodes—some happy, others gloomier. It's hard to keep them straight, but I know one thing. If it weren't for Draco, we wouldn't be airborne on this nearly six-thousand-mile flight from Zurich to San Francisco while carrying Russian diplomatic passports issued with aliases. He'll never know how much this means to me.

***

My thoughts are returning to the beginning, when the CIA recruited Henri and me during our last year of university, 1965. We thought it sounded exciting. We got married, trained, and were awaiting deployment when a new director envisioned a role for us that took advantage of our unique attributes. Henri was distinguished, pleasant, and amiable as well as staggeringly wealthy, we both came from old-line blue-blood families, and I was striking. We were A-listed just for showing up. So it was off to Paris to flitter and flutter with the beautiful people, the idle rich, ambassadors, ministers, and tycoons. Henri adopted a Bertie Wooster[9] persona, while I became a social butterfly. Our assignment was vague—gather any information we thought was worthwhile. We quickly learned that our new friends' lips were loose enough to sink fleets of ships; they had no sense of confidentiality in matters of business, government, money, or the bedroom. Sometimes Henri and I worked together, other times alone. We first met Arseny Draco at embassy functions and became casual acquaintances. It was hardly the swashbuckling career we'd pictured, but it was fun.

Then in 1970, we were reassigned to the Riviera for June through September. So we kept our Paris flat, packed our bags, and set out with our little one and his au pair for Saint-Tropez. Our instructions were the same, except we were to focus on Le Milleu and the drug-trafficking hub in Marseille. Draco was on the Riviera at the same time and sought us out. When we reported this to Langley, they replied that he was KGB—a comer—and had us cultivate him. We all recognized that we were players in the cloak-and-dagger game but became friends anyway. Despite that, we never spoke out of turn or became confused about our loyalties. This assignment went on for three years. Henri and I pursued our goal of developing intelligence, helping the French and our Bureau of Narcotics and Dangerous Drugs to thwart the heroin smuggling that threatened our national security. Meantime Draco, for his part, assisted Le Milleu in continuing its operations. These were exciting times—the French Connection era. In 1972 we aided in seizing a half dozen illicit heroin-processing laboratories alone. And French drug arrests went from under one hundred in 1970 to over three thousand in 1972.

Then life became complicated for me. That last year, when Henri was on assignment in London, I had an affair with Draco. He was a regular overnight guest. It was easy to be discreet, because Denis and his au pair had a separate room. Happy memories. Then it was back to Paris full-time until the summer of 1982, when Denis went to high school and we were reassigned to Moscow. By this time we were deep-cover, reporting to the director of the CIA.

We continued to run into Draco, but I never renewed our assignation because I loved Henri and it was too confusing. Then in the spring of 1995, he called. It was a short message. "I have assets in Marseille. They report an investigation is beginning into Denis for a sexual assault." I took him seriously, since Draco had used the word *asset*—the clearest sign he'd ever given me as to who he was. I pulled strings at Lawrenceville and got Denis out of Paris. He wasn't very happy. Later, I realized that Draco seemed to have dropped from sight after the FSB was formed in 1995, although I encountered him once in a while. Then, after the reorganization of our clandestine services in 2005, we began reporting to the director of national intelligence under even deeper cover, if such a thing was possible.

Denis's voice rouses me from my reverie. "Are you awake, Mother?"

"Just thinking. Did you finish your book?"

"Yes, not bad . . . better than a run-of-the-mill mystery."

"I didn't know you liked them."

"A friend of mine got me started last year."

"It won't be long now. Draco arranged for a car. It shouldn't be more than ninety minutes to the winery."

We're going to stay at a guest house at a winery near Sonoma that Henri's father invested in back in the 1950s. I hope this will give Denis and me a chance to sort things out. I've been on a six-month family leave. Maybe I should retire; I'm nearly seventy. If I did, Henri wouldn't be far behind, because I always take the lead.

I return to my reflections. When Draco called in January and we met at Bosco Mishka's, I was glad but suspicious it wasn't for old times' sake. I was correct and shocked. Not about Denis's health, because it seemed like he was recovering. No, I was shocked about how he'd turned out. Fleur Petit jumped out at me. We'd been vacationing in Saint-Tropez in August 1986 before Denis started Princeton. Then Draco's call in 1995 about Marseille—obviously, the hooker Denis mentioned in his note. And what he'd written about me hurt.

But long ago, I accepted my blameworthiness for what I've done, and Henri has forgiven me. I even think I understood why I lost it when my friend seduced Denis. She screwed any man with a dick, so I was mad at her but furious with Denis. For Christ's sake, I loved him, and I felt betrayed. *How could he?* I thought. *It should've been me. I wouldn't have denied him.* So he had to be punished.

Eventually, I realized how unnatural and unhealthy it was. I was able to stop after about two years, about the time we were transferred to Moscow. It was hard, but I was strong and powered through. I soothed myself, thinking, *You're not the first parent to lust for their child and stumble.* I believed I was past all of it until his note.

I was bowled over! I'd been so self-centered that I had repressed how it might've affected Denis. Now it was obvious: he hated me and had been taking his revenge.

Draco had realized I wasn't handling the situation. Thankfully, he jumped in. We got Denis out of hospital and back to his hotel, and I took a separate room. We planned to travel by rail from Russia—far less security than airports. So in a few days, Arseny drove us to Moscow's Kievsky Station, providing Russian passports and tickets to Berlin, where we would change for Zurich. Then we were on to a clinic north of the city that the FSB used for plastic surgery and fingerprint removal. And now, nearly six months later, we're using an oligarch's private jet.

***

I look up, thinking, *Denis is as handsome as before, just different. He won't trigger facial recognition.* And then the pilot announces, "We're on our final approach to SFO. Wheels down in twenty minutes."

Denis and I begin getting our bags together after the jet taxis to a remote service hanger and the flight crew begins opening the exit door. When I look up again, I see the director of national intelligence entering with two operations officers behind him.

"Mr. Director, I didn't expect to see you here."

The director steps between Denis and me. I'm confused. I hear fragments of conversations between the operations officers and Denis, then handcuffs and Miranda rights. And now the director is putting his hands on my upper arms.

"Margaux, you can't interfere. He'll be safe. I'll help with your bags. My car's below."

By the time we come out onto the airstairs, my training is pushing through. I assess the scene beneath me: at nine o'clock, two uniformed men, replacement flight crew; at eleven o'clock, a fuel truck approaching from a distance; at noon, the director's car; at two o'clock, Denis being maneuvered into the back seat of a large black SUV with tinted windows and government plates; and at four o'clock, before a similar SUV, two armed US marshals flanking two handcuffed men. As we start down the stairs, I turn to the director.

"I don't understand."

"Arseny swapped Denis for two KGB lifers."

THE END

NOTES

1. Adapted from *Casablanca*, a 1942 Warner Bros. film directed by Michael Curtiz and based on Murray Burnett and Joan Alison's unproduced play *Everybody Comes to Rick's*.

2. Oscar Wilde, *The Picture of Dorian Gray, Lippincott's Monthly Magazine*, 1890.

3. Joseph Conrad, *The Heart of Darkness*, Easton Press, 1980, page 105.

4. Charles Dickens, *Christmas Books: A Christmas Carol in Prose, Being a Ghost Story of Christmas*, Folio Society, 2007, page 16.

5. Lingchi: A form of torture and execution used in China from roughly 900 until the early 1900s, also known as death by a thousand cuts or slices.

6. *The New Oxford Annotated Bible*, New Revised Standard Version, Michael D. Coogan editor, Oxford University Press, Inc., 2001: Luke 15:7.

7. Anna-Lou "Annie" Leibovitz is an American photographer known for her iconic portraits of celebrities.

8. "Footprints" or "Footprints in the Sand," poem, circa 1964, disputed authorship.

9. An amiable English gentleman of the idle rich class, appearing in the Jeeves and Wooster short stories and novels by P. G. Wodehouse published between 1934 and 1974.

AKNOWLEDGMENTS

With thanks to my wife, Ann, for her encouragement, support, and tolerance of my terrible spelling, numerous typos, and frequently humorous homonyms; my sister, Pamela H. Rappolt; and my friend, Michael F. Shepherd, who encourages me and is always my first beta reader. And a special thanks to Rachel Keith for her first-rate copyediting combined with excellent comments and suggestions.

ABOUT THE AUTHOR

Joe Hodgkins and his wife of over fifty years, Ann, live in Morris County, northern New Jersey.

 He graduated from Fordham University's Rose Hill Campus in the Bronx and is a member of the Fordham Alumni Support Team, FAST, representing the university at college fairs and nights held by local high schools. After attaining his undergraduate degree in liberal arts, he attended New York University's Graduate School of Business Administration in Manhattan.

Hodgkins was a senior manager in both commercial banking and corporate finance. He was a member of the Commercial Finance Association, now known as the Secured Finance Network, and was a frequent presenter at continuing education seminars for the New Jersey Society of CPAs and the New Jersey Institute for Continuing Legal Education on topics such as crisis management, asset recovery, and secured lending. He took early retirement in 2002.

He is currently a eucharistic minister at his local Episcopal church, where he also served as treasurer and chairman of the finance committee. Hodgkins has been active in Freemasonry for nearly forty years and has been an Officer or Grand Officer in all bodies of the York Rite. In 2015 he received the First Masonic District of New Jersey's Distinguished White Apron Award for his service and contributions to the Craft.

Other interests include traveling with Ann, reading, and handgun target shooting.

Made in the USA
Coppell, TX
28 January 2023

11866995R00225